The Storymaker

Jeff Katzman

The Storymaker
Jeff Katzman

A novel
The characters, events, institutions, and organizations in this book are strictly fictional. Any apparent resemblance to any person, alive or dead, or to actual events is entirely coincidental.

 **SDP Publishing**

Published by SDP Publishing, an imprint of SDP Publishing Solutions, LLC

Developmental Editing: Julie Mars
Copyediting & Proofreading: Neysa Jensen and Karen Grennan
Cover Artist: Rebekah Smith
Cover Design: Howard Communigrafix, Inc
Interior Design & Layout: Howard Communigrafix, Inc.

For more information about this book contact Lisa Akoury-Ross at SDP Publishing by email at info@SDPPublishing.com.

SDP Publishing
Permissions Department
36 Captain's Way
East Bridgewater, MA 02333
or email your request to info@SDPPublishing.com

Library of Congress Control Number: 2012945437
ISBN-13: 978-0-9829256-0-7
Printed in the United States of America

For my family, near and far away

Acknowledgments

When I began this book, I planned to write a tale describing psychological processes in the workplace. As I wrote, deeper thoughts came knocking at my door. I'm left with a very different book. About love, life, and taking a risk. In the end, perhaps it is about business and how we can discover the humanity in everyone we greet at work each day.

Many people, both recently and long ago, have encouraged my growth toward these values and have shown me what it takes to put together a book. Alphabetically, they are:

The Arbinger Institute, whose thoughts about human connections moved me deeply and helped shape my thoughts about relationships; Dr. Leonard Bearne, who introduced me to the realm of depth psychology and who will forever be my personal hero; Dr. Patricia Coughlin, who showed me the role of psychological defenses in blocking our vitality and what to do about them; Dr. Cynthia Geppert, who has encouraged my passion for stories and shared a curiosity for depth thinking in the workplace; Dr. David Graeber, who encouraged me to keep writing and whose friendship and mentorship over the past decade have been fundamental in my life; Neysa Jensen, who gave this work a final few reads and helped to find the best words for Marty's story; Dr. Sam Keith, who welcomed my ideas at work at every point in my career; Myna Kolb, who first introduced me to the world of improvisational theater at *The Second City* training program and to whom I am forever grateful for her teaching on spontaneity; Dr. Tom Krapu, whose insights about relatedness have been invaluable for me; Julie Mars, my editor, who took the characters in this book quite seriously and unleashed my joy in writing; Drs. Mary Main and Erik Hesse, who taught me the fundamentals of human attachment; Doug Montoya, Kristin Berg, and others at *The Box Theater*, who embraced my crazy musical productions and helped me put them up on stage; Pari Noskin, who further challenged me in the development of these characters and mentored me about writing fiction; Dan O'Connor and the group from *Los Angeles Theatersports*, who taught me the rules of play; Lisa Akoury-Ross and her staff at SDP Publishing, who escorted me through the publishing experience; Dr. Dora Wang, who has been a model of a physician-writer; Dr. Joel Yager, my training director, colleague, and life consultant, who has underscored the importance of following my passions;

And ...

Veterans I have known, who taught me about overcoming life's adversities and shared with me the impact of war;

Generations of psychiatry residents who have afforded me the opportunity to teach;

My parents, for a life filled with love and adventures, and for ongoing encouragement with this project;

My siblings, for ongoing support through life's challenges;

My father-in-law, who took my ideas for writing seriously and insisted that I get started;

My mother-in-law for her demonstration of a life of humor and courage;

My grandfather, whose art for storymaking in his B movies served as tremendous inspiration;

And an old friend whom I miss, who is nothing like any character in this book, but whom I wish were alive to read it;

And most of all ...

My wife and family, who have helped me to live a life honoring emotional experiences, and whose companionship is fundamental to my life.

Table of Contents

Prologue

I've come to know a couple of different ways to make a story. The first kind comes from the head. It's a form of make believe, and it can be a lot of fun. It's about pretending and playing. But it can be dangerous if you're not careful. It can also be used to deceive another person and sometimes used to fool ourselves. It can be told to take control of a situation or to mask over difficult feelings. This is the account of one such storymaker. Though I sometimes grew weary of his fiction, I wish he were alive to tell me one last tale.

I know about another kind of storymaking now, too. That's a story that bubbles up from somewhere deeper, a sacred place within us—a spot that knows a more fundamental truth. A story created by the heart. When you let that tale in, then you know you're truly living. It's a story that can alter your experience of who you are.

That's the kind of story that came to me, Marty Grossmark. I decided to write it down to recall the events of the past year. It's a piece of storymaking that changed me a bit, so I don't want to forget it. It's my story that helped me to feel rather than to self-punish. To play rather than to stagnate. To follow an impulse and see where it goes. So I honor the tale now that came forth from within me to recall and write down how to love.

Part

I

About An Island

The Blog

Dr. Bradshaw gazed at me from across his conference table with steely blue eyes. "I have two Congressional inquiries and a letter from the Inspector General. I want Dawson fired."

"Dawson. Dawson …"

"Henry Dawson. He's an emergency room doc." He squeezed his hand gripper tightly.

"I don't know him," I answered, straining my memory.

"That's right. You wouldn't. He's been a perfect employee. He even won physician of the year a while back." Bradshaw's tall, muscular body and neatly shaven silver hair created an intimidating presence for most people. The embroidered logo of the Pacific Veterans Rehabilitation Hospital on his perfectly pressed white coat and his Chief of Staff ID badge further underscored his authority to me.

"What did he do?" I mustered the courage I knew was required in dealing with Bradshaw.

"He wrote a blog on his website. I'll forward you the link." His voice was smooth and calculated. He got up from the conference table and towered over me as I remained seated. I smelled the musk in his cologne mark the air around him as he passed behind me to take a seat at his computer. The light accentuated the gel in his hair as he glanced at his emails. He squeezed down on his hand gripper and read for me with a chilling mockery in his voice. "We must bring our soldiers home. The only way to truly prevent Post Traumatic Stress Disorder is to prevent the unnecessary exposure to war." He continued, crossing his arms in annoyance. "Treatment takes a very long time, and the best medicine is primary prevention—to remove the stressor and withdraw from combat."

"He wrote that?" I admired Dr. Dawson's courage, though I saw the problem.

"Yes. I've put him on administrative leave, Martin. Paid."

"I'm sorry."

"Oh come on. That's not why we pay you. I don't need sorry."

"I'm just saying ..."

"That it's going to cost a lot of money and now we're short staffed in the ER. I need you to move quickly on this one, Martin. I need to fire him expeditiously so I can post the position."

"It may be a Hatch Act violation," I told him. I was happy to be useful. "At least at first glance. Seems like he may be using his federal position to influence political agendas." I knew this might be a stretch, but I was thinking on my feet to satisfy Bradshaw.

"Right. That's what I thought. I've drafted this response to the inquiries." He found a document on his desk and raised his eyebrows, indicating that I get up and retrieve it. He had composed a benign bureaucratic note indicating that the facility had placed Dr. Dawson on leave while the case was being investigated. I knew where this was headed.

I took a breath. "This could drag on for a while. You know how it is. He'll probably file an EEO. Or claim age discrimination."

"Or race." The gaze of his eyes was too intense to bear. "He's African American. With an affiliation at the medical school. Full professor. "

"Oh. You're looking at freedom and tenure issues. Constitutional issues—free speech and press."

"We're not going there, Martin. And I don't need you giving me a list of problems and concerns. I need you to find me the law that justifies firing him."

"Right. I can't promise anything fast. I'm telling you this takes time to get it right. Maybe you can get a temporary hire to replace him. Locum tenens or something," I answered, my voice trembling a bit as it trailed off.

"We can't afford that. We have a hiring freeze. You know that. I can't afford to use taxpayer dollars for a doctor to sit at home. Just tell me how to get through this one as quickly as possible." He got up from his desk and returned to the conference table.

"I'll try. But you know as well as I do that nothing happens quickly with federal employees."

"Oh come on. No excuses here." I sensed his frustration with me. "I expect some action. He broke the law. And I have enough to do without this added pressure from Washington. Isn't this why we pay you lawyers? Why does it always have to drag on so long?"

"Okay. Let me start by reviewing the law. First I'll make sure we have a case."

"Martin, we have a case. See these inquiries? Washington says we have a case. So we have a case."

"Do you have a problem with what he wrote?" I asked.

He paused, squinting his eyes. "Are you asking me what I think about war? Or if I believe in PTSD?"

"I just wasn't sure which part of this really disturbed you."

"Oh be serious. I don't like war. Who does? And of course our patients suffer because of it. But that's not the point now, is it?"

But for me, it was. At that moment in my life, I felt differently. I didn't believe our patients came to the hospital as a result of combat after all these years. I saw them as generally rough characters who were likely damaged in some way before they ever got to a battlefield. In some sense, I resented them, as they just added to the humiliation I felt about my job. I had worked hard to get through law school, but had landed at a federal rehab facility. I was even suspicious that some of our patients feigned their symptoms to have free food and a nice place to stay. That's what I believed, though I kept my thoughts to myself.

"What are you thinking?" he asked.

"Oh … nothing." I knew what I was thinking, but the year that followed would prove me wrong. Life was about to teach me some valuable lessons.

"The part that gets me is that we're on the radar now. That's all. Dawson put us on notice in Washington, and we need to get off. They don't do well right now with articles challenging the war efforts. And he broke a law. Plain and simple."

"Right. I'll just sort out our best defense." The last thing I wanted to do was spend my time justifying how to fire another federal employee. While my colleagues from UCLA represented movie stars, I was surrounded by federal employees. And what's worse, I had become one myself. But it was a living, and my kids needed me to make it work.

Dr. Bradshaw grinned and changed his tone. "And while you're doing that, I'm going out to a very fancy dinner this evening."

I relaxed a bit with the shift in focus. "Sounds nice. Where are you going?"

"Greyson's on Sunset. It's a new spot with a top chef. And I've met quite the lady to escort." Bradshaw's history with women had reached near legendary status at the facility. Four past wives, and many beautiful women along the way, including a top model whom he had brought to the fundraiser gala last year.

"What's the occasion?"

"I'm in love," he answered. "I'm dating an actress who's a real hottie." He grinned at me. "It's hard to think of anything else. She's a piece of heaven, really. Recently separated and in need of consoling. She appreciates my wisdom, and I'm helping her find the nerve to divorce. Her husband's a joke. Makes less than she does. But you know, leaving is difficult."

"Right," I answered him. Leaving. I didn't like that word.

"What about you? When are you getting back on the horse, Martin? It's been a while now. What, five years? Six? Longer?"

"I'll get back on when I'm not spending my time figuring out how to fire federal employees. Then maybe I'll think about it again. For now, I'm good." I struggled against the anxiety that this new line of questioning created.

"That's a nice try, Martin. Any excuse to avoid the world. That's how it is for you, isn't it."

"No, I'm just not quite ready to date yet."

"I should say not. Try going shopping for yourself. A few new ties might help you get your groove back. Look at that one—it has an old coffee stain, and I've seen you wear it for years. We all have. You might try pressing your shirts, too.

Heaven knows we pay you lawyers enough." I saw his back fillings as he smirked at me.

"I'll take your thoughts under advisement."

"The gym would help, too."

"Right."

"Don't take offense. I'm just trying to help you out."

"No offense taken."

"Okay. Thanks." Bradshaw raised his eyebrows and smiled at me. "I'll talk to you later in the week." He returned to work at his computer. I sat still at his table. "That's all I have, Martin. Have a good day."

I had missed my exit cue.

My Anniversary

I lay in bed at 5:15 in the morning after a restless night, disturbed by the conversation of the prior afternoon. As I considered the case that had just been assigned, I realized what day it was. August 14. I calculated the years through the fog of my sleepy mind. Today would have been twelve. Happy Anniversary, Lara. Happy fucking anniversary. Once again I recalled the image of my wife leaving for Pagosa Springs, Colorado. It had been nearly seven years since she waved goodbye on the back of a motorcycle, gripping the pelvis of a man she called Major. I assumed that referred to the size of his organ. He could probably keep it up for hours. Lara had finally found the real man she was looking for to take her on true adventures. I remembered Major on the motorcycle. Sweaty white T-shirt, oil stained blue jeans. Six-two and a mass of muscle. Worn leather boots, a black leather jacket. A full head of brown locks flowing from his head to his shoulders. Rough worn skin with a full beard. Piercing green eyes and a wild, wicked smile.

She left the three of us stranded in our small yellow wood rot home in Culver City, a community in West Los Angeles. Lara left me, the home, and full custody of the kids, Nick and Sammie. Sammie was less than a year old when Major pulled up that day, and Nick was only two. Lara had a trust fund left to her by her father and said that was all she needed when she handed me her house key. Major flashed a peace sign as they left for a mountain cabin in southern Colorado. That was my story. Happy Anniversary, Lara.

I looked at the clock. 5:30. I had a familiar tired, wired feeling and wondered how I would make it on five hours of sleep. I donned my worn bathrobe over an old half marathon T-shirt and torn boxer shorts, and I found a pair of holey athletic socks to cover my cold feet. I enjoyed this time of day when people were still sleeping. It reminded me of my high school track and field days, when I was out ahead of the pack. My shoulder bumped into an old Van Gogh poster as I shuffled down the hallway. Most people in my law school cohort had original art to hang on their walls. But I had no room for extra purchases, not even new socks. So "Starry Starry Night" still graced my hallway with the other posters I had bought in college. A Rothko, a Matisse, a Dali. Not originals, not framed, just worn and frayed. But better than empty walls. The only real treasures I had were still sleeping.

The freezer was nearly empty, but I maintained a stock of gourmet coffees. It was my one pleasure, along with an early smoke. I was tired, and the buzzing in my body was intense, an anxiety that I just couldn't settle. I poured the Kona beans into the grinder and filled the stained coffee pot with water.

I caught a glimpse of myself in the bathroom mirror. My wavy brown hair receding with a touch of gray. My pale complexion. I stuck out my chest to stand up straight and tall. But I couldn't hold the pose. I wished I could stretch myself beyond five foot nine. I noticed new crow's feet at the corner of my eyes and dark circles stretching down my face. I could see why Lara left. I looked a good ten years older than 42. I looked like I was dying, and no wonder. I was.

I finished my pee and went back to the kitchen for my favorite mug, twenty years old now, blue and white, with a faded Bradbury University insignia. I sipped quietly as I stared at the room. Piles of unfinished business. There was Sammie's trip slip to be signed, notice of strep in Nick's classroom. Nick's homework packet, the cable bill, a request for a UNICEF donation, an offer for another credit card, a business card from a gardener offering to mow my lawn.

I would get to it tomorrow. That's what I told myself. In between learning about the Hatch Act. I fantasized about a room upstairs, a room above the house where I could look out over the world. My own private study, my own private space, where I could smoke without a hassle and listen to my Best of the '70s CD without interruption. Gilbert O'Sullivan. "Alone

Again, Naturally." A tree house, where I could escape for just a moment and lose myself to the poetry I had studied in college.

I went out front to watch the dawn dissolve into day. The air was cool, and I sat on the porch steps sending smoke rings into the air, wondering how my life, once filled with adventure, had evolved to this. I watched the glow of the street lights disappear as the darkness faded. I was still haunted by the image of Lara leaving. The first car passed, and I knew my time outside was nearing an end. I thought of Emily Dickinson and privately muttered her words.

A little road not made of man,
Enabled of the eye,
Accessible to thill of bee
Or cart of butterfly
If town it have, beyond itself,
'T is that I cannot say;
I only sigh,—no vehicle
Bears me along that way

Morning

Nick was shuffling about early. His asthma had kicked up, and he had a slight wheeze. He was working on a logic problem well beyond my comprehension. Nick wasn't the boy I had imagined raising. He wouldn't play sports, not since he had been slammed in the face with a high fly ball in his first tee-ball game. He told me then through blood soaked toilet paper that he didn't want to play anymore. I figured it was okay, that he could be a runner like me. But then his asthma kicked in. Nick was content to do logic problems and had taken a keen interest in chess. He liked to write long original stories of travel to faraway lands. He was skinny, and his jet black hair always seemed a little greasy and out of place. The glasses he got last year seemed thick for a nine year old. One day I knew he would be beaten up. And he would be wheezing too hard to run away.

His sister Sammie was different. She was my little tiger. She had inherited my speed and a bit of my Teflon coating. I thought she'd probably be a lawyer like me one day. She could negotiate most anything, usually with a smile and an earnest explanation of her side. For now, she did her fighting on the soccer fields. She wore her team jersey around much of the time, and with this, she made me proud. She often scored four or five goals in a game. I cheered wildly on the sidelines, though Nick was often with me and I knew this enthusiasm was difficult for him.

There was a lot to do each weekday morning. Dishes from the dishwasher to the cupboards. The kids' lunches. Breakfast. The beds. Bits of leftover homework. I cut corners where I could. Lunches were usually a prepackaged meal, and I would toss in a piece of fruit and a juice box. Breakfast was a waffle in the toaster. That was cooking. But we were out of everything that morning. No more oatmeal. No more pop tarts. No more bread to toast. That left just cereal. And we were fairly empty in that department as well. I shook the Cheerios box—it was light and filled with crumbs, hardly enough to fill a bowl.

There was just one box of cereal that I had bought months ago. Little Lemurs. I had heard the checkout clerks talking about it, so I grabbed a box. Then I saw what it was—strawberry and banana puff balls. Gluten free, whatever a gluten was. I could never bring myself to give it to the kids. But that morning, I was out of options.

I heard the familiar screams from the back of the house. The kids were up.

"No, it isn't! It's mine! You lost yours! Give it back!" screamed Sammie.

"This is mine and you can't wear it!" Nick answered.

I stormed back to their bedroom. They were fighting over a school T-shirt. I was too tired for this.

"Damn it, do we have to do this every morning?!" They looked at me. We were off to a bad start.

"It's mine, Daddy. And Nick won't give it back." I looked at her locks of dark hair, the replica of her mother's. She gave a little pout that would melt the heart of any father.

"Nick, is it hers?"

"No. Look. It has a stain on the front from when I was painting. But fine. You can give it to her. That's fine." He stormed off to his room. I was too tired to follow.

"Okay, Sammie. Looks like you can wear it."

Nick overheard me from down the hallway. "I didn't say that!" he screamed. "You just like her more!"

"Nick, come on. That's ridiculous. Get dressed and come get breakfast."

"Then tell Sammie that she can't wear the shirt!" he screamed from his bedroom.

"Fine, I won't wear it."

"Is it yours or Nick's?" I asked her quietly.

"I don't know," she replied to me sincerely. "I think maybe Nick's. I just want to wear it. I can't find mine."

As was often the case, Sammie had lured me to her side. I would do anything for her, and they both knew it. Sammie carried her mother's charm, and I was drawn to it. Most of the time the three of us got along fairly well. We generally resolved things by separating and ignoring each other. And we tried as best we could to make it through life together.

Nick and Sammie got themselves dressed, and so did I. I turned up the shower water as hot as I could. I grabbed a towel and dripped water across the bathroom floor. I stared at the shirts in my closet. I hadn't bought new clothes in seven years, and the fraying collars were getting tight. It had been years since I had exercised, and I had put on a good ten pounds. I had five suits, one for each day. Bradshaw seemed to know that. I wondered what he'd say if he saw my wardrobe. My ties looked old and worn hanging across the bar in my closet. I kept them hanging in a noose tie, so the knot would always be in the same place, to preserve them as long as I could. That morning, on August 14, 2010, my closet looked like a gallows.

The kids made their way to the kitchen, and just as easily as they had settled into fighting, they began a new conversation. Nick was explaining chess to Sammie, and she was interested. I was not. I turned to the cereal box to disappear from the conversation that I somehow found humiliating. The back of the box caught my eye and I started to read. About the island of Madagascar, the only natural home to ring tail lemurs. And the problems they faced from humans hunting them and turning them into pets.

As Nick explained the concept of castling to Sammie, I imagined a pet lemur, swinging around our house, making a mess of my piles of paper. I wondered how they trapped them. I wondered how you got one. Then I looked up at the clock and saw 7:25. We had to go in five minutes.

"Hurry up and eat, guys."

They didn't listen. "Well, I don't get why you would want to do that," Sammie said to her brother.

"To protect the king. It forms a wall around him so no one can get to him."

"But then he's stuck, and he can't move."

"You don't need to move him. You need to protect him.

Then you can use your other pieces to get your opponent's king."

Though I didn't much care for chess, this particular discussion caught my attention. To form a wall around the king so no one could get to him. That's what I had done. It had started when my mother died, then my father. And then my best friend, Danny. I had built a wall around myself, and no one could get to me. Not Lara, not my old track friends, not my three sisters. I lived in my own private world. I guess I had been castled. Protected by Nick and Samantha.

"Come on and eat. We have to leave."

"What is this stuff, Dad?" asked Nicholas.

"Just something I picked up at the store. Strawberry and banana puff balls."

"What's it called?" asked Sammie.

"Little Lemurs," I answered.

She laughed. "Little lemurs? What's a lemur?"

"It's a monkey that lives on Madagascar," I answered.

"Where's that?" she asked.

"Madagascar? It's an island near Africa."

"Well, it's good," said Nicholas as he spooned it into his mouth.

I rushed them along. "We've got to go guys. You can bring whatever you want in the car."

They finally heard me. Sammie grabbed her pink backpack and got her Dora the Explorer lunchbox from the refrigerator. Nick got his books and grabbed a calculator on the way out the door. I opened the car doors, and they shuffled into the back seat.

I got in the car, still entertaining myself with the thought of a pet lemur. In my mind, I named him Elliot. I enjoyed the image of him swinging around my kitchen. He threw around the laundry. He shit on the table. He threw the oranges and broke a window. I thought maybe I could tame him. I saw him pounding out the bump in the kitchen linoleum. I saw him organize my piles of papers, finishing my Unfinished Business. I imagined him reciting Robert Frost. Or Dickinson. Or Cummings. I was transforming him into a personal assistant, the most civilized lemur in the world. The ultimate pet.

The Jeep Cherokee had a heavy dust glaze that turned it blue-brown. There were papers covering the passenger seat. I knew some were important and belonged in my briefcase. The back seat was worse. Old banana peels, pretzel crumbs, water bottles.

Nicholas pulled out the calculator and gave it to Sammie.

"Quiz me on my multiplication. I'll say a fact, and you put it in and see if I'm right."

"Okay," she answered. Sammie was munching on cereal balls. She had brought the whole box into the car.

"Alright. Put in 18 times 6," Nick instructed.

I looked behind me. "You guys need to strap in."

And they did. I reversed the car out of the garage once I heard the click of the seat belts.

The Intersection

I saw Jane, our next door neighbor, watering her plants as we pulled out. She was peacefully focused on her task, surrounded by the beautiful flower beds thriving around her. She had lived there since we moved in thirteen years ago. Her yellow shirt lit up the street like a bit of sunshine on an otherwise gray day in L.A. I figured Jane to be about my age, but her worn face gave her an added sense of wisdom. It seemed she did nothing artificial. No creams or salons, no manicures or fancy clothes. And her natural radiance was alluring to me.

The juxtaposition was noticeable. My chaotic home, piles everywhere, dead plants gracing my backyard. My insomnia, irritability, and multiple tasks each morning to get us going. There she stood, so calmly, enjoying the simple task of watering her plants. Jane never seemed rushed or in a hurry. I didn't know much about her. Only that she worked part time as a teacher at a nearby elementary school and that she grew up in Carson City, close to Lake Tahoe. Her mom used to have a story time for the community in a large teepee at their home. She once wondered if Nick and Sammie had any experiences like that. I told her no—that they liked stories, but that they didn't hear many. And there was no teepee around.

Jane brought over harvests from time to time, and the fruit was spectacular. I supposed I could do that, too, if I had the time. I mean, if you could hang a fruit for every employee I helped fire, I would have an orchard. I always thanked her for the gifts and then told her how busy we were. In Nick's language, she was the opponent's queen, and I was castled in. I would quickly shoo her from the front door. I never let her in. As the sounds of math problems rang through from the back seat, Jane caught me staring. She gave me a big smile as our car backed up from the driveway. I waved, did a three point turn, and went on my way.

I pulled away and drove up to Coombs Avenue. It was a beautiful day, and joggers were running on both sides of the street. This was the L.A. crowd, and they all looked beautiful. Some were teenagers, some must have been 75, but no one looked a day over thirty. A young woman in her early twenties came running down my side of the street as we puttered up to Coombs. Tight sports bra, bright orange shorts. Long blonde hair. She looked up and smiled at me. I felt a little better, like I was part of the world for a moment. Then I wondered who she would be sleeping with that night. Some Hollywood executive from the nearby studios. Or maybe Bradshaw. I got a surge of envy as I turned the car to the right and got my customary glimpse of the Veterans Memorial Park. I had good memories of the place. I raised Sammie and Nick on the playground there. I used to try to run there with Nick in a stroller. But after Lara left, my life grew too hectic, and I had given up running in favor of smoking a half pack a day.

Fresh dew on the bright green lawns reflected bits of sunlight. Begonias, pansies, and roses bloomed everywhere in Culver City, the seat of Hollywood studios. These beautiful people kept in shape exercising each morning. I felt bad just looking at them. The memory of my haggard face in the mirror came to me as I saw people of all ages walking dogs or chatting in pairs on a return from their visit to the local coffee shop. No one seemed to be as rushed as I felt every morning of my life.

I drove down Coombs and stopped at Lindblade Street. This was the course I drove each morning to get the kids to school. I passed through the stoplight at Lindblade. There was a house that I liked there. It was different from the rest. It was built of adobe and looked like it belonged in New Mexico. I wondered what it looked like inside and on some days was half tempted just to ring the doorbell, like I might have many years ago. In the backseat, "11 times 14" from Samantha. "154" from Nick.

We pulled up to the stop sign at Braddock. I pressed on the brakes for a moment and no one was coming, so I drove through. It was 7:54, and school started at 8:00. The light was green up ahead at Garfield. I could sense the fatigue from my sleepless night slowing me down a bit, and I was trying to overcome it. My eyes wanted to shut. I wished they had felt that way the night before.

I passed through the green light still imagining knocking on the door of that adobe home to see what it looked like inside. That's when I saw a car coming from the right, and I didn't understand it.

"Whoa … Shit." I said aloud. I accelerated, trying to get through the intersection so he would miss me. I looked for the briefest moment into oncoming traffic and saw there was nobody coming. I leaned away from the other car, as if leaning would keep me from being hit. The jeep swerved with me, heading across the double yellow line. My instincts took over. No more time for thinking. He was coming too fast.

I heard a loud slam as my car was hit, and we started to roll. The left side of the car lifted off the ground. I recall breaking sounds. Scraping. Crunching. The windshield shattering. Then I was on my head, suspended from the ceiling for just a moment like an amusement park ride. The car tilted again, the left side of the vehicle sliding along the asphalt. Glass breaking. I gripped the steering wheel and tried to hold on. And then four tires on the ground with a little bounce. Smoke wafting up from the front of my car, dancing.

The car had stopped. For a second I sat there. The windshield was gone, much of it in shards on my lap. I saw Sammie's pink lunch box hanging from the rear view mirror.

There were no more math facts from the back seat. No sounds at all.

"Sammie! Nick!" I cried. I knew I had to turn. I imagined two dead children, cut with glass, in pools of blood. I imagined unconsciousness and strewn body parts.

I turned my head and looked at them, strapped squarely in their seats. They stared right back at me. There was no blood. There were no bruises. They were both in one piece belted in against the blue leather of the back seat, still and quiet.

"Are you okay, guys?" I unbuckled myself.

"Yeah, we're fine, Daddy," Nick answered.

"We're okay, Daddy," Sammie said. She smiled at me for a second holding back tears.

"Let's get out of here." I opened my door, and it fell lose from the hinge. I went into the street, and opened the back door on Nick's side. I reached in and undid his belt, pulling him free. Then I reached across and dragged Sammie to me.

"Careful, guys. There's glass everywhere," I said as I rushed them out.

"Daddy," Sammie cried, holding me tight around the neck as I excavated her from the car.

"What the fuck are you doing!? You fucking asshole!" I heard someone scream.

"I'm sorry." I mumbled to the unknown voice. I felt Nickie holding onto my leg and I pulled him close.

"Not you! That asshole kid ran that light. He slammed right into you. You spun over twice. You should all be fucking dead! Look at that asshole!" The man came running to us. So did another woman. We moved from the street to the sidewalk.

"I have a phone!!" she screamed.

"Call 911!" the man answered. "Call 911!"

From the sidewalk I saw the car. It was spun around 180 degrees. The roof above the front passenger seat had caved in completely. Had someone been sitting there, they would surely be dead. The window on that side had shattered as well. The tires were all flat. There was oil spilling from the car and steam rising from the hood. The mirror had been knocked from the side. There were bashes and dents all over, and the windshield was completely shattered, little glass pieces hanging like small icicles, most of it gone. The car had hit right behind where Sammie was sitting. If I hadn't accelerated, he would have plowed right into her.

"We're at Coombs and um ... Garfield," the lady said on the phone. "Okay. They're all here on the sidewalk. They walked out of the car." She turned to the man. "The paramedics will be right here."

"Fucking asshole kid. Where is he?" asked the man. With his long gray hair, moustache, and bandana, he looked like one of Major's friends.

Sammie broke into tears. She started to scream. Then Nick followed.

"It's okay. We're okay." I wanted to walk away now. I didn't care about anything except getting out of there and pretending that it had never happened.

I put my face down to Sammie and looked into her eyes. "Listen to me, kiddo. You're okay. You did amazing. Okay? There's no reason to cry. We're okay."

"What the hell?" said the man. "His car's right there, but I don't see the kid. I don't know where he went. He drove right through the fucking intersection. His light was red."

His light was red. Nothing was my fault. I couldn't believe it. I assumed it was my fault. I always assumed everything was my fault.

The lady came and sat next to Sammie and Nick. "You guys are like heroes. How did you know how to survive a car accident like that?"

Sammie smiled at her. The lady wiped away Sammie's tears. "We just did it." She got a little proud.

"Maybe you have super powers," the woman said.

I felt some strangely loving feelings in my chest. "They do. This is Nick. He is one of the smartest boys in the world. He must have figured out how to hold on and stay in his seat as we were spinning around. And Sammie here, she figures out how to make it through anything."

I heard the sound of sirens. A large firetruck arrived at the intersection. Paramedics jumped out. They ran over to us. One of them had large stuffed animals in his hand. He gave a polar bear to Nick and a Cheetah to Samantha.

"Here you go, guys," he said. "Look what you did! You made it through a big car accident!"

The other one had a blood pressure cuff. "Everyone gets only one accident in their lives," he said. "Looks like you made it through yours. Congratulations, you guys. You don't have anything to worry about from here on out."

"That's right," said the first.

"I still haven't had mine," said the lady joining in. "I have to drive around nervous. You guys can rest easy now." Sammie was smiling now.

"I need to take your blood pressure, okay?" said the paramedic. The kids were joining in now.

"Sure," said Nick, more heroically. "I've done that before at the doctor's."

"That's right. Same thing."

I thought of the mess in my car, now that my children were well attended to. I went to start collecting what belongings I could. I walked out into the street. Police had arrived now, and they were redirecting traffic. Orange cones, yellow tape. I went under the tape and opened the passenger door.

"Sir, what are you doing?" said the officer. "You need to get away from the car."

"Oh, sorry. I just want to try to get my stuff."

"Well hurry and grab it and get away from the car. I don't know what that smoke is. It could catch fire any time."

I nodded my head and grabbed what I could. I took my briefcase. It was on the floor of the passenger seat. I took Sammie's lunchbox from the rear view mirror. I grabbed her pink backpack from the back seat. Nick's backpack had flown to the front seat, under glass. I shimmied away the shards to get it. I didn't care if I cut my hand. The loose pages that had been on the front seat were everywhere. I searched for my cell phone but couldn't find it. Glass everywhere. And under the glass in the back were hundreds of pink and white cereal balls.

"Sir, you need to move away from the vehicle." I walked back toward the kids who were encircled by the paramedics and the lady. But before I could get there, a boy stopped me at the sidewalk. He was young, about fifteen. He had dark hair, a dark complexion. I didn't know who he was or where he came from. He looked worried, a bit stunned. He wore a white undershirt and a pair of green pants with a hole in the knee. They were smeared with a fresh black stain by his front belt loop.

"Excuse me, mister, can you give me a ride home to my mom?" Then I knew who it was. It was the boy who hit me. This was crazy. Was he on drugs? I looked around for the police. No one seemed interested in him.

"Oh, look, I'm sorry. My car's a bit of a mess right now. See? I don't think it will make it to your house." He looked at me. I got pissed and turned away. I passed a police officer coming to question the boy.

Sammie was recovered, fully engaged in conversation with the lady while Nick stared off into his own private world. I was relieved that no one was crying. I knew that I had many tasks ahead. We should document a doctor's visit. I would need to rent a car. We had no way to get home. I would have to call someone. I could not imagine leaning on my sisters. I tried my secretary but she didn't answer. I left a message on the machine.

"Hey, Dorrie, something has come up and I won't be coming in today. I'll see you Monday morning. I don't have my phone but you can call me at home if it's urgent." I couldn't bring myself to say what happened. I was trying hard to pretend that it hadn't.

I knew of only one person who was home.

"Can I use your phone?" I asked the lady. And I called Jane.

Afterwards

Jane told Nick and Sammie about an accident she had been in.

"Marty, why don't you just let me take the kids back to my house? We can color, I'll make them lunch."

"They need to get checked by a doctor."

"They seem okay," she said. And they did. I knew that down the road, an insurance claim would be worth more with every doctor's visit we accumulated. And that we should document everything right now. But for the kids, there was nothing to record. I had an aching pain in my left shoulder and neck, and I knew I needed to be checked. But the kids were fine. At least physically.

I couldn't seem to get through this one by myself. So I took Jane up on it, and she took the kids home. I got a rental car—a white Volvo. Not your typical rental, but I was willing to pay the difference at that point for safety. And I went to my doctor, Dr. Megg.

The drive to his office was nerve wracking. At each intersection, I was certain that a car was coming at me. Though I saw each vehicle slowing to a halt, I imagined them driving right into me. This happened in every intersection. I pulled over for a rest and a breath. The experience continued, as I slowed down to nearly ten miles per hour at each green light. Even small alleys had me slowing down and swerving to the left. I had developed a fear of intersections. I pulled into Dr. Megg's office, anxious to tell him what had happened. I had known him for ten years now, and I knew he would be beside himself with my story.

I dressed in a gown. Weight: 181 pounds. Ten pounds up over last year. Blood pressure: up. I was sure that must be from the accident. Pulse: 115. I was led into the exam room, where I waited. Dr. Megg was a shrunken man, nearly seventy. Bald, glasses. He usually had a smile for me, but not today. He was very busy and a bit distracted.

"What can I do for you, Mr. Grossmark? Looks like your weight's up a bit. Blood pressure, too."

"I was just in a car accident. A bad one. A kid ran a light and ..."

"You want me to check you out?" he replied. I thought I saw his eyes roll. "What happened?"

I began my account of the accident. He looked in my ears, my mouth, and my nose. He felt my neck.

"Turn all the way to your left. Okay good, now to your right. Good. Maybe a little decreased motion to the left, not bad though."

"It hurts there, on the left shoulder." He felt it. I wanted to finish my story.

"Wouldn't hurt to get some plain films. Maybe try some ibuprofen. See how you do."

He didn't want to listen to me. He put his stethoscope to his ears and listened to my chest. I never finished the story. A car accident, big deal. He was in no mood for my story.

"If it persists, we can try physical therapy. You need to get your weight down, though. I don't like it creeping up like this."

Dr. Megg had been one constant in my life. It had been good to know I had a doctor who knew me. But today I was just another patient. A nuisance and a bother. I couldn't imagine he'd be helpful if this ever went to court. I had wanted him to hear my story. I wanted anyone to hear my story. But there wasn't anyone who would care. I thought about my sisters. About Dorrie, my secretary. And Dr. Bradshaw. Truthfully, I hadn't shown much concern about their lives, and I couldn't imagine they would care about mine.

"Anything else?" he asked.

"Well, yes, actually. On the way over, when I was driving, it seemed like cars were coming at me from the right. They were stopping, but in my mind it seemed like they kept rolling toward me."

"That'll go away," he responded. "It's normal following an accident. Sometimes it lingers. Then it's Post Traumatic Stress Disorder. But it won't. Not after just a car accident.

Why don't you get dressed, and I'll leave the X-ray request and prescription at the desk."

It was just a car accident. No big deal. Maybe it would be PTSD. Like the veterans at the hospital where I worked. The ones Dr. Dawson had written about. I hadn't cared a damn about their experience. For a moment I wondered how our doctors treated them. Were they as burnt out as mine? I imagined they were worse—they were federal employees. He left me alone in the office. I took off the hospital gown and put my clothes on. I shoved my tie into my pocket and left the office.

I stopped by Spellman's Bakery on the way home to grab some treats for the morning. It had been a while since I had visited, and it would be good to see Frannie, the owner of the bakery.

"Marty!" Frannie greeted me. "Where have you been all my life?"

My heart warmed when I saw her. Frannie was easily over 80, with dentures too big for her little mouth. Her hair and red apron were smeared with flour. She was a small woman with a raspy smoker's voice and a slight Texas drawl, and her squared off little body seemed toned enough to still jump into a rodeo ring. Her smile gave a glow to Spellman's that had kept customers coming for decades.

"I've been busy. You know, work and the kids. I was in an accident, Frannie. A bad one."

"Well then come over tomorrow night. Everyone misses you. I'll sing you a great number."

"The car flipped over. It rolled. I was with the kids."

"Oh, honey. That's terrible. Even more reason to come to the club. Tell me what I can get you. The kids want some rugulah?"

"That'd be great. Maybe a dozen."

"I've got a new song I'm singing. Come hear. It'll take your mind off the accident."

She searched for the best pastries, coughing while she worked. I glanced at the door to my left. It was closed during the day, hiding what was reserved for Saturday nights. Only the smell of cigarettes gave a clue to what lay beyond. Behind the locked door was a large windowless room with black walls and glittered party strands hanging from the ceiling. I could envision the small black tables and chairs surrounding a stage. I had stumbled in on a whim a few years back, and I visited a couple of times a year—generally when I was feeling lonely.

Deep inside the bakery, Spellman's was a smoky, alcohol free karaoke parlor for the elderly of West Los Angeles, and I was enchanted from the moment I discovered them. I must have been the youngest in the room by a good thirty years. On my first visit, the room was jammed, each patron holding a rhythm instrument of some kind. They surrounded a dapper old man singing "Moon River" in front of a wall sized monitor. He wore a bow tie and a felt hat, performing like this was his finest moment. Surrounding him, each person shook a shaker of some sort, keeping time to the music. Frannie was my favorite, holding a small black plastic egg that she waved back and forth with her thin but determined arm, slightly off the beat. She welcomed me in that night, begged me to sit next to her, and handed me her extra egg. As the years passed, I could always count on seeing her there. I didn't have many friends at that point in my life, so the karaoke council of elders was my one place of connection outside of my two kids. A refuge from the dreariness that my life had become and a place where I felt strangely alive again. But it had been nearly a year since I had passed through the door to my left.

"I can't. The kids ..."

"Get a sitter," she told me, and looked up from the pastries with a smile. "We really miss you."

"I miss you, too." I smiled. My eyes softened for a moment.

She handed me a pink box. "Good. Then it's settled. We'll see you tomorrow night! Maybe you'll finally get up and sing."

"One day, maybe."

"I'm glad everyone's okay. Someone must be on your side." She smiled at me, and I waved goodbye.

I picked the kids up from Jane's. They had drawn pictures with her. Nick had drawn the three of us hanging upside down in a car, hanging in the sky by a cloud. We were about to fall back down to the ground. And his mother was there, on the ground, on the corner of the page with her back to all of us, staring at the edge of the paper. Sammie's picture was a little more hopeful. She drew a picture of a fireman giving her a stuffed cheetah. And another one of Jane standing with her and Nick eating ice cream cones.

I brought the kids home, and we watched television and ate frozen lasagna. None of us ate much, and Sammie fell asleep with her head on my chest. Nick dozed off on the other end of the couch. It dawned on me that I had broken a promise. It had been my job to make sure that no more bad things happened, and I had violated the contract. They had been touched by the outer world, and now they knew that it was filled with bad things. A dangerous world that could come crashing through at any moment. And Dad couldn't stop it. He couldn't stop it when Mom left, and now he couldn't stop it again. I scratched Sammie's head and wondered what would have happened if I hadn't swerved. I tried to fend off the feeling, but it was there. Somehow, I had done well. I had strapped them in. I had averted catastrophe. Frannie was right—someone out there was on my side. Someone wanted us to live. I think that's when I decided that I would. That I would live. And I carried them off to bed.

Knocking

I had dozed off without medication and was in a deep sleep when I felt a tapping on my shoulder.

"Dad, I can't sleep. I saw something."

I was confused. "Nick, you need to go back to sleep."

"I can't. I saw something. It was like a gorilla. Outside my window. Can you come look?"

"There's nothing there. Just go back to sleep."

"Dad, really. Can you come?" I got out of bed, and we walked down the hall to Nick's room.

"He keeps banging on the window. Like he wants to play or something. He's outside in the ivy. He keeps running back and forth. I thought it was like a dog. But it's not. It's some kind of ape or gorilla or something."

"I'm sure it's just the wind," I responded.

"No, Dad, I saw him. It's not the wind."

We walked into his room. I flicked on the light, and we peered out the window.

"There!" Nick screamed. "See him! He's waving!"

"What? Where, Nick?" I looked into the bed of ivy, but there was nothing there.

"He's gone! He just disappeared. Like he waved goodbye when you came in."

"I don't think there's a gorilla out there."

"There's not now! He left when he saw you, Dad."

"Okay, then. Go to sleep, Nickie. He's gone. We all need to get some sleep."

"But Dad, he's gonna come back! As soon as you leave!"

"Come on, Nick. You're nine years old. You ..." I stopped myself. I looked at him. And I decided to do something different. Sometimes I wonder what course my life would have taken if I had just told Nick to go to bed. But I smiled at him, and I put my hand on his shoulder.

"Okay, kiddo. I'll sleep with you in here. Let me go get a

sleeping bag." And off I went. I found the camping supplies on a shelf in the garage. I had kept them stored away since my travels with Danny, my best friend from college, but I had never used them with the kids. I found my old blue mummy bag, the one I had taken with Danny to Nepal, Africa, Indonesia … all over the world. I hadn't used it in nearly twenty years. Nick had followed me into the garage. I looked back and saw him in the doorway.

"I don't want to be alone in there."

"Right, sorry kiddo. I was just getting a sleeping bag. Do you want one? Would it be better to be down on the ground, in case he comes back?"

"Maybe. But I've never used one before. I don't know how."

"It's easy. I have this one here." I took out the other sleeping bag. It had belonged to Danny. His mother had given it to me at his memorial. Along with his knife, which I had lost. The sleeping bag had been in storage up on a shelf. I couldn't believe I was about to unpack it.

"This is a good one, Nickie. It belonged to an old friend of mine. He let me have it when he didn't need it anymore. He used to tell me it was magic and would keep anything away."

I threw it to Nick, and off we went into his room. We unstuffed our bags, there at 2:30 in the morning, to begin our camping journey right there on Nickie's floor. And as Nick unrolled his sleeping bag, a book thumped onto the floor.

"What's this, Dad?" I looked on the floor, and I knew what it was. I hadn't known that I had been given that, too. It was Danny's old journal from when we traveled. He used to write in it late at night when we drifted off to sleep. I felt anxiety race through my blood the moment I saw it.

"Oh, that's my friend's old journal." I picked it up and put it by the head of my bag. The old leather binding smelled sweet after years without air.

We spread out our bags next to each other. I got into mine as Nick watched, and then he mirrored my motion.

"I like it in here, Dad."

"Yeah, it's fun. Maybe we can do it outside one day."

"No—the gorilla."

"I mean in a while. Once we know he's gone for sure. We could use a tent, you know, to protect us."

"A tent? He could just knock it down." Nick was getting sleepy as we chatted.

"Well then maybe something stronger."

"Like a motor home?" he muttered as he fell off to sleep.

The image made me smile. "Maybe just some kind of really strong tent. Like a teepee."

Nick fell off to sleep. I didn't think any more about the car accident. Or Dawson's case. I thought about Danny. I had managed to keep him far from my mind for years. But the memories marched back in, one after another, with the unrolling of his sleeping bag. One image from Gbamandu, West Africa. Another from Cheskham, a village in Nepal. Another from Alaska. I looked over at my son fast asleep, safe from the gorilla outside, and I drifted off to sleep.

I woke up early, about 5:45. The dawn light through the window gave the journal a glow. Quietly I moved from my bag. And I opened it.

July 2, 1985

We climbed these steps all day. I think I could live in Nepal.
I like my new tweed hat. I get lots of comments about it on
the trails. The Sherpa are pretty funny. They run on up the
mountain, then they smoke cigarettes at the top. They call
them "stamina sticks." Marty tried to lecture them about the
ills of smoking. They just laughed at us. The others in our
group were a little grumpy today, especially Bernadette who
is pretty overweight. I don't know if she'll make the whole
week travel to Cheskham. Today we sang as we walked.
I was trying to remember the lyrics to an old song. "Thank
You for Being a Friend." I'm not sure why that song came to
me today. Marty remembered that it was Andrew Gold. He's
a freak about '70s music. We kept singing as we stepped
up the mountains. There were prayer carvings on the rocks
every so often. As we walked through small villages, the
children all smiled and said "Namaste." It didn't seem like
they wanted anything from us except to say "Namaste." Their
smiles were cool. Between villages we would sing. Between
us, Marty and I figured out most of the words, and made up
a few new verses. "Thank You for Being a Friend." I can't
get it out of my head now. We sang the last line over and
over again as we walked up the steps. That's one thing I love
about Marty—he'll just sing and doesn't care where he is or
who's listening. He never seems to get embarrassed. It was
cool getting drunk on a song. Like you would "A Hundred
Bottles of Beer on the Wall." But it was "Thank You for Being
a Friend" as we stepped up and up the mountain passing
smiling Namastes.

The Next Day

Nick was relieved the gorilla didn't return that night. It was Saturday morning, and we had nowhere we had to go. Sammie talked all about the accident. She seemed on top of the world that we had survived. Nick wanted to think about anything else, and he immersed himself in the chess set.

"Then Dad said, 'Whoa!' and I saw this white car coming into me."

"Sammie, can you stop? I'm trying to figure out this move. If your rook is over there, and your bishop there…."

"Then I can barely remember it. Daddy, what happened next?"

"I don't remember much either," I answered her. I looked for something for breakfast.

"Nick, do you remember spinning around?" she asked.

"No! Can you shut up? I need to figure this out."

"What do you guys feel like for breakfast?"

"I want cereal, Dad," answered Sammie right away. "That new kind—the Little Leprechauns."

"You mean lemurs? The Little Lemurs strawberry and banana balls?"

"Yeah, those."

"Those are all gone. You brought them in the car. They were all over the backseat." I kept looking in the pantry.

Sammie got quiet at the thought of the lost cereal, and Nick tuned into the conversation. "Is a lemur like a gorilla?" he asked.

"Not quite. They're a little different." I kept searching the pantry. I saw nothing. Just some old flour. Sugar. Baking soda. I had bought this all some time back when I had an inkling to cook.

"How about pancakes?" I stared at the sack of flour as I awaited their response. I knew that I could never make pancakes from a box. My father would have wrung my neck. We had few family traditions, but pancakes on the weekends had been one. We had always looked forward to it. Dad would make them exactly the same each week. Though he had become more reclusive after Mom passed away, he always came to life when he made pancakes. He would tell us stories over breakfast. One series was about Sheriff Fred, the great nine-year-old superhero who would capture the bandits of the wild west. He had told that story just for me. I had never made any pancakes for my kids. And I hadn't told any stories. I always had too much to do.

"No thanks," Nick answered me, lost in his chess pieces.

"Nick, come on and help me. Grab the measuring cup."

"Dad …"

"You need to eat breakfast. You have all day to do that."

"I'll get it, Dad!" Sammie was excited to help. She knew exactly where the measuring cup was. And as she got into it, so did Nick. We went to work. Sammie got out the big metal bowl. She slid it up onto the small kitchen island. There were four old gas burners there which I had never cleaned. At first, Nick watched. I called out the recipe from my mind, and Sammie ran around laughing as she collected the ingredients. Flour. Sugar. Eggs. She grabbed the stepstool from the laundry room so she could reach the mixing bowl. She held the bag of flour up to pour it into the measuring cup. Like magic fairy dust, the flour floated into the air and bowl simultaneously and covered Sammie's long dark hair.

"You're making a mess, Sammie! Let me do it!" Nick exclaimed.

"No—you didn't want to help!"

"Well now I do because you're making a mess!"

"It's okay, Nick," I interrupted him. "Do you know how to crack eggs?"

"Yeah. I can do that." He proceeded, getting shell bits in the eggs and picking them out with his fingers.

I heated the pan, and we poured the pancakes. We made a mess. Batter on the burners, on the tile, on the floor, on their PJs. We were laughing a kind of laugh that I hadn't felt in quite some time. And for the first time in years, just above my breath, I sang Elton John as we cooked.

The pancakes came out okay. Nick was inspired, and he set the table with enthusiasm. He took out the finest plates we had, stored in the lower cupboards. I was surprised he knew where they were. The Blue Garland pattern, with blue cornflowers dancing around the rim tied together with raspberry vines. Lara thought they were a bother to clean so we never used them.

I brought the first plate to the table, and the kids sat down.

"So Dad," Nick said in a confident voice. "Tell us a story."

"Okay." I surprised myself. I hadn't made up a story since I was very young. But something was ready to come out of me. "What do you want to hear about?"

"Lemurs!" answered Sammie. "Like on the cereal box."

"Lemurs? Okay. Well I don't know so much."

"Yes you do, Daddy," chimed Samantha. "Just tell us."

"But I really don't."

"Tell us what you know. And make up the rest. We'll try to figure out if it's real or not," answered Nick.

Nick wanted a story. So far I had been successful. I had strapped them in. I had swerved the car. I had unwrapped Danny's sleeping bag and driven the gorilla from the ivy. I had discovered secret ingredients in the pantry and found myself singing a '70s tune. This was a very different kind of breakfast.

"Okay," I answered. I thought a bit. I did know a little about lemurs. I had visited the Duke Lemur Center in North Carolina at one point in my life. And I had read the back of the cereal box. I recalled a few facts. And the rest I was going to have to make up.

"Well, let's see. Lemurs live mostly on Madagascar. It's an island off of Eastern Africa, off of Mozambique. The island used to be part of the mainland. But it separated millions of years ago."

"How did it separate?" asked Sammie. "Did someone cut them apart?"

"No, oh no. It was through erosion. Just a natural process

of how the earth moves around. You know, like we have earthquakes."

"Are we going to separate out from the country?" Sammie seemed a bit nervous. I knew I had better be careful with my storytelling.

"Yes. We are. People talk about it all the time," Nick responded. "Southern California is going to disappear under the ocean one day."

"No! Daddy is that true?" Sammie looked frightened, as she grabbed a pancake in her hand and shoved it in her mouth.

"No. We're talking about processes that take millions of years. So let me keep going…." I paused and watched them eat. I was lucky to have such an audience.

"So back when they separated, the lemurs floated away on the island that we now call Madagascar, where they could be free and powerful. They were at the top of the food chain, with no one to threaten them. The rest of the lemurs left in Africa had troubles. Gorillas and apes ate their food. And the lemurs couldn't survive very well. But on Madagascar, they were safe and happy."

"I like it there," smiled Nick. "No gorillas or apes. That sounds like a good place."

"Right. It was. And as time went on, it became a beautiful island. Palm trees up against a beautiful beach. And right in from the coast, there was a little special forest called Paden's. Paden's Patch. And you could get there from the beach. Right at …" I looked over at the table and my eyes caught the china. "Right at Blue Garland Landing."

I came to sit down with another plate of pancakes. I started to eat, and Sammie was impatient. "Who lives on the island now? I mean in Paden's Patch?"

I swallowed a bite. It was much better than the frozen waffles we had been eating each morning. I looked around at the kitchen. Flour, batter, eggshells, packages. A mess. It looked like my pet lemur had indeed leapt right off the cereal box. And I guessed it was time to tame him.

"Well, the lemurs, they went through a lot of evolution. And they got real smart. In the most recent generation, there were four brothers and sisters. Elliot was the main one. He liked to think a lot. And he had a brother Carlos, and Jasper, and a sister Rosalie." I was thinking quickly. I didn't know where this was coming from or where I was going.

"I think this part isn't true," smiled Nick.

"It is now," I answered him smartly. "And so the lemurs had a good life there, there in Paden's Patch. Since there were no gorillas or apes to worry about, they could swing freely in the forest. But they did have some problems. It seemed like every lemur had some special characteristic that got in its way."

I took another bite of my pancake and let my imagination go wild. "Elliot was a very smart lemur. He liked to read a lot … he especially liked poetry, like … Frost. He liked Robert Frost."

"What?" challenged Nick.

"He liked poetry," answered Sammie. "Robert Frost. Just listen, Nick."

"That's right. He did. He lived in a big tree house that shot up above the forest. It had big bay windows, and he could see everything down below. On this particular day, it had rained for over a week, and he was getting bored inside."

"So what was his characteristic?" asked Nick.

"Who, Elliot? Oh, he was a thinker. Sometimes he spent so much time reading and thinking that he forgot how to play. And he could scare himself with his thoughts. Particularly when he thought about evolution. He had heard about other lands where gorillas and apes could hurt lemurs. And he had read about what lemurs become when they evolve. So he thought it was safer to stay on an island than to risk changing too much."

I continued my tale. As I narrated, the kids stopped questioning me and enjoyed my voice. I talked as we ate and cleaned up. For the moment, I forgot about Lara, Dawson's case, and the car crash. I became absorbed with the lemurs in Paden's Patch.

It had rained for seven days and all the animals in the forest had grown restless. The world had become very small for Elliot all alone in his tree house. More than anything, he wanted to jump out his window to swing. But since he couldn't, he just allowed his mind to play …

He pictured himself bursting through his maple wood door, clad in his finest bright red bathing suit, swinging through the trees and howling to awaken the others. Elliot was a good-sized lemur with a well toned body. His body was dusky gray, his face and ears white as snow dotted by auburn colored eyes beneath a black facemask. His fur was coarse. Most in the troop looked similar, distinguished by the rings around their long tails.

He imagined howling as he launched through the trees, every lemur staring up at him. He swung through the branches, drenched with rain in his new red bathing suit. That would be a hoot. Certainly that would surprise the others. He wasn't known to be carefree, and he wasn't known as a playful swinger. Elliot the thinker. That was his reputation.

The storm grew louder. Elliot sipped his Kona coffee and paced to the sound of the rain. He gazed around his study. His bookshelf displayed his heroes. Plato. Kipling. Locke. Descartes. Dr. Seuss. Frank L Baum. Orwell. Rousseau. Darwin … Some of these books he had collected, left behind by visitors to the forest. Others had been given to him by his father, Max. Elliot saw his favorite and took it off the shelf. He didn't need to open it as he knew the poems inside by heart. He often had imaginary conversations with the author and thought of him as a special friend. He looked at the worn cover and could scarcely make out the letters. F-R-O-S-T. He sank back into his desk chair with the comfort of his companion. He recited his favorite out loud to the last line … "One could do worse than be a swinger of birches." As he closed the book, he tried to recall the last time he had gone swinging and wondered why he had stopped.

Carlos' Search

We had finished our pancakes, but the kids didn't move from the table. I took the dishes to the dishwasher.

"Keep going," said Nick.

"No, that's enough for this morning. I'll finish it another time."

"Daddy, you just started. That's just about Elliot. What about the others?"

"Yeah. You said there were four. Tell us about another one."

I had a lot of work to do. I had to read up on Dawson's case. But I was having fun. I looked at Sammie and Nick, and I flashed to our rolling in the car. I saw the glass in my lap, and Sammie's lunch box on the rear view mirror. I recalled turning my head to look at the back seat, not knowing if they were dead or alive. They were alive. Thank God they were alive. The case could wait. Bradshaw could wait. I would research that night. My children and I were enjoying a moment together. I thought for a minute, and I moved on to Carlos.

...The rain slowed, and Elliot was ecstatic. He stared out his window and laughed as he saw his brother outside.

"I should have known you'd be first. I'm surprised you stayed inside at all," he muttered to himself.

Carlos threw up fists of mud as he dug deeply into the rain-soaked ground.

Elliot unlatched his window and climbed down his tree. He jumped toward his brother, tackled him, and they rolled across the muddy jungle floor.

Carlos protested. "Stop, Elliot. Stop. Look at me now. Five minutes outside and I'm a dirty mess. You have some kind of nerve. You know I'm busy."

Elliot heeded his words and stopped. "You've searched there before, Carlos. You should write down your tracks. You'll never find it if you don't mark where you've already looked. Anyway, you've searched for four years now. It's time to play a little."

"No, Elliot. I have no time to play. I only have time to search. And search I will until I find my knife." Carlos moved away and resumed digging. Elliot walked in circles around him.

"You've become a boring monkey, Carlos. The troop all talks. It's all you do now. Dig and dig and dig."

Carlos continued on his task. "I have a purpose Elliot. Unlike some of us, I don't just sit around and read great books to impress the others. I need to find my knife. That's all. I just need to find it. So stop bothering me."

"Suit yourself."

Elliot found a pile of pecans under the tree. He cracked one open and spit the shell at his brother. Carlos noticed nothing.

"For all you know, someone found it and carried it far away," Elliot said with a laugh.

"I don't think so."

"Father didn't give you that knife so you would spend your life searching."

Carlos smiled at his older brother. For a moment he forgot his digging. He flashed to their younger years learning to swing together and mashing apricots in their mouths. He recalled their teasing Rosalie together. And he recalled the tragic loss of their mother to the trappers that dreadful afternoon …

Carlos leapt in the air and landed squarely on Elliot. The two rolled around through the mud laughing for all to hear. For a moment, Elliot forgot about his books and Carlos forgot about the knife. They hooted and howled together as the last rain drops fell.

But then, like a marionette on a string, Carlos stopped tumbling and brushed the mud from his poncho. Without another word he lay down on the ground to resume digging with renewed fury.

Dorrie

Monday morning arrived. The ache in my shoulder clamped down on my mood as I drove myself to work after dropping the kids off at school. Every intersection remained a threat. I tried to override this with mind games—talking to myself, focusing sharply, ignoring what I thought I saw—but none of it worked. When a car appeared on my right, I slowed to a near stop, right in the middle of the intersection. Though the approaching car slowed, I imagined it continuing through the intersection right at me, as if I saw two images simultaneously.

I was in a bit of a panic by the time I pulled into the driveway leading to the large expanse of the Pacific Veterans Rehabilitation Hospital. I had spent the weekend lost in the story of an island and had neglected my task of researching Dawson's case. I amused myself as I imagined telling Dr. Bradshaw about my friend Elliot, the poetic lemur, and I saw his face turn bright red. Today I had better close my office door and get to work. At the minimum, I thought he might be sympathetic to my accident, as he had endorsed Dawson's idea of the impact of a trauma.

I gazed at the buildings of the Pacific Veterans Rehabilitation Hospital. I watched patients walking in hospital gowns amidst the low buildings and cottages that housed different physical and psychiatric rehabilitation programs. I passed the memorial park dotted with fountains, a duck pond, and the large horticulture garden.

I pulled up to my office—a small white cottage with a red tile roof. I got out of my car and walked through the small receiving area graced with an unused fireplace. On the wall, a framed poster from the Monterey Jazz Festival—a lonely trumpet on a chair perched on the ocean sands with seawater soaking the legs. I turned down the corridor to the right to greet Dorrie, my secretary, seated behind her desk just outside my office.

"Good morning, Mr. Grossmark. Dr. Bradshaw has called twice already this morning. He said he's waiting for your brief."

"Tell him I was in a wreck," I answered.

"A car accident?"

"Yes," I answered, walking into my office. Dorrie followed me in. I generally tried not to waste my time talking to her. I had a lot to do each day, and I didn't see the point of friendly banter.

"Is everyone okay? Oh, I feel terrible. I got your message and I was going to call. But you sounded like you wanted to be left alone."

"Oh, thanks. Yes. Yes, we're all okay. More of a hassle than anything else really. The kids and I got T-boned on the way to school. That's where I was Friday."

"Sir, I'm really sorry I didn't call …"

"Well we're all okay," I answered. The back of my neck throbbed and I grabbed it.

"Are you sure you're alright?"

"Yes." My tone was sharp. "I'm really better if you don't make a big deal about it. To me at least. Just call Dr. Bradshaw and let him know what happened. Tell him I was in an accident. But that I'm recovered from my trauma and working hard now on his case."

"Oh, I will, sir."

"Is Jerry coming today? You scheduled that, right?"

"Oh, he's been waiting over in Human Resources for you at Mr. Greenson's office. I told him I wasn't sure if you would be in, so he was considering leaving."

"Why over there?" I snapped at Dorrie, a bit upset. "I always meet with people here."

Dorrie turned a bit red. "I'm sorry, sir. He had to do some work in HR with Mr. Greenson and said you could meet him over there."

"Well tell him I'm here and they can come on over." I went into my office and stared out the back window. I looked out at the horticulture program and saw a veteran pushing a wheelbarrow down the dirt path leading to the garden. I watched him for the next few minutes until he disappeared from sight.

Dorrie interrupted my gazing. "Jerry Martin can't make it. He said he'd be back at the end of the week and you can talk then."

"The end of the week? Come on, Bradshaw is all over me. I need to talk to him about Dawson. We have notice that he's representing him."

"He said he had to go to his son's football game."

"He told you that? Okay, I give up."

"Dr. Bradshaw said he was very sorry to hear about the accident. He wanted me to let you know that he was happy you were well enough to be at work."

"I don't know if I am. I feel like I'm losing it here."

"He said he'd meet with you whenever you had the information he needs."

"Okay. See if you can make an appointment with him for next week. And I'm sorry for losing my cool."

"That's quite alright, Mr. Grossmark. It's nice to see you passionate!" She returned to the work at her desk.

I was sorry. Dorrie did the best she could with managing my tasks. And now, after the accident, my patience had grown even thinner. I generally tried to avoid getting too personal with anyone at work. I had heard her talking about her son at one point with some sort of medical problem. I didn't have room to know about that, so I kept her at an even greater distance.

I wondered why Jerry Martin had told Dorrie where he was going. He put work aside to go watch his kid. That caught my attention. But I felt bad, too. My kid didn't play football. My kid saw gorillas out the window and played chess. He figured out math problems in the back seat of a car, and he had asthma. I figured one day his kid might beat up mine. Jerry must be a better father than I. He had produced a football star. And I ... well, while he watched his son practice football on weekend mornings, I was telling lemur stories.

Revolutions

I came home in a bad mood. Nick and Samantha knew when I was irritated about work, and they generally stayed away. I boiled spaghetti noodles in a large pot and poured on a jar of marinara sauce. I boiled some frozen corn. We ate quietly together that night. I tried to engage them in small talk.

"How was your day, Nickie?"

"It was good."

"Anything new?"

"No."

Sammie said the same as we twirled noodles on our forks. Nick broke the stalemate.

"Are we telling the story tomorrow, Dad?"

"What story?" I answered.

"The lemurs, Dad. Carlos and Elliot," answered Samantha.

"Oh, I thought we finished it."

Nick was appalled. "Finished it!" he said loudly. "We barely started!"

"Yeah," agreed Samantha. "All we know is about Elliot wanting to play and being scared of revolutions."

"That's evolution," I corrected.

"Same diff …" said Samantha.

"No it's not," Nick corrected her. "Revolutions are like what we had in the car, when you go around and around. Evolution is when things change."

"Right, that's right, Nick." I smiled.

"Anyway, that's all we know. And Carlos is looking for a knife." She twirled the spaghetti on her fork into a huge ball and shoved it in her mouth. I felt my mood changing.

"Okay. You're right. We haven't gotten very far. But we have to wait for Sundays. That'll be our story time. Okay?" That's how it had been with my father, and it felt like I was resurrecting an old family rhythm.

"We have to wait a whole week?" Nick protested.

"It'll give us something to look forward to."

"Well, can we tell it with pancakes?" Sammie asked.

"Always." I smiled back at her. "Always with pancakes."

Nick and Sammie fell asleep in front of the television as I cleaned up dinner. I got changed for bed, brushed my teeth, and tucked myself in. I found Danny's journal on the night stand, and I opened it.

July 6, 1985

Today was a blast. The Sherpas took Marty and me to a lake in the morning. There was a huge tree with a rope hanging from a branch. They grabbed the rope and did flips into the water. I felt the water—it was freezing! Not to mention it was a ten foot drop from the branches. I told them that we would pass, but Marty grabbed the rope and went for it. That's another thing that's really cool about him. Sometimes he just loses all fear and dives into life. Marty ripped off his shirt and did a Tarzan yell from the vine with a front flip into the water. Then I went for it, too. It was freezing but an awesome way to wake up! On the way back down, the Sherpas asked me what I did in the States. I said I was a doctor and that I studied the effects of smoking. That's how I knew they should all stop. Marty cracked up. He once told me he got perturbed when I made stories, but I think he sort of likes it, too. This time he joined in, telling them I had earned a national award for my work. We talked about that most of the way back to Cheskham, and the villagers were impressed with my status. We talked about it around the fire at dinner, and we drank this stuff they call Raksi, a kind of Nepali wine. After a while the story got out of control. By the end, Marty had me as a world traveler, hired to stop smoking in every sector of the world. He had me ordained as a knight in England and a winner of the Nobel Peace Prize. He's good at telling stories once he gets going. There's a hot Nepali girl who perked up in the conversation. She spoke mostly Nepali, but a little English, and she was impressed with my accomplishments. She admired my hat while we drank. I wouldn't mind some action before the trip is over. I feel bad telling lies for sex, but not really. It's just part of the adventure. Besides, three months of celibacy on this trek sounds painful. I'm having trouble after only two weeks. Been thinking of Mom selling houses and telling Dad where to go. Sit at this house, go get this, go get that. I feel bad for him, but that was his choice. Not mine. I'm never getting myself in a situation like that. I can't imagine life without adventures.

A Visitor

Sunday morning finally arrived, and the kids woke up ready to go. They had retrieved the ingredients before I stumbled into the kitchen. I joined them, and after a few minutes, we were laughing together as we spilled pancake batter on the counters and kitchen floor. There was an excitement between us as we shared this pancake making, and we all wondered where our story would go next. We cooked, sat down to eat, and I continued where I had left off ...

Elliot looked up when he heard the three loud chimes on a pan. Rosalie had prepared a meal.

"Breakfast, Carlos. Let's go. I smell pancakes."

"I'll be there in a bit. I have a good feeling right now about this place."

"Carlos, you haven't eaten in days. You'll starve. I'll have to scoop your bones off the forest floor. That's if the vultures don't get to you first."

"I said I'll be there in a bit. I'm busy, Elliot. Just leave me alone."

"You could at least think about Rosalie. She probably cooked up 175 pancakes just for this morning. You should show your respect for ..."

"You can go ahead and have mine. Tell her I'll be there next time."

"Oh I give up then. Keep digging. And enjoy the vultures."

Elliot left his brother, and the smell of Rosalie's pancakes grew stronger as he stumbled through the jungle. He stomped through the puddles as he came upon them, just to stomp. He enjoyed the feeling of getting a little wet and even a little muddy. He quoted his friend Frost out loud.

"Then he flung outward, feet first, with a swish,
Kicking his way down through the air to the ground.
So was I once myself a swinger of birches.
And so I dream of going back to be."

Sammie interrupted my story. "You made it about pancakes 'cause that's what we're eating." Her jet-black hair was a bit of a bed head, and syrup covered her face, dripping onto her Winnie the Pooh PJs.

"And who was this Frost?" asked Nick. "I don't get how Elliot got his book?"

"Who was Frost?" I smiled as I dug into another pancake. "He was a famous poet. Certainly by the time I was nine I had memorized most of his poetry."

"No you hadn't! You're such a liar," Nick retorted between bites.

"Well he was a really good writer, and he wrote a lot of really good ideas. You know, Two roads diverged in a yellow wood ..."

"So how did Elliot get his book then? Did they have a school there?"

"No," I answered him. "His father, Max, found it on the forest floor. It had been left there by a team from Duke. There's a special center there that studies lemurs. One of the explorers liked to read poetry at night to help him fall asleep. And he had a collection of Robert Frost poetry. You know, to keep him company on his travels."

"You're lying again, Dad. There's no special lemur center in North Carolina."

"Okay smarty, then Google North Carolina lemurs," I replied.

Sammie asked, "Are there any more pancakes?"

"No, but I can make some."

The doorbell chimed.

"Who could that be at eight on a Sunday morning?"

"It might be Elliot," answered Nick. "He may think this is Rosalie's Kitchen." It was the first time I had heard him laugh in years.

"Okay. Okay. Get the door and see who it is. I'm going to make your sister more pancakes. At least she appreciates me."

"I'll have some, too," Nick said as he went to the door. "It's Jane. Should I let her in?"

"Jane? It's too early. We're in our PJs...." I was embarrassed. The kitchen was a disaster. Batter decorated every counter, egg whites drizzled across the floor and stove, flour dusted here and there. I had never let Jane in. I had never let anyone in. But this storymaking had left me feeling expansive. And out it came. "Sure, let her in."

And in she walked, dressed like she had been gardening already that morning. Her hair a bit damp—perhaps from a shower, perhaps from watering, or maybe the morning dew falling upon her. Her face a natural glow in the frame of the doorway—her large brown eyes, her wide face, and a smile that melted my porcupine quills. She had no makeup, no manicure, and as she stood just inside the doorway, my kids ran to her side. The pied piper from Carson City.

"Dad's telling us about Elliot. He lived in an oak tree on an island and got stuck there in a rain storm," said Sammie wide eyed as she escorted Jane into our home.

"Oh, is that right? Was he a castaway? Was he living off the land?"

"No," answered Samantha sincerely. "He was a lemur. He was really mad because he was stuck in his oak tree. He liked to say poems, and he was scared of evolution."

"Oh I ..."

"And then there was another lemur named Carlos," Sammie continued. "He was Elliot's brother, but they lived in different trees. He had a knife and he couldn't find it. And Elliot wanted to have a play date with him but Carlos was too busy looking for his knife. Then they smelled pancakes from

Rosalie's kitchen. She's their sister. Daddy's making more pancakes if you want one."

"Well, thanks. I was just stopping by to let you know that next weekend is the big garage sale."

"Cool," responded Nick. "Last year I made twelve dollars from my old junk."

"Jane, I'm sorry for the overly enthusiastic greeting," I said, ready to tell her that we were really busy.

"Don't apologize. Your children are charming. I brought you these tomatoes from my garden. They're growing like weeds. Here you go. It does smell really good in here. Your dad's a good cook, isn't he?"

"How do you get your tomatoes so big?" asked Nicholas. "Ours always die after they pop up."

"You must water yours," I said with a smile.

"And fertilize. If you want, I can take care of yours next summer and get them going. As long as I'm doing mine ..."

"Maybe you could teach us how," I responded and returned to cooking.

"Would you?" Sammie asked.

"Sure thing," Jane responded.

Jane was kind in her offer to help, though I felt my guard go up as she walked into the kitchen. I poured three more circles of batter on the grill. The experience of a woman in my home brought the memory of Lara back to me. As the pancakes thickened, I saw Lara in my mind, on the back of the motorcycle, off for Pagosa Springs. We hadn't seen her since that day. Lara didn't believe in technology, so we couldn't email her or call her on her cell phone, not that she would answer. At first, the kids had wondered who their mother was, so I found Major's number. They left messages on Major's answering machine but gave up after a few months when there was no call back. I told them that Major probably didn't give Mom the messages.

The kids chatted with Jane as I recalled Lara.

A couple of years ago, Lara started writing letters about

once or twice a year. I knew the kids missed having a mother, but the memory was too painful to mention it much. I never thought her letters would be helpful, so I threw them away.

While I pondered Lara's departure, Sammie and Nick brought Jane up to speed about Elliot the thinker, Carlos the searcher, and Rosalie's Kitchen. She basked in their enthusiasm, and I wondered what light in my home could make her face glow so stunningly. I agreed to resume my story for an audience of three.

Rosalie's Kitchen

For the most part, the lemurs fended for themselves. They ate leaves and ants and foraged for apricots and pecans. But on Sundays, Rosalie cooked pancakes for the troop. Her mother, Rama, had cooked more often than that. Rosalie continued the tradition once a week, but she often resented the lack of appreciation.

Today she started early with a bit of enthusiasm. But as she stirred many vats of batter, her mind drifted … "They won't even clean up. They'll just leave me with the mess. 22 plates, 22 forks, 22 knives. Why do I bother?"

The lemurs rarely used utensils, only at Rosalie's breakfasts. Mother Rama had always insisted, trying to create a civilized troop. Rosalie tried to keep her mother's tradition alive. She had some kitchen-hands who helped her. Samaya was the most enthusiastic. She was from another family in the troop. But Samaya's love of cooking often left Rosalie wondering if she was perhaps a direct descendant of mother Rama.

On this Sunday morning, Rosalie was visited early by Lionel, her brother Jasper's mischievous accomplice. He was entertaining, and many of the female lemurs enjoyed his company. He was dapper, always looking for a good time, and he usually made one happen. This often came at the expense of the others, but to Lionel that was part of the game. He had started the "School for Swingers" with Jasper, the youngest of Max and Rama's four children, and together they created a gang that enjoyed bullying the other lemurs.

Lionel swung into Rosalie's kitchen, wearing a tweed hat, a woolen vest, and a pair of mud-soaked tennis shoes. He did a double flip entrance into the kitchen from a vine hanging high above.

"Awfully good day for swinging, Miss Rosalie. Perhaps you should consider a romp in the tree tops with me. Too much work in the kitchen can ruin a day."

"Who invited you in?" Rosalie asked him.

"Smells mighty good. Looks like it tastes …"

"Don't even think about it! Just get out of my kitchen."

"Ah, Miss Rosalie. Maybe I could just get a kiss and be on my way?"

"Are you kidding me?"

"No, Rosie. It's my dream. You being so beautiful and all. You can't blame a gentleman for his confession. Or leave him empty handed."

"Swing on back out of here. Now."

"Your chance to kiss the most handsome lemur in Paden's."

Rosalie paused a moment. "Perhaps if you close your eyes I could give it a try. You are quite romantic after all, swinging into my kitchen like this."

Lionel closed his eyes and puckered his lips. "Your wish is my command."

Rosalie scooped a fist of mud from the forest floor. "You are simply irresistible. Here, now. Here you go." She pressed the pile of mud onto Lionel's lips. "Oh Lionel … what a great kisser you are."

For seconds he enjoyed himself. Then he opened his eyes, tasted the mud, and spit.

"Now get out of my kitchen!" Rosalie yelled.

Lionel squealed in laughter enjoying Rosalie's spirit. "I knew you had it in you ol' girl. You're quite a prankster, aren't you! We ought to join forces!"

"Get out of here! No flapjacks for you!"

"Okay, I'll leave. But I know you're sorry to see me go! No flapjacks today. Just mud on my face. Good one, ol' lady. Good one!" Lionel grabbed a vine and swung himself out to the top of the trees. From up above he called. "I love you, Miss Rosalie. I love you!" An apricot landed in Rosalie's vat. "For you my love! I love you!"

Rosalie grabbed her spoon and returned to stirring. She watched the apricot swimming in the batter and wondered how it would taste. She knew that all work in the kitchen was no life. But it was her destiny and obligation. In some way, she was sorry to see Lionel go. Rosalie stirred with a ferocious banging and felt the apricot bash up into bits against the side of her bowl.

Magic

I stopped there, wondering where Lionel had come from. He seemed to have been unleashed by the audience of my next-door neighbor. I was a bit embarrassed. I preferred my usual presentation of the guy trapped inside a tree house, lost in thought. Or the guy out searching for something buried long ago. Or the one working without appreciation. I knew I was no Lionel. Lara would never have left a Lionel. He was the adventure she was looking for. He probably rode a Harley.

"I didn't know you could cook, Martin. These pancakes are really special." Jane said.

"I'll get you another one," said Samantha.

"Can you get me one, too?" asked her brother.

"No, you get them then," she spouted back.

"Okay. Jane how many do you want?" asked Nick.

"No! I'm getting them for her."

"We call this the Samantha Nicholas show." I smirked at Jane. "You can't get involved in it. Just enjoy the action."

"Stop it, Dad," shouted Nicholas. "We're not fighting. Just discussing."

"Oh really!"

Jane smiled again. "Well I appreciate the discussion. Your children are lovely, Martin. I'll get the pancakes. More syrup, too?"

The kids smiled at me. "Yes, thank you," answered Nick.

I was stunned. They never said thank you. Jane's spell was taking hold, and I grew nervous. For a moment, I wondered who she really was, what she wanted, and why she lived alone. My suspicions ran wild. I was embarrassed about my response, but it was automatic and beyond my control. I wanted her out of my kitchen, though it seemed that that was getting more difficult to accomplish by the moment, and I would be outvoted two to one.

"So what happened to Carlos?" she asked.

"Um … I'm not sure," I answered. "Look, I've got a deposition tomorrow. I hope you don't mind if …"

"Oh no worries," Jane answered me. "The kids and I will clean up. We can hang out so you can work. I don't have much going today."

"Oh yes, Daddy!" answered Samantha. "Go do your work. Jane will watch us."

"No, I don't think that's …"

"We're fine," Nick added. I was surprised. He didn't take to strangers well. Not since one took his mom away.

"I thought I might take the kids to the zoo. You've inspired me to learn more about lemurs."

"I don't know." The kids had absolutely nothing to do. But Jane was pushing it here.

"We'll clean up, Dad. You can go do work. We're going to the zoo." Nick had never offered to clean up before. Maybe Jane did have some energy to loan to my household. Nick and Samantha appeared content to spend the day with our neighbor. But I was nervous. The three of us had made it this far on our own, and adding a fourth person to the mix would make it complicated. Besides, I had sworn off relationships the day that Lara drove off, and I wasn't going to put myself in jeopardy again.

"Look, I don't know. I was thinking later we would start working on the science fair projects."

"They're not due for a month," answered Nick.

I thought about just saying no. But my children were already carrying their plates to the sink. They scraped them and put them in the dishwasher.

"Want to come, Martin?"

Perhaps she was a witch. She had powerful magic. Maybe she did voodoo next door, and she had pinned a little doll of me. I smirked at my thoughts and wondered how they spun these tales so quickly. I saw her stirring a brew in a pot late into the evenings, yet I watched as she lovingly helped my children clean up. And the warmth of her smile melted my reluctance.

"I really do need to prepare for tomorrow."

"Take all the time you need. I can get the kids dinner."

I paused. "That would be great. I could really use the time tonight."

Fly With Me

Frannie greeted me at the door inside Spellman's. "Marty! You came!" Her small body was draped by a flowing blue gown that sparkled as she moved. Atop her gray hair she wore a sequined tiara that glittered in the light, and her ravishing smile made her look even more beautiful. "It's my birthday tonight!"

"I'm sorry I missed last week," I told her.

She took my hand and brought me to her table. Her hand was cold, but it was full of life, and she clutched my fingers and held on as she guided me to the table up front. I caught the fragrance of her perfume—a scent of orchids I recalled from a trip to Thailand, and it complemented her animated presentation.

There must have been eighty people at Spellman's that night, all over seventy. Six sat at Frannie's table, waiting for the next singer, sipping various sodas. "Here, sit here. Take this. I'm about to sing." She handed me two sandpaper blocks to rub together to mark the rhythm. I set them on the table as I sat in the last seat.

"Everyone, you all know my boyfriend Martin?"

I looked around at the faces, some familiar, some not.

"Oh yes! Marty it's good to see you!" answered Claudine. I remembered her. "Frannie's been missing you honey! We all have!"

"Thanks. It's good to see you. It's been hard to get here." I felt my heart warming. I was happy to be there.

"Get a drink, Martin. Oh! This is my old friend, Horty. Have you met? She was in pictures with Elvis." I had never seen her before. I would have remembered her. She had perfect skin doused in pancake and pink dyed hair poofed high above her head.

"Pleased to meet you," I answered as I shook her hand, still holding onto Frannie with my right.

"You too, sweetie. You come here often?"

"No, just sometimes."

"He comes to see me when he's lonely. He's my boyfriend. Isn't he just gorgeous!" She moved her frail arm around my shoulder, and I loved the contact. "Roy Rogers, honey?" Frannie knew that Cherry Coke was my favorite drink.

"Sure." I took out a cigarette and lit up. "I didn't know it was your birthday. I would have …"

"Every day's my birthday, Marty. That's what I decided. I thank God I'm alive every morning I wake up. I call every day my birthday. You should, too."

"You got that right, sister!" Horty chimed in, raising her soda glass.

"Marty was in a bad accident last week!" Frannie said to the table. "With his two kids! Who are the most precious children in the world." She coughed a couple of deep coughs that caught my attention.

"So it's your birthday, too!" Horty turned to me.

"Waiter? Get my boyfriend here a Roy Rogers," Frannie called.

"And now, Francine Neighbors singing "Come Fly with Me," called the MC, a dapper old man wearing a tweed jacket and a heart-dotted white shirt.

"Oh, I'm up, Martin. You got here just in time." She got up from her chair and shuffled slowly to the platform.

Horty moved over close to me. "This is her best number. Have you ever heard her do it?"

"No, I haven't." I was so happy to be there.

"She should have sung in pictures. She missed her calling." Horty stood up and yelled, "Happy Birthday Frannie baby!" The crowd clapped and waved their rhythm makers through the air.

"Do you sing?" Horty asked me.

"No. I mean I used to sometimes. Never in public though. I just like to come in to listen sometimes."

Frannie went to the microphone, her tiara shining in the

light, her gown shimmering as she moved. The music began, and the crowd went wild. Horty pointed her finger at my sandpaper blocks, and I remembered to move them together. Frannie took the microphone from the stand. She glanced in my direction, and the karaoke began. Frank Sinatra. And in her raspy voice, a little off key, she began to sing.

She was stunning. I was mesmerized by her presence, as though she sang to my bones. The others cheered, shaking their instruments to keep the rhythm. Frannie worked the crowd, having memorized the words. Each time her voice cracked, I admired her even more. She didn't seem to care. Nor did anyone else. As I listened to the lyrics, I thought of Danny and the adventures we had taken. I missed him. I missed a lot of people. But on that evening in Spellman's, I was thankful to be with this fine company.

Another Visit

More than a week had passed since the accident, and I found myself wondering about the boy who hit us. "Can you give me a ride home to my mom?" He had totaled my car. Why would he ask me for a ride home? The question rattled inside me, as Nick and Sammie shared stories about the zoo. They talked about the animals, the ice cream, and how they loved being with Jane.

"The lemurs were the best," Samantha said.

"There were four of them," Nick continued. "They were swinging around in this large cage."

"What kind were they?" I asked them.

"They were all ring-tailed," Nick answered.

"Their tails were black and gray and white striped. One kept looking at me," Sammie added. "I think he knew we were telling stories about him."

"I think that one was Elliot," Nick chimed in.

"No, I think it was Rosalie," said Samantha. "She was telling me about Lionel and how she secretly liked him."

"We won't know until next Sunday, right? We can't tell the story at night. It's just for Sunday mornings, with pancakes," I said.

We had a quiet evening, the kids went to sleep, and I crawled into my bed. The television was on to keep me company, an infomercial on a cable station. My mind quieted and I dozed off. It was two in the morning when I felt a tapping on my shoulder.

"He's back again," Nick said, standing at the side of my bed. His face looked white as he stood by my bedside, paralyzed.

I was disoriented. "Who's back?"

"The gorilla. He's back. Outside my window. He's knocking and he wants to get in. And he's laughing at me."

"Nick, there's no gorilla. Just go back to sleep, kiddo." I tried to roll over, but Nick wasn't going for it.

"Dad, come now! He's trying to get inside!"

We walked down the hallway, past Sammie asleep in her room, and past the clanking of the heater. I led the way into Nick's room and turned on the light. He ran to the window and peered behind the shade, now appearing a bit more empowered.

"He's gone again!" Nick cried.

"Nick, there's no gorilla out there. It's just the wind. Let's get back to bed." I guided him to lie down, but his body was rigid.

"Stay in here, Dad. He only comes when I'm alone. Please?"

I was frustrated with my anxious little boy. Perhaps the stories of Madagascar were too much. Maybe the car accident was lingering. One thing was certain—he was calling for his Dad right now. So out came the sleeping bags, and we chatted as we unstuffed them.

"Dad, who was your friend? The one who gave you this sleeping bag?"

"Oh, Danny? He was just a good friend. From college."

"So why did he give you his sleeping bag?"

"I told you. He doesn't need it any more. I mean he didn't need it. I mean when he gave it to me." It was late and I was getting confused. I still always thought of Danny in the present tense.

"He got a new one?"

"No, he just didn't need it anymore. He stopped going camping."

"Where did you camp?" We crawled into the sleeping bags. Nick was enjoying this. The gorilla was long gone.

"We went to West Africa. Nepal. Lots of places. Alaska. Ecuador. Indonesia, Thailand—we went to an island called Komodo. Where they have these big lizards called Komodo Dragons."

"Are there any on Madagascar? I mean in Paden's?"

"Oh, no. Remember, there's nothing to be frightened of there. No scary animals to worry about. The lemurs are at the top of the food chain. Just man. That's the only thing they had to be afraid of."

"What could man do?"

"Man could trap them and bring them to a zoo. Or turn them into a pet I guess."

"Would they kill them? Did they hunt the lemurs?"

This was activating Nick. "No, they just wanted to own them. You know, to play with them."

"You could have a lemur as a pet?"

"Well, these lemurs you could. You know, because they were so well behaved. These were special lemurs. They could read poetry, cook pancakes, and teach swinging lessons...."

Nick had fallen asleep. He felt safe thinking about Paden's. He wasn't afraid much of trappers. Just gorillas. And this island didn't have any.

I was flooded with images of camping with Danny as I lay in my bag, wondering where my spirit of adventure had gone. My mind churned over images of times with Danny until I fell into a deep sleep.

A Dream

I was up on a bridge over a large ocean. There were waves below me and a boat in the distance. A voice was calling to me from below, and I turned down to see who it was. There he was. Danny. Swimming under the bridge. His head was bobbing up and down as he struggled not to drown. He called my name, again and again. As I leaned over the bridge, I felt a force pulling me down. It was hard to balance. A force wanted to pull me into the sea. I saw Danny struggling. "Don't come down here, Marty. Don't come down from the bridge. It's too cold, Marty. The water's too cold. Live." Just then a car came rushing toward me, driving at top speed. Now I was in my jeep. The car slammed into me and sent my car spinning. I rolled into the side of the bridge and started to spin off of it. I heard screams from the back seat. And I woke up in a panic.

Nick was next to me, asleep. I was so thankful to hear each little breath. Each little snore. The crickets chirped outside. I wondered what Nick really saw out the window, and why he saw it. I prayed that it was normal, that it would stop, and that his high-powered mind was not somehow getting out of control. My foot moved up against his. Through the sleeping bags, I felt the warmth of his little foot. His human foot. I felt him living. I felt me living. And I was so very thankful that we were both alive.

Out Elliot's Window

I bought a new car with a five-star crash rating. The kids felt good knowing this, since we reviewed the safety records together. But I continued to perceive cars in intersections plowing into me from the right.

I had a bit more energy at work. The pressure was growing around Henry Dawson's case. The facility had received a letter from the Inspector General wanting to know if he had written this blog on federal time. We needed to provide evidence of an investigation, and we had two weeks to get back to them. We got two new letters from our Congressional representatives inquiring about his internet post. The frenzy of the case seemed out of proportion to the act. I was a bit dumbfounded by such a response to an obscure little blog.

The weekend was a well-deserved break. Jane rang the bell on Sunday morning and invited herself in without hesitation. Sammie and Nick were already preparing pancakes. We poured the batter, we flipped the pancakes, and we served them up on our fine china. I began right where I had left off.

Elliot sat back in his old leather chair and gazed at his book collection. He looked with pride at the books he had collected through the years. He heard a howling out in the forest. He knew the sound well. It was Nikko.

Elliot worried about Nikko. He reached back up to his book shelf for his favorite, for Frost always had the answers. Like a fortune cookie, he opened his worn leather book. *The Oven Bird.*

> *"The bird would cease and be as other birds*
> *But that he knows in singing not to sing.*
> *The question that he frames in all but words*
> *Is what to make of a diminished thing."*

Mr. Frost always got it right. Elliot returned to his chair and held his book tightly in his lap, listening to Nikko's howls. Elliot knew that he and his siblings had stopped singing long ago. They were all busy and in that way had become diminished. He with his books, Carlos with his searching, Rosalie with her cooking, and Jasper with his swinging. This had grown worse for all of them since mother Rama disappeared. But Nikko was different. He didn't have a distraction, just a quiet confidence that allowed him to keep singing. Though his song was different than the others, minor and off pitch.

Nikko wasn't born in Paden's Patch. His mother was from another troop. Carlos had found an abandoned baby lemur crying under the canopy of a small palm tree. He had tried to go about his business, but couldn't ignore the cries. So Carlos brought him back to Paden's Patch and to mother Rama who cared for him. And Carlos tried to be his father.

Nikko wasn't quite like the other lemurs. He was faster. He was bigger. His arms were longer. And his legs were longer, too. Most striking of all was his tail. The other lemurs all shared a gray body and a beautiful tail marked by a series of rings. Not Nikko. His body was dark black. To Elliot, Nikko looked more like the humans he had seen in the forest.

In many ways Nikko was similar to the others. He slept during the night. He enjoyed eating laurel leaves, though not as much as he enjoyed Rosalie's breakfasts. But in this one very important way he was quite different. To the human ear, the others communicated through sounds like the purring of a cat. Not Nikko. While he could make that sound, he enjoyed creating a roaring sound in the day. And in the evening his hooting was a minor note that only he could make.

The other lemurs sometimes gossiped about Nikko. Rosalie wondered where he came from, who his parents might have been, and why they had left him under a bush. Sometimes she scared the others. "Why did they leave him to die under a bush? Perhaps he carried a disease. Or a curse," she would suggest. Rosalie always washed the plate he used on Sundays with a little extra soap. Just in case.

Nikko wasn't aware of the gossip. He wasn't aware that he was treated differently. But he was alone much of the time. Carlos was so busy searching for his knife that he had no time to play with his adopted son. Nikko had given up trying to get his father's attention, just like all the lemurs had. There was no distracting Carlos from his searching.

Jasper enjoyed wrestling around with Nikko on the forest floor. So did Lionel. They would roll and laugh as they contorted into various positions. But as Nikko grew, he became too big and strong for their games. He would leave them sore after a wrestling match. So they left him alone.

That night Elliot listened to Nikko's cries. The eerie sound wafted past a full moon that lit up the forest. No one understood these special sounds. What was Nikko crying? The moon cast a shadow on a figure lurking hunched over on the forest floor. There he saw his brother, Carlos, bent over, searching. It had been fourteen hours now with no break. Elliot wondered if Carlos would ever go to sleep. He watched his brother dig as he listened to the ghostly cries of an unanswered son. And though the sounds disturbed the ear, he admired Nikko's desire to sing.

Madagascar

I knew just a bit about lemurs. I had been an English major and knew more about Frost. I knew that I could keep telling my story, but with Jane present, I felt the pressure of validation. The kids were asleep, and though I knew I had case law to read, I filled my time learning about lemurs.

I had gotten some details right. Madagascar had been part of Africa and broke apart. Lemurs lived there 60 million years ago, and when monkeys evolved some 40 million years later on the continent, they couldn't cross the ocean over to the small island. They outcompeted and killed lemurs in mainland Africa toward near extinction. The largest species is the Indri. Humans have been the greatest threat to the lemur population on Madagascar.

I looked around at my lonely home from my computer in the study. The peeling wallpaper, the worn art posters. From my study it looked like a museum displaying artifacts from my earlier days. Two large African wood carvings I had purchased from a local carver in a village. A game of Kallah he had constructed as well.

I recalled the African village of Gbamandu, where the children gathered every night in a circle. Tine, a wise woman with leprosy, pounded on an old metal jug with her burned hands for the children to dance. They chanted under the moon on the large field. I knew the song well and felt it well up in my chest all these years later. I stopped my computer searching of Madagascar to sing softly with Tine in my mind.

"Ba Ma Sa Ke De Oh, Ba Ma Sa Ke Di Oh, Ba Ma Se Keh Wah."

"Ba Ma Sa Ke De Oh, Ba Ma Sa Ke Di Oh, Ba Ma Se Keh Wah."

The chanting brought me to memories of my travels with Danny. My mind drifted from the living room artifacts to my early memories of my friend.

It started when I was a freshman at Bradbury College, a small liberal arts college in northern Maine. Danny visited my dorm room the second day of school. He was a sophomore, and he let me know that this room had been his the year before. We talked a bit, and he said that he was from Malibu, not too far from where I grew up in West Los Angeles. We laughed about our similar circumstances, and he told me that this room had been a good home for him and would be for me. We talked about various good courses to take during freshman year. Before I knew it, he had invited me for dinner. We went to a local pizza joint, and we shared ideas about where we wanted to travel in the world. That was the beginning of our friendship. By October, we had made a pact that we would visit a new part of the world each summer, and we spent the school year planning our trips in the Bradbury coffee house

I recalled our first planning session. Danny had brought a large foldout world map to help figure out adventure number one. He was a large presence—six foot two with broad shoulders and a muscular build. He had a thick head of bright red hair and a slightly ruddy complexion. His pink cheeks dotted the tips of his slightly cockeyed smile, and his large green eyes seemed to pull in anyone who crossed his path. Danny dressed differently than the rest of us at Bradbury. He never wore collared shirts or sweaters. That day, like always, he wore a T-shirt and jeans. forest green with the insignia—Durango Outfitters. Sometimes the shirts were plain, sometimes they had a logo. American River Rafting Adventures. Mammoth Lakes Treks. Mountain Gear. As always, he wore hiking boots and looked as though he was ready to hit the trail. "Location, location, location!" Danny exclaimed. "That's what my mom says. It's all about location." He let out a sigh with the mention of her.

"She sells real estate. What does that have to do with ..."

"She knows what she's talking about. Life is about where you want to be. So where do you want to go first?" Danny's gaze drifted off with the mention of his mom, as though he left me for a moment for some private place.

"How about Mexico?" I answered him.

"Mexico!" He was back. Why would you want to go to Mexico?"

"You know. For our first trip. Seems like it's not too far. We could see the Mayan ruins."

"Marty! You're thinking like a tourist. Let's get one thing straight. We're not going to see things, or to see people. We're going to mix in. To be part of it. The crazier, the better." He pulled out a folded brochure from his back pocket.

"Look at this," he continued. "I picked it up in the student center. You go with a group. You meet Africans and work together on a project."

"Africa?"

"Yeah, Africa." He looked over my shoulder and noticed a girl behind me at the other end of the coffee shop. "Look at that. Do you know her?"

I looked over my shoulder. "Who are you looking at?"

"That one. With the red hair. She's hot."

I had lost him now. He was on an adventure in the coffee house. And as we talked, he continued his gaze over my shoulder.

"So what is this program?" I asked.

"I don't know. I don't really care. It gets you to Africa."

I opened the brochure and started to read. I got excited about the adventure and doing something helpful, like building a schoolhouse or a water purification system.

He continued staring. "I was thinking maybe Liberia. Or Sierra Leone. Or the Ivory Coast?"

"Are you worried at all though? I mean … malaria, typhoid, dysentery …"

He was still staring over my shoulder while he talked to me. "Why don't we close the map and just write down all the bad things that can happen wherever we go. Then we can wind up this summer, I don't know, volunteering in the library?"

I smiled at him. He knew that I was scared, but that I desperately wanted an adventure. And he knew how to get me through my fear.

"We can start in Nepal, then. You'll like that. It's a lot of exercise. We can do Africa after that. Here she comes. Watch this."

The girl passed our table. Five foot six, black hair, large lips, large breasts, dark rimmed glasses. Danny looked up, and he began.

"Hey, wait a minute … don't walk by. Aren't you in my class? 19th Century U.S. History?"

She smiled at him. She held an empty coffee cup and was going to get a refill.

"Oh, I don't think so. I'm a graduate student. Anthropology."

"Anthropology? Really? I'm an anthropologist."

I kicked Danny under the table. He was lying again. I had seen him do it many times. He called it storymaking, and he had encouraged me to try it.

The girl smiled at Danny. I could tell she recognized his lie but appreciated it nonetheless.

"Oh, really? What's your area?"

"I'm studying the behavior of college students here on campus. I'm comparing it to the villagers of Africa. We're comparing educational systems."

"You're comparing this university to an African village?"

"Oh yes. My research partner and I. This is Martin. I'm Daniel. We're here just briefly in an exploratory capacity."

She was charmed by his storytelling. I was honored to be included in the tale. They spoke for another five minutes before she left us to fill her coffee. They never exchanged phone numbers. But that wasn't the point. Danny was into novelty, and adventures, and though he seemed critical of his mom, it seemed to me that he would be a great real estate agent himself one day.

It was 10:30 at night. I indulged myself in my memory as I stared away from my computer toward the wood carvings in my living room.

I wondered what happened to the girl in the coffee house. Had she become an anthropologist? At that point, the idea seemed thrilling. She had probably pursued her dream. I had wanted to continue to study English, but I knew where that might lead. I would be teaching English. For my father who had built his department store metropolis out of nothing, it was clear what the expectation was for my future, and off to law school I went. He had offered for me to take over the family business, but when I declined, he cautioned me that I had better work hard at something else to make a living. So I did.

Lara didn't much care for Danny. She told me he was irresponsible, and that he should focus on making a living. She wanted my full attention, and she and then the kids came to define my time. So Danny and I drifted apart.

Danny met Jody during sophomore year. He kept studying U.S. History and got a Masters' degree at Bradbury. He and Jody stayed together, despite her sporadic objections to his mingling with other girls. After graduation, Danny and Jody took lots of adventures. She took my place. They went camping all over the world. Jody didn't mind getting dirty, and she was charmed by his extroversion. They settled back in California, and Danny got a job teaching at a high school in Los Angeles. As time passed, Danny and I had less and less in common. Though we lived close by, we hardly talked to each other. We had drifted into our new lives. I lost myself in my law school studies and then in Lara. Danny left me messages a couple of times a year. I stopped calling back, mostly due to Lara's cynicism. Eventually he stopped calling.

I returned to my computer scrolling and read more about lemurs. I read about the different species. I read about the Indri, and its particular human qualities. I read of old legends involving the Indri lemur and its place as a sacred animal. There were many stories of the first Indri, most involving the relationship of a father and son. One involved a father and son venturing into the forest together, where the son was transformed into a lemur. The minor pitched cry of the Indri is analogous to the wailing of the father in the forest for his lost son.

I wondered what it really looked like in Madagascar. What would it be like to walk down a dirt path and bump into a lemur? Would it run away? Would I run away? Would it stay for a bit if it knew that I was telling his story?

I logged off the computer and made my way to my bedroom. The house was quiet, but my mind raced with thoughts of lemurs and faraway lands. I changed my clothes, brushed my teeth, and turned on an infomercial. Nothing was slowing my mind. I glanced at Danny's journal on my nightstand, and I opened it. His words had a way of helping me fall asleep, like we were back talking again in our sleeping bags.

July 19, 1986

The trek in to Gbamandu was crazy. When we got here, the villagers knew that we were coming to deliver supplies that we had carried with us from the States. They sacrificed their only cow for us. That's a big deal in an African village. Today we got to meet with the Village Council. These guys get the women to do all the work while they sit around and get drunk on palm wine. Marty and I tried some while we played on a drum that Tomba Komanda made. It has a good sound. What a trip! Drinking palm wine, hanging in the village, and pounding on a drum over the village. A good part of me is ready to stay right here in Sierra Leone and never go back home.

I'm a little worried about Marty. He seems distant, even on the greatest day in the world. He got a post card from his dad, and he has seemed down ever since. He told me he felt guilty because his dad was home all alone. I wish my dad would care enough to write me a letter. I can't imagine him doing that. He's too busy sitting in open houses for my mom trying to sell homes.

As we were getting into our sleeping bags, Marty asked me if I believed in God. I thought maybe he asked me since I took a religious studies class. But maybe he asked because of his mom. I don't know what it would be like to have your mom die. Maybe he's wondering where she was now after death. I guess my real mom died, too. But I never knew her. So that seems really different.

I told him what I thought. I told him that I didn't know if there was a God. But that if there were, I bet that woman pounding on the tin can down there had met her. They call her Tine. She has no hands—from leprosy. But she still drums all night long. The kids all dance around her until they fall asleep in a big circle right there on the field. She's in touch with some kind of energy that lets her play for them all night. And she seems like the source of life for everyone else.

We are sleeping in our mosquito nets in a structure reserved for guests. Marty's fast asleep. I feel like shaking him and asking him why he asked me that. And what he's thinking so much about. It's happened a couple of times on this trip—his drifting off to a private place. Not like the Marty who swung into the lake last summer. It's like sometimes he lives in a private world, all shut in. I just want to break in and find out what the hell's going on in there. Most of the time he's like a cool brother and a blast to be with. More fun than my own. That's when I love him. But he can get pulled into this thinking place and I don't like that at all. And it's happening more often now.

I'll tell him that if there's a God, I'll bet Tine has met him. That's why she can play those rhythms all night even though she has no hands. Though I should probably think some more about his question. I should probably figure out if I do believe in God. If he presses me some more in the morning, I think I'll say yes, I do. Because of his mom and everything. That's what he would want to hear. I'll say that I do. But I'm not sure. The only thing that I'm sure that I do believe in is having adventures like this one.

Giovanni's Pizza

On the way home I had picked up food from a small Italian restaurant on a corner in our neighborhood. I held the pizza box in my arm as I wrestled my way out of my car and struggled to get the mail from the box. Most of it was junk—offers for a credit card, throw away law journals, a UCLA Law School alumni magazine. There was a small blue envelope sent from Pagosa Springs, Colorado.

I threw my briefcase on the floor of the kitchen, juggled the pizza to the island, and opened the letter.

Martin—
Joan Baez came through today. I can't believe she can still sing so grand. Major and I spoke with her after the concert. Oh Martin, it was so beautiful. Right on the dock at the edge of the lake. I remembered when you and I had seen her at Mel's. So I just had to drop you a note. Say hi to the kids for me.
Warmly,
Lara

I ripped the note into shreds. I imagined her emerging naked from the water, Major sliding in between her legs, the two rolling on the pebbly shore. Joan Baez singing in the background, the two making love, with no cares as to who was watching. I ripped with all of my might, and my elbow knocked the pizza box open onto the floor.

"Shit!" I bent over to pick up the pizza, cheese side married to the linoleum. Nicholas stood watching wide eyed at me and my mess.

"Dad is that dinner?"

I tried to cover my rage. "Yeah, Nick. Sorry. I don't know how it fell."

"You knocked it with your arm. What's that letter?"

"It's nothing. Go tell your sister dinner's ready."

"Then why are you ripping it up so much? It's from Mom, isn't it?"

"Yeah."

"Did she write anything for me?"

"She said to say hi."

"Why doesn't she ever write us letters?"

"She's busy, Nickie. She just writes me with official stuff."

He turned his head to the pizza on the floor.

"Nickie, I'm sorry, I don't …"

"Why did she go away?"

"She changed, Nick. She just changed. Sometimes people do. They decide they're going to give up everything and go on a wild adventure."

"Are you going to do that one day, too?" He had tears in the corner of his eyes.

I looked at my son. I felt a new anger flood across my chest. If I were to see Lara right then, I would smack her across the face. I distracted myself with words to quell the energy inside me.

"The only adventure I'm ever going on is with you."

"I'm not going on any adventures."

And a new feeling came. In a moment I thought of losing him. I thought of the wailing I would do if we walked into a forest and he were turned into a lemur forever. I was overwhelmed at the thought of his leaving me one day. I wanted to tell him about the dangers of adventures and evolution, just so he would stay close. But I struggled to overcome myself and to hold the tears in my eyes. And I did what a good dad should.

"Well, they don't have to be bad you know. They really don't."

"Well, if they make you leave people, they're bad." Tears fell down his cheeks. I was starting to hate how much I loved him. Maybe Lara had left because she was afraid of this feeling. Maybe she didn't want to feel how much she loved the kids.

Though that might have been generous of me. I pulled in Nick close to me and he wept.

"Sometimes they can be bad. When they hurt people. But adventures can bring you closer to people, too. Sometimes they help you find out new things about yourself."

He backed away and looked at me. "Not if they take you far away. Then they can't bring you closer to people."

The doorbell rang. I had hoped it might. I had even ordered an extra-large in hopes that Jane might come by.

"It's Jane!" screamed Samantha, running from her room to the door. She was wearing her soccer jersey—bright blue and white stripes. She played for the Blue Tigers.

"Well don't just open it. Ask who it is."

"I know it's her. I called to see if she could come over."

"You called her?"

"I have to turn in my sales form to school tomorrow! I need six more points to get the soccer ball trainer."

"Sammie, I'll buy something. You can't just ask her to buy things. "

I opened the door.

"Hi Jane. I'm embarrassed. Samantha just told me that she called you."

She was beautiful. She was grounded, as though part of the earth herself. With each visit now she seemed even more stunning. A sort of beauty I had not been accustomed to perceiving. She brought no harvest tonight. Just herself, nothing fancy. She wore a pair of shorts and a shirt that read Santa Monica Mountains Conservancy. And she had manicured her nails. A natural milky color, but it was not like her. She smiled, and it changed the mood that Lara's letter had created.

"Don't be silly. Sammie's selling stuff I want."

I was a little ashamed. "Oh well, come in, then. I don't want to interrupt a pitch."

"Let's see the catalogue, Sammie."

"Really, you don't have to buy anything," I told Jane. "I feel bad …"

"No, no. You know, I know what it's like. It's the same at my school. It's important." She smiled.

I left the two of them at the dining room table, and I returned to cleaning melted cheese and letter fragments off the floor. Nick watched the girls in their negotiation. He had wiped his tears and was trying to join them.

"Where do you teach?" Nick asked her. He was asking questions that I hadn't bothered to consider. I was still wondering why she had manicured her nails. My hands were mired in pizza sauce.

"At Cheviot Elementary and George Washington. Just part time. I do special projects there for the schools. I run the garden, arts programs, stuff like that ... so I know the schools need this money."

"If we get money at our school, we might be able to get a grass field.

"You don't have grass? Where do you play now?"

"On the cement. There's a little area where we play soccer."

"Don't you get hurt when you fall?"

"Sometimes I get like a skinned knee. Like this one." She showed her the open scab on her leg.

"Sammie, that looks terrible!"

"It doesn't really hurt. It just stings sometimes when I bend my knee."

"Marty, did you see this?" she called to me. "I can't believe they let them play soccer on asphalt!"

I was nearly done picking up the paper pieces. "I know, it's crazy isn't it?" I had no idea what they did at recess. But I pretended.

"Is it bleeding?" I called as I got out the plates.

"No, Dad." Sammie was smiling at Jane's concern. She tried to redirect Jane to the magazine. "See that's why we need the money. For the field. "

"Marty, do you have any Neosporin? I don't like the look of this."

I was transferring the pizza to the plates. "I think we're out."

"Yes, we do," Nick answered. He left the table, went to the small drawer in the kitchen, and found a rolled tube of antibiotic cream. He gave it to Jane, who carefully checked the date.

"It's still good." She squeezed some lotion onto her finger to rub onto Sammie's skin.

"Does it sting?" Sammie asked, still smiling at Jane's concern.

"Not at all. It'll make it feel better and prevent an infection." Sammie rolled up her pant leg, and Jane rubbed it on. Sammie smiled widely as she did.

"There now. See that little red area around the sides? We don't want that to get bigger. You watch it, okay? And put some of this on every morning."

The two returned to reviewing the catalogue as Nick quietly watched on.

"What's wrong, Nicholas?" asked Jane.

"Just a bad day," he answered her.

Sammie chimed in. "We got a mean note from our mom. She moved to Colorado. But I think she's coming back soon."

"Oh, I'm ..."

"She doesn't usually write letters. I think that just means she's missing us."

Nick got up and went to his room. "Tell me when dinner's ready."

"It's ready!" I called back at him. He came back to the table, sat down, and he and I began to eat. We both struggled to catch the cheese before it slid down off the crust. The girls continued to look through the magazine.

"Samantha, how did you know that your mother wrote ..."

"I was spying, Dad! That's why I want these Super Spy walkie talkies. I only need six more points. Then I get the soccer trainer and the walkie talkies!"

"Then I don't think we should get them," I smiled. "You seem to be good enough at spying without those."

"Stop it, Daddy! You're going to make Jane not buy something!"

"Don't worry, Sammie. I need quite a few things. First these gardening gloves …"

Sammie interrupted her. "I like your nails. Did you paint them yourself?"

"No … I had them manicured. I just decided to do that today. I haven't done it in years." I thought her face flushed a bit. For a moment Jane seemed embarrassed.

"Will you take me for a manicure?"

"Sure, that would be fun. We could have a girl's day out."

"Really! Daddy, can we do that?"

"Sure you can."

"I like your soccer jersey, Sammie? What team are you on?"

"The Blue Tigers. We're undefeated." She smiled even more brightly. "That's why I need the soccer trainer. So we can stay ahead."

I told Sammie to come eat three times, but she was lost in conversation with Jane. Nick and I were quiet as we ate and listened. He was hurting badly inside. He had a mother who had left him when he was too young to remember. He had a sister who could steal the attention of visitors in our home. Though we had managed to drive the gorilla from the window, he had returned. Nick needed more from me. He needed me to get rid of the ape for good. And he needed me to find a way to be with him. As for Sammie, I thought that she was fine. That's what she had always led me to believe. She was negotiating for a soccer trainer, for walkie talkies, and for someone to take her for a manicure. But my little goal scorer wasn't so okay. It hadn't dawned on me, but soon I would learn that she was rattling inside, too.

An Indri Cry

I was back sleeping in Nick's room. I enjoyed being close to him, and I took pride in keeping the gorilla away. Sunday morning, the kids were up and bounding with energy. They made pancakes on their own now. The doorbell rang at eight, and we knew who it was. I enjoyed Jane's visits. She had a bit of magic to her, though I was growing concerned about my attraction to her. I had promised myself after Lara left that I would make it through this world on my own. The risk of letting someone in is that they can leave. But the growing attachment I had for this semblance of a family was overcoming me, at least for a few hours each week. The pancakes and lemurs were holding the four of us together. We sat at the table enjoying the meal prepared by my children, and I began …

Rosalie ran her kitchen like a drill sergeant. She gave out instructions, and her helpers followed. "I need silverware on the table," she would say. Or, "You're moving too slow! I need 25 more pancakes in the next ten minutes!" And, "Careful with those plates! My father brought me those and we can't break another one!"

There were 22 lemurs in the troop, and only they were allowed entrance to Rosalie's. Carlos had skipped the past few months, so there would be a few cakes left over. It was Sunday morning in late August and Rosalie and her crew had cooked up quite a feast. She was resting under the shade of a Baobab tree under a hot Madagascar sun, enjoying the sound of the larks calling up high. The guests gathered to form a line. But what began as a pleasant and orderly breakfast was interrupted by a hooting call from the tree tops. Rosalie recognized the sound but was too tired to move.

Jasper swung down from the trees and took a big cut in line. The others were outraged, but Jasper didn't care. He wanted his pancakes and saw no reason to wait. Jasper toppled over the plates as he searched for his favorite. From there he went straight for the woven basket. He took four pancakes from the top of the heap with great enthusiasm.

A rumbling sound came from the back of the line. Like an ocean wave, the lemurs pushed forward, toppling the neatly stacked dishes down to the ground with a crash. As the plates fell onto the dirt, Rosalie rose with alarm. Two plates that her father had given her were shattered. Furious, she filled her chest with air and let out a series of calls that sent the others cowering behind the trees.

"The kitchen is closed today. Goodbye and have a nice week."

"Oh Rosalie!" laughed Jasper. "Loosen up, sister! You don't want your hard work to go to waste!"

"You broke my dishes, Jasper. I'm tired of you and your sidekick Lionel. I'm tired of cooking. I may close the kitchen for a month!"

The others muttered in dismay. Some ran for the nylon basket and scooted from the kitchen with pancake in hand.

"I'm certainly not ever cooking again for you, Jasper! Make your own pancakes for once!"

"Oh come on, Rosalie …" he laughed.

"Find me two new plates and I may reconsider. Until then, I don't want to hear from you."

The others whispered and hooted around the brother and sister quarrel. Above the cackling, a sound wafted from the West. It was familiar to them all, as no other lemur in the troop could make that minor note. But the sound that morning was particularly loud and disturbing. From the distance Nikko's mournful call came in long thirty-second spurts. The commotion in the kitchen stopped.

Elliot was the most alarmed and followed Nikko's call. He had good energy to swing now with two pancakes in his gut. He knew this was no ordinary cry. He had heard Nikko's sounds through the years, but this one was different. The tone was lower with a minor pitch that sent a chill through Elliot's body. And Elliot's concern grew as he realized the sound was coming from a clearing very near his oak tree.

Elliot couldn't believe what he saw. He had warned of it, half in jest, but he never thought it would happen. He looked on at Nikko hunched over his father's body. There lay Carlos, fallen and breathless, face up and eyes wide open as though he were still searching. Nikko howled, the sound of a wailing Indri lemur. His large body across his father's, face down to the dirt as he moaned.

Elliot's body grew cold as he watched on. He wanted to help Nikko, but he couldn't move. He watched from beyond the clearing, too stunned to help. As he watched the young Nikko filled with grief, he tried to stop his thoughts from racing.

Elliot's mind couldn't stay with his brother. It was too much. He found himself wondering about his books. He tried to call forth Mr. Frost. But there was no voice back. Staring on at the eyes of his dead brother, he wanted more than anything to feel. But that ability seemed to belong to the young Indri lying across Carlos' lap.

Elliot's horror was interrupted by the reflection of an object at the base of his oak tree. Perhaps it was the alignment of the sun in that moment that made it sparkle. He wondered if he had ever looked at his tree from that angle. Certainly Carlos hadn't or he would have found it. It was not buried after all. It was right there all the time. A faded brown knife with a spoon, a fork, and a can opener exposed, reflecting the sunlight beaming through the treetops. From the rust on the blades, one could see that it had likely been at the foot of Elliot's tree for quite some time.

Leavings

Carlos was dead. Something from within had taken over and killed him—presumably a dark part of me announcing its presence publicly. I had surrendered myself to a story and completely lost control of it. I got up from the table to shake my discomfort and tried to ground myself in dishwashing. It was quiet now in the kitchen. Another moment of great fathering for Sammie and Nick. I figured it was no use. I was better off not letting anything out from inside of me.

I wiped my plate clean of syrup and stacked it in the dishwasher. I cleaned the blue bowl, put the milk back, and switched the disposal to flush the egg shells. I grabbed Nicholas' plate, then Samantha's. I picked up Jane's, but she wasn't done. I looked at the other plates—no one was done. I was taking away breakfast ready to send everyone on into the day.

The kitchen remained quiet. The kids saw my distress. Jane did, too.

Samantha looked at me wide eyed. "What happened to Nikko?"

"I don't know, sweetie. I think he went back ... and lived happily ever after."

"How could he live happily ever after?" Nick challenged. "That's not a story. What happened to Nikko? You said he was making those sounds."

"Look, I have to do some work, guys. I'm sorry. It's going to be a busy few weeks for me with this case. I told you about that. Do you have homework?"

"It's Sunday morning. I don't have homework over the weekend," Sammie answered. She was so confused, and I couldn't help her.

"OK. I know what happened," smiled Jane. "The lemurs all looked at Carlos. And when they looked at him they saw his finger move ..."

"No they didn't!" I barked. "Damn it, he was dead. That's the end of the story. He died trying to find the goddamn knife. He wasted months and years. He gave up eating pancakes. And he never found Max's knife. The one and only thing his father had given him." Jane's attempt at storymaking had disturbed me. Though I was overwhelmed by the story, I knew somehow that Carlos needed to die. If I were ever to move on with life.

"Okay, Martin. Okay. He was dead."

"And he wasn't resurrected. And there was no happy ending. The vultures came down and they ..."

"Stop it, Martin. Stop it right now. I'm taking the kids to the beach, okay? You do your work."

"No, I didn't mean for ..." Guilt welled up inside of me. I was sorry for snapping at her, for ruining everyone's Sunday pancakes, and for miring the innocence of our story with my own unconscious.

"Kids, go get a bathing suit. Martin, we're going to the pier. We'll be back at 3 or 4. I'll bring over dinner after that."

"No, don't worry, the kids are fine ..."

Samantha and Nicholas lit up. "To the pier? Can we go on the Ferris wheel?" asked Samantha.

"Yes, absolutely," said a determined Jane.

"Okay," I said, disoriented. "But don't worry about dinner. I ..."

"I made it last night. After all these Sundays I've intruded, it was the least I could do."

She was trying to work her way into my home. Soon it would be decorated with frills and curtains and God knows what else. But as keenly as I perceived that, I had a growing sense of needing Jane.

"Okay, thanks. If I get ahead, maybe I'll come and find you."

"Great."

The kids rinsed the dishes in the sink. They followed Jane, the Pied Piper. I wondered about her music and what song she played. Maybe they could hear something that grown-ups like me just couldn't.

As I watched Jane guide the children out the front door, a feeling in my chest rushed in. A hot energy, like I was on fire, with an impulse to call out, "Don't you fucking leave me." I was angry as I watched them walk away. I bit down on my tongue and distracted myself from the feeling. I got a broom to sweep the morning dust from pancake making. But I couldn't block the image of Carlos, searching for his knife, too busy to play, and dying from a lack of pancakes. Pecked at by vultures, ripping at his flesh on the forest floor. The energy in my body intensified, coursing up my neck and into my arms.

Then a new image came to mind. It was Major, flashing me a peace sign, and Lara content as she rode away from me and the kids. The fury I had tried to bury for seven years bubbled to the surface, and I used my imagination to direct it at the real source of my anger. I imagined the bike, skidding off the road, slamming into a tree. Major's head snapping from his neck like a bowling ball thrown up the street. And an unfortunate car, driving up the street, slamming over the couple, leaving only blood and bones.

Then the next flash came, as if the memory of one person's leaving brought on thoughts of another. My father dead in the garden after pulling weeds on a hot summer morning. My sister had found him lying there. Then she blamed me for it. All three of them did. For being so out of touch. We hadn't spoken for a couple of years after I married Lara. The truth was, he had sworn off doctors all his life. It was an enviable way to go. At one moment busy in the garden, in another moment somewhere else. No suffering, just gone at the age of 59. As I thought about my relationship with my father ending in a deadlock of silence, I felt sad about his death for the very first time, and a wave of grief enveloped me and washed away my rage. My chest softened deep inside as tears came to my eyes, and I let them flow down my cheeks rather than hold them back.

I watched out the window as the kids walked to Jane's and disappeared from sight. Then another, more hazy, memory.

My mother's long struggle with breast cancer, ending when I was seven years old. I didn't want to think about this leaving. Unlike my father, she had suffered a great deal, but I had paid her little attention. While I played with my friends in the neighborhood, she became weaker and more emaciated over a two-year period. The sicker she got, the more I stopped visiting her in her bedroom. I went days, even weeks, without going in. Dad told us not to worry, that she would be okay, and that she needed to rest. I knew my father would take care of her, so I trusted the situation to him. But then she died. My father couldn't save her after all. She died in her bed in my father's arms.

I recalled my numbness at her funeral. I had felt bad for my father who was alone then. It seemed that everyone there was looking at me. I didn't shed a tear, but instead sat in my seat and thought up my first story of an alien city to keep myself entertained.

I rarely thought of my mother's death. It had been over three decades, and I had never visited her ashes, settled in the bottom of an urn off the 405 freeway, very close to my home. I slapped my knee sharply as the memories came to me, chastising myself for my behavior. My parents were good people, and I had loved them very much, though my actions spoke differently. I didn't know what crime they had committed to make me so indifferent these many years. I wondered if it was simply that they had left me too soon.

I watched as Jane backed her car out of her driveway. Then came the image that I didn't want to think about. Danny up on the bridge in Pasadena. What had he been doing there? Why didn't he call? More tears flooded my sight.

Danny had been the person to help me with my leavings. First it was alien stories in my head. Then it was running with the team. Then it was traveling the world with my new friend. Danny was my family then. And though we had lost touch, he had helped me navigate a particularly difficult point in my life, when I left home for the first time without a mother to say goodbye to me.

I wondered for the millionth time why Danny had jumped. He and Jody had married shortly after college, and I had imagined that they were living his dream life. Though for some reason he had left her and everyone else in his life one night to stand at the edge of the Colorado Street Bridge. The image grew stronger. Danny up on the bridge. A stranger meeting him up there, trying to talk to him. Danny nodding his head as though he had made up his mind. Turning. And jumping. Found dead at the bottom of a river bank. Sometimes I wished that I could have been the stranger. I spoke to Danny in quiet moments after the suicide. I practiced what I would have said. But I could never convince myself that my words would have been strong enough to stop him.

Jane was driving off. I ran out the front door as fast as I could. "Wait a minute!" I hollered. Jane saw me and stopped the car. "Can I come along?"

Dorrie

I shuffled slowly down the hallway toward my office. I noted the peeling paint, the industrial scent copy toner, the stale coffee, and the slight caving of the roof overhead. My job seemed meaningless to me against the backdrop of storymaking on Sunday mornings, and I was too preoccupied with the image of Carlos to care much about the Hatch Act or Dawson's case.

Dorrie greeted me. "Good morning, Mr. Grossmark ... I left a note on your desk. Mr. Hauser called from payroll. He needs to talk to you. Sounded pretty urgent."

"Can you call him back and let him know I'll get with him in an hour or so."

"Sure. You know you have a meeting with the Chief of Staff at nine."

"Can you call him for me? Tell him that I have to pass this morning. It's not important. Just our weekly briefing. He cancelled the last two weeks anyway."

"Do you want me to find another time for ... are you okay, Mr. Grossmark?"

"Who, me? Oh, yeah, I'm okay. Just trying to figure something out ... thanks."

"Sure thing. Would you like me to get you a cup of coffee?"

Jack Siegal, an enthusiastic paralegal on staff, passed us in the hall.

"Morning, Martin. Morning, Dorrie. Meetings in the hallways now?"

"Morning, Jack," I answered as he rushed past us. I wondered what kept him going.

"Sure. A cup of coffee would be good," I said to Dorrie. "But I can get it."

"Don't worry. I'll get it." She disappeared to the break room.

I was frozen in place. I looked at the poster of a lone trumpet sitting on a chair. I wondered if anyone would ever play it. I thought about Carlos and the knife that he never found. I wasn't sure if I could make it through the day without Carlos. Maybe I was losing my mind. Maybe this was a mid-life crisis.

Dorrie found me again in front of my office. "This might help you." I noticed Dorrie that morning, really noticed her. Her gold hair with gray roots. The worn lines on her tanned face.

"Thanks. You know, I'll call Dr. Bradshaw. I think I can make it to that meeting." I smiled at her and walked into my office. Then I imagined Carlos again. It was a brief resurrection. I imagined him digging. It was good to see him. He was more vibrant than ever. But no sooner did I have him digging than I saw the vultures in the sky. I could try to bring him back to life, but he was dead. He was gone.

The experience recurred throughout the day. Like a magnet, I was seized by a seductive force and lost focus on my office tasks. I saw Carlos lying dead on the ground. And then his thumb would move. Or his ankle or his neck. My attempts to bring him back to life varied, but they all ended the same. With a last breath from a lonely lemur who returned to a lifeless state. My story somehow needed Carlos to die. As much as my mind tried to keep him alive, I spent the whole day killing him.

The experience grew more intense through the afternoon and haunted me as I walked to Dr. Bradshaw's office. He spoke to me about an incompetent nurse he wanted to fire. But I couldn't focus. I thought of Carlos. Poor dead Carlos. Ripped apart by vultures. Fur, skin, blood, bones, all torn into a buzzard smorgasbord. Dr. Bradshaw began to discuss the Henry Dawson case. I let him know that the deposition with his counsel was pending. He was frustrated with the slow pace. I wondered if he could tell that I was focused on a dead lemur on the floor of a clearing in Paden's Patch.

"Marty, we're paying for him to be out at this point. He's probably writing more letters from home. Jesus, he's probably part of a sleeper cell for all we know."

And I laughed. "A sleeper cell? What do you mean?"

"I'm kidding. I'm trying to get your attention. You seem distracted."

Samantha

I stopped by Spellman's on the way home. No one was at the counter.

"Hello?" I called to the back. I rang the bell on the counter.

"One minute, please," answered a voice. It was Frannie, and she coughed after she answered me. After a few moments, she appeared at the counter in her apron.

"Martin!" She beamed at me. "What can I get you today?"

"Oh. Something for dessert. Anything, really."

"I've made fresh mandelbrodt. You want to try a piece?"

"I don't know what that is. But sure."

"Martin. Mandelbrodt. What do you mean you don't know what it is?"

"I never heard of it."

"My oh my. You must try some then. It's in your heritage. The finest Jewish cookie around."

"I don't know much about Jewish things." I was embarrassed. "We're not that observant."

"I know that, honey." I wondered what she meant, but didn't say anything.

Frannie handed me an almond toasted cookie that looked like a biscotti. "Try that," she said with pride.

"That's really good," I told her.

"Next thing you know, that son of yours will be lining up for a Bar Mitzvah."

"Maybe so," I said.

Frannie packed me a box of the cookies. I passed a small men's clothing store on the way home. I was half tempted to look inside, but I told myself I had too much to do to waste any more time.

While the kids did homework, I tried to steal a moment to work on Dawson's case. As I sorted through case law, I was having trouble finding support for the stance of the institution. I knew I had to keep digging. The last thing I wanted to do was to cross Dr. Bradshaw. Never mind the Inspector General and the host of other federal authorities sending him inquiries. Though I was frankly having trouble supporting any kind of action against this physician.

We had a quiet night, and the kids enjoyed the cookies.

"Where did you get these?"

"Over at Spellman's. Same place I always go for a pink box."

"They're awesome!" Nick exclaimed. "What are they?"

"They're called Mandelbrot."

"Mandelbrot?" Sammie asked. "What kind of cookie is that?"

"It's a Jewish cookie," I answered her.

"Oh. We're Jewish, right?" she asked.

"Yes, silly. We're Jewish," I said. I was ashamed by her question. I had provided little sense of spirit or religious affiliation for my children. It hadn't been a big part of my growing up, and I just continued to sidestep the issue in my parenting.

The reality was, the kids weren't really Jewish, since Lara was Catholic. But I didn't want to get into that, as it would involve mentioning their mother's name. I preferred to just pretend the whole issue didn't exist. Sammie went to bed early that night, and I slid into a sleeping bag in Nick's room to protect us from the ape out the window.

I woke up later than usual the next morning. Nick was snoring softly as I snuck out of his room and made myself some coffee. I peeked into Samantha's room to see if she was up. Her bed was empty. I shook the sheets trying to find her. I looked all over the house for her. I opened every door, softly calling her name so as not to awaken Nicholas. I wondered if she was hiding. I searched every closet. I looked under every bed. My panic was mounting and I called for her more loudly.

Nick woke. He had no idea where she had gone. I called the police, and they were on their way. I ran outside in my bathrobe screaming her name.

"Samantha! Samantha! Samantha!"

I couldn't think. My mind raced, imagining the very worst. Maybe an abduction in the middle of the night. The world on our street spun, as there was no answer to my calls. I ran into the house and slammed the front door.

"Nicholas, get in the car. We need to go find her."

"But what if she comes home?" He cried and screamed with me. I pushed him along into our garage and into the car.

"Just get in ... We're just driving around the block. I need you to watch for her."

"Dad! The gorilla!" he screamed. "What if he took Sammie away?"

"Nick, there's no fucking gorilla! Put your seat belt on."

Nick was terrified, and so was I. We pulled out of the driveway and I smashed squarely into the mailbox.

"Daddy, stop. Stop!" yelled Nick.

"She didn't say anything to you? Did she tell you she was going to leave? Tell me Nick!"

"She didn't, Daddy. She didn't say anything. Just good night when she went to bed." Nicholas cried harder. We were in quicksand together and I couldn't find anything to grab.

"Nick, think. Where would she go?" I straightened the car and tried again to back up out of the driveway.

"Daddy, stop. Wait!" he cried. "Stop the car!"

"Nick, we need to find her ..."

"She's right there! I see her. On Jane's porch. They're walking this way."

There she was. I couldn't believe it. She had slipped over to Jane's without telling me. We drove into Jane's driveway, and I watched as Samantha turned her face down toward the asphalt. I jerked the car into park, turned it off, and jumped out.

"What are you doing?" I yelled to Sammie.

"It's all okay, Martin. It's okay," Jane responded. Sammie said nothing.

"What happened? I was so scared, Sammie! Are you okay?"

Nick stayed in the back seat watching on.

"I'm not sure what happened exactly, Martin. I rolled over this morning and I found Samantha lying next to me in bed. She said ..."

Samantha wouldn't look up at me. "I woke up this morning, and I went over. I just went in Jane's doggy door."

"Honey, why in the world would you leave the house like that?" I tried with everything I had to restrain my anger. She wouldn't look up.

"Samantha, honey ..." my rage was dissolving. "What's wrong?" I went to hug her and she wouldn't. She stood like a pencil in my arms as I lifted her. Finally she looked up and met my eyes.

I held onto her as tightly as I could. I wanted to squeeze her so she could never leave again. Her eyes got tearful. "Samantha, I'm sorry. Whatever it is. I'm sorry. Tell me why you went to Jane's house."

"I didn't know where else to go."

"Why did you have to go anywhere, kiddo?"

"I had a nightmare, Daddy. I had a nightmare about Carlos. He was in the field. But he was covered in glass. I don't know where it came from, but there was glass everywhere around him. And cereal balls. And he was dead." She was crying. I had never seen her cry before, not since she was an infant. Not even when she fell on the soccer field. "Then when I woke up, my knee was stinging really badly. I thought I had glass on me. So I kept wiping it to get it off."

"Why didn't you come get me?"

"I tried, Daddy. But you weren't in your room. So I got scared. I went into Nick's room, and I saw you in there. But you were asleep."

"You could have woken me up!"

"My knee was stinging really bad. So I just went to Jane's because I knew that she could help me. I brought the ointment so she could put it on. I crawled through the doggy door."

"You just went outside?"

"I thought Jane could make my knee stop stinging."

"But you didn't even wake me up, sweetheart," Jane said calmly.

"Well, you were sleeping, too. So I just got into your bed.

And when I did, the stinging stopped."

I knelt down to Sammie's level. Tears flowed from her eyes. "Sammie, do you promise you'll wake me up next time?"

"Can I sleep with you and Nick? I don't want to be alone in my room. Nick says there's a gorilla that can take us away."

"Sure you can. We can have a campout. And we'll stop telling the lemur story. I'm sorry that it got too scary." I was relieved to be talking to her. "Ten Daddy points off for me. I'll think of another kind of story to tell."

"No, Dad. We can't stop the story!" I hadn't heard Nick get out of the car.

"It gave your sister a nightmare, kiddo. And you're still afraid of that gorilla."

"I'm okay, Daddy," Sammie stared at me. "I just got sad for Carlos. That's all. I'm sad that he went away."

My eyes watered up looking at her. "Me too, kiddo. Me too."

I turned to Jane. "I know it's not the weekend. But you want to come over for some pancakes this morning?"

"Sure," she answered. "That sounds like a good idea to me." The kids were excited.

"But we'll be late for school," Nick answered.

"It's okay," I answered him. "I think this is more important."

A Knock From A Nephew

I left the car parked in front of Jane's home and we shuffled toward the house. My neck ached. Jane promised that she would help cook. I was growing wary of what came from the recesses of my mind, and I couldn't kill another lemur. I couldn't let that happen to the kids again. Like I was back in the Jeep, driving through the intersection, I had to defend against the oncoming traffic that was threatening the sanctuary of our kitchen. Though it's tough to be careful and spontaneous simultaneously. Storymaking could be risky business.

We got out the pan, found the ingredients, and went to work.

"I got some chocolate chips to add to the batter, guys. What do you think?" I could imagine my father's disapproval. He made them exactly the same each Sunday and would have never altered the recipe. But I followed my impulse.

Sammie lit up. "Chocolate chip pancakes! Yes, Daddy. Let's add them."

"Won't they melt all over?" Nick asked.

"There's only one way to find out, isn't there?"

Sammie was in the pantry. "Where are they, Daddy?"

"They're on that high shelf. I'll get them. You can't reach."

"Yes I can." She climbed up the shelf just like a lemur. She wasn't sad anymore. She was strong again, and a bit more playful. "Got 'em!"

I heard a crash in the pantry. "Oh gosh!" Sammie yelled. I ran to see what had happened. She had knocked a few soup cans over to the floor. I grabbed her from behind and held her. I lifted her up, and I put her up on my shoulders.

"Daddy! What are you doing?"

"No more trouble from you, Missie! I'm going to keep you right here where I know where you are."

She was laughing. "Put me down."

The doorbell rang. "Jane's here!" Sammie yelled. She was

laughing. "Put me down, Daddy." I walked over to the door and opened it. Jane smiled at us in the doorway.

"Morning." I smiled at her.

"Morning again to you. And look at you way up high. Is there enough air up there?"

Sammie was still laughing. "He won't put me down."

"I don't blame him. That way he knows you're close by."

I put Sammie down. We all went to work, and the chocolate chips melted into a mess, just as Nick had predicted. But they were delicious. As we ate, I felt a surge of creativity and playfulness, and I began.

At dusk, Nikko carried Carlos' body away to a field by the Southern end of the Sekio River, just above Miriam's Falls. This is where he decided to bury his father. Others followed him, including Carlos' family—Elliot, Rosalie, and Jasper. They watched as Nikko dug a hole and placed his father gently inside, kissing him on the cheek before laying him down to rest. Nikko covered Carlos' body with dirt, digging from the ground as his father had. The others watched on, saying nothing. It was a quiet time, and not a word was spoken.

The following morning, the lemurs tried to go about their routines. Rosalie cleaned the kitchen. Jasper and Lionel continued to swing. And Elliot returned to his books. He moved about trying to settle himself, but he found it impossible. Then came three knocks on his door. He peered out the peep hole at the darkest of the lemurs.

"Good morning, Nikko. How are you this morning? Would you like some coffee? I've made far too much..."

"No, Elliot. I would not. I've been spending time thinking after laying my father in the ground. I have some questions."

"Why certainly. Any way that I can help you, you know I'm most happy to." Nikko followed Elliot and sat down on a large pillow while Elliot poured himself another cup of coffee.

"Would you like something to eat? I have some apricots I've harvested from the north side of the river. There's a tree there that is quite prolific this year."

"I'm not hungry. I am filled with questions about my father."

"Yes. I'm sorry. Your father was very special. I am having quite a time of it, too. He being of my own blood and all."

Nikko paused. "Those are curious words, Uncle Elliot. Is he not also of mine?"

"Oh, that's not what I meant."

"So you take it back?"

Elliot was quiet.

"You don't. Was my father not of my own blood?"

Elliot paused. "Certainly he spoke to you of …"

"He spoke to me of very little. From the time I can recall, I have only one image. That is of him searching for something near the foot of your great oak. "

"So he never …"

"Told me what he was looking for? No, he didn't. Told me why I am darker? No he did not."

"Well certainly the others … Rosalie, Jasper … they must have told you something."

"It seems no one has bothered. I know that I am a different sort. I am darker. I am larger. My cry sounds different."

"You are faster, you are stronger, and your intellect is keen."

"What is it, Elliot? What can you tell me?"

"Nikko, I don't see this as my responsibility. Perhaps Rosalie can share if you were to help her out in the kitchen."

"She hardly talks to me. And Jasper and Lionel swing the other way when they see me. I need to know the truth about my father. And about me."

Elliot sighed as he looked at the great Nikko. Elliot knew he deserved to know the truth. But it would be difficult to hear.

"Carlos was not your father, Nikko."

Nikko paused. "I figured that. He didn't act like a father. Always lost in his own searching. But then where did I come from? What do you know about me, Uncle Elliot?"

Elliot rose from his desk chair and stared at his great books. He wished the answer lived in the pages of a great work, and that he could just hand it to Nikko to read. But he would have to tell him himself.

Elliot joined Nikko and took a seat on the pile of pillows. He mashed an apricot in his mouth as he spoke. "It was during monsoon season. It had been raining for days, as you know it can here. When the rain cleared, Carlos came out from his wooden tree house. And as he climbed down from the branches he heard a baby lemur crying. He was wrapped in a worn cloth. Well, Carlos didn't know what to do. So he …"

"So he brought me to his tree house?"

"Not exactly. He did take you. He saved you, Nikko. We don't know where you came from. There had been talk of a darker troop, a tribe of Indri lemurs that live beyond the waterfall in Argon's Forest. Carlos picked you up, and he brought you to me. I knew nothing of babies. So he brought you to our mother. To Rama."

"I see."

"Rama knew that Carlos couldn't possibly care for you. So she took you into her home. You grew on coconut milk, and you and Rama were inseparable that first year. But I'm sure you don't recall."

"No, nothing. Where is Rama now?"

"It was four years ago. You were one, Nikko. I was nine. Rama was playing with you in the clearing. She stumbled into some bushes at the west end. She hollered that she couldn't get up. Her howling sounded through the forest. Carlos came running from his tree house. I met him at the bottom of my oak. We ran toward her calling."

Elliot continued as Nikko listened carefully. "Then came the sound of the trappers. Maybe eight or nine of them. 'Over here. We got one over here!' Carlos and I stopped in our tracks. You were there, in the middle of the field, frozen in fright as the men approached. Our mother had been caught in a trap in the bushes. The men were coming for her, and they would have taken you, too. If ..."

"If what? If what, Elliot?"

"Carlos was able to get to you. He saved you. He ran for you, out in the clearing. He grabbed you into his chest and scooted with you toward the bushes. But the men had already gotten to Rama. She shouted for Carlos to run away. She hollered like only a mother can. And he listened to her. And faster than I had ever seen him move, he danced away from the clearing and disappeared with you into the treetops."

"And Rama?"

"We don't know. I found a jacket the next day. I can get it for you. I put it in the closet thinking it might one day be useful." Elliot rose and went to his closet. He pulled out a dull olive rain poncho with the red lettered words MOFINKO TRAPPERS. He held it out for them both to see.

"I never knew what to do with it."

"Did you follow the men?"

Elliot was ashamed. He and the others were afraid of the world beyond Paden's Patch. But Elliot knew that adventure and exploration were in Nikko's nature. He would never be afraid of what was beyond, for it was from the beyond that his story had begun. Of course he would have tried to find her.

"Nikko, we couldn't chase them. There were many men. They had guns. We were too frightened. And in one moment, her howling ceased. Though we never heard a shot. That I know. We never heard a shot."

"But I don't understand. She was your mother. Why wouldn't you follow her?"

Elliot didn't have an answer. He only knew that they could never leave Paden's Patch. It was here that evolution had stopped and they could never compete with what lived beyond the island.

"I don't know. I don't know the answer to that question."

Nikko sat thoughtfully. He wasn't critical of his uncle. He just sat figuring it out.

"Then did Max take care of me? He was her husband after all."

"He had already gone. Oh at times he came back, but most of the time he was gone."

"Where was he?"

"I don't know, Nikko. Nobody does. He was often lost in his own world. He would come and go. At times bearing gifts for us children."

"Gifts?"

"These books for me. Plates for Rosalie. Equipment for Jasper."

"Equipment?"

"Swinging gloves. Ropes to swing. Bouncing tennis shoes. A hula hoop."

"Where did Max get all of this?"

"He found it. Objects of evolution, from humans who camped in the forest. He wanted everything for us children, so he spent most of his time looking for these things."

"Where did he go?"

"After Rama disappeared, he seemed to as well. He came back a few more times. Then he just never returned. It has been quite some time now. He just stopped visiting."

"What did he bring Carlos?"

"Oh, well, he ..."

"Did he bring Carlos anything?"

That was the moment that everything changed. Elliot realized that there was only one way to keep the spirit of his brother Carlos alive.

"He did, Nikko. He did. But he brought him only one thing. I needed a lot of books to keep reading. Rosalie needed a lot of kitchenware. Jasper frequently required new equipment. Father knew that Carlos needed only one object to keep his fears at bay. But it was gone before you were old enough to remember."

"What was it?"

Elliot hesitated. He knew that he could not hold onto it, but he certainly enjoyed having it around. For Elliot, it was a way to hold onto his brother. But he knew that he could not keep Carlos in a drawer. Carlos' spirit deserved an opportunity to live. Elliot went to his cedar desk. He had placed the knife in the back of the bottom drawer, wrapped in a piece of faded blue cloth. He reached for it, and he held it in his paw, gripping it tightly. Elliot brought it to his lips and gave it a kiss.

"I will see you later, my brother," he spoke to the knife. "For now you have places to go."

"What is it? What's in the cloth?"

"It's a knife, Nikko. It's a knife that my father gave to your father, Carlos."

"A knife? He was searching for a knife all those years? He starved to death for that? Why would he, Elliot? I don't understand."

"I believe that he wanted you to have it, Nikko. That's all. That's all that was important to him. To protect you on your adventures. He felt that since you came to us from somewhere else, that among other things, you carried the gift of adventure. It's a spirit that none of us have. That's why we stay right here. But your father … he knew that you would take an adventure one day. And he felt it important that you have the knife to protect yourself. He felt it was the least that he could do."

Nikko was quiet as Elliot continued.

"Your father lost it when Rama was captured, when he ran to save you. In one moment he lost his two most valuable assets, his mother and his knife. Really, his mother and his father. Just the other day, after Carlos died, I saw it there. It had been there all these years, leaning up against my oak tree. The rains of the previous two weeks must have washed away the forest floor enough to expose it. The sun was shining just right when I looked, and I caught a beam off the blade."

Nikko walked over to the window and looked out to the clearing at the bottom of the tree. As he gazed, Elliot placed the knife wrapped in cloth deep into Nikko's paw. Nikko grasped it tightly, as if to accept everything that came with it.

"So you must have seen him. My father. Searching all those

years under the hot sun. Digging and digging. Did you try to stop him?"

"I tried. But I couldn't. I tried to play with him. I tried to bring him to Rosalie's each week. But he wouldn't come."

"Did you help him search?"

The question pierced deeply. Elliot had never considered that.

"I didn't, Nikko. I didn't. In fact, truth be told, I never thought of that."

Part
II

Across
A Sea

Jane's Response

Later that afternoon, the kids followed Jane over to her house. I worked a bit more on the case. I would be meeting again with Jerry, Dawson's attorney, and some details of the law were escaping me. I struggled to discern if he had actually violated the Hatch Act. The VA systems had gone into motion, and Dr. Bradshaw expected I would fall right in line. But I was losing my conviction that Dawson had broken a statute. The accusation was that he used his VA position for a political cause, but as I read his blog, I had trouble understanding how his writing was political. He was speaking about his experiences as a clinician, like a dermatologist might write about the dangers of the sun after treating so much skin cancer. In a sense, he was saying to be careful of the sun. But in this case the sun was a war, and that was the cause of the problems he was treating. It was starting to make sense to me. Primary prevention. If there were no trauma, then there would be no aftermath. And my ongoing experience at intersections was rapidly changing my idea of the impact that such events can have.

The kids had moved to Jane's backyard. I could hear their voices through my study window. I heard the flapping of material and a thud at one point. My shoulder ached, and I sat back from my computer to listen to their voices.

"Nick, see that handle over there? It's easier to hold if you grab it."

I couldn't imagine what they were doing. It sounded like a big parachute flapping in the wind. I remembered playing with one when I was in grade school.

"Grab that stake, Sammie. If you push that corner into the ground, we'll have an easier time."

"What's this made of anyway?" I heard Nick ask.

"It's buffalo hide."

I went to the window and couldn't believe my eyes. The

three of them were erecting a huge teepee. I watched in amazement as they worked.

"I got it in," yelled Sammie.

"Good girl. Now Nick, pull your side out tight. See these wooden poles? We need to put them up one by one from the sides. Then we'll grab them and hoist them up the center."

"It's got cool designs," said Nick excitedly. It looked like real buffalo skin. Tan colored with some red markings, and thick brown sticks holding it up. The breeze caught the material with a sound like rolling thunder.

"How will it stay up?" asked Sammie. "It keeps falling over."

"Don't worry. I'll show you. Come by me and grab this pole. Nick, can you lift your side up?" Jane was hard at work, and the kids were by her side helping in any way she directed. "This is the part that's a bit difficult … okay one, two, three … push." I saw the top of the teepee rise into the air. They had erected a beautiful teepee, right in Jane's backyard, in the middle of Culver City.

"Wow!" screamed Samantha with electric enthusiasm.

"It's so cool," Nick added as he jumped to see the top.

"Hello teepee," Jane said. "Happy to see you."

I gazed in amazement at the teepee towering over the sidewall of my backyard. It sprung from Jane's green grass, adorned by roses, pansies, and geraniums in pots around its circumference. I went outside to the dead yellow grass of my backyard. The voices had muffled. They were inside the teepee, and I listened on.

"Your knee looks better, Sammie. It's not as red as last night."

"I know. I think the lotion worked on it. It doesn't hurt anymore either."

"What do we do with it now that it's up?" I heard Nick ask.

"What do you want to do?" asked Jane. "We could play a game. We could rest. We could …"

"Bring some stuff in?"

"What are you thinking about, Nick?" Jane asked.

"We have some sleeping bags at our house. But ... do you sleep in this?"

"We could if you want."

I listened to Jane talking to my children. They were content, swapping ideas back and forth. Nick seemed to have forgotten about gorillas. Sammie's knee had stopped stinging. For the moment, they were both at peace in her garden. There were no cars crashing through, no motorcycles taking her away, and no trappers abducting her. I felt content as I listened to them chatting.

I closed my eyes, and I recalled a scene from long ago. It was misty and remote, but it was there. I was in the kitchen of my childhood, with my best friend Margaret. We were to have a lemonade stand, and we made it in a blue plastic pitcher. My mother was stirring it for us with an old wooden spoon. I could hear her voice.

"How much do you want to charge?"

"I don't know, Mom."

"Maybe ten cents a glass," I recalled Margaret saying.

"It's a hot day," my mother answered her. "People will be happy to see you."

My mother was stirring and stirring. I could hear the gentle slap of the large spoon against the plastic pitcher. Around and around I heard it churn. And I hung on to those words. 'Happy to see you.' Against the muffled chattering of voices wafting from the teepee.

Then another image came crashing into my head. As uninvited as his car in the intersection, he came again for a visit. I saw him on the curb, a fifteen year old boy. He was staring at me with eyes wide open. "Can you give me a ride home to my mom?"

July 24, 1987

This seems a little crazier than anything we've ever done. I wonder if we hadn't seen that National Geographic special on the Komodo Dragons if we would be here. Probably not. But that's usually how Marty and I do our adventures. Just hear about something and go. So here we are drifting on a boat from Flores, which is a small flight from Bali. There's a lot of quiet. It gives me too much time to think. So that's why I'm writing. Today I was thinking about my real parents, and what they might have been like. I don't like it when my mind goes there. I get up against this empty space and it scares the shit out of me. I can usually start thinking of Mom and Dad and be thankful that someone rescued me. But today all I can think of is that I'm from Amarillo, Texas, and that my dad gave me away after Mom died having me. It's a bad feeling, and I can't make it stop. I keep hearing the water lap against the side of our little boat. The guide seems like he knows what he's doing. He said when we get to Komodo, he'll bring us to his friend. They have to kill a goat for us to bring to the dragons as a sacrifice. They're considered holy spirits. We'll see.

Different Sort of Pancakes

Sunday morning came again, and I was tired. I sat down in my recliner and wished that I could close my eyes for the weekend. The doorbell rang, and Sammie let Jane in. She was carrying a plastic bag.

"Morning, guys. I brought these over from my tree." She took some large fruit from the bag. I wasn't sure what they were.

"Oh thanks, Jane." I closed my eyes. I wasn't up for a Sunday morning. With the mood I was in, I would likely kill off another lemur or two, just to end the story and go back to sleep. The kids had spent the afternoons that week playing in Jane's teepee. Dawson's case was heating up, and I was appreciative of their distraction.

"You're tired," Jane said to me. She took the red and black plaid blanket off the couch and laid it over me in the recliner. "Just close your eyes. I thought I'd try and see what would happen if I added these pomegranates to the pancakes."

I didn't want to open my eyes, but I was alarmed. "Pomegranates? In the pancakes?" I thought of my father, every week the same pancakes. It seemed more sacrilegious than marrying outside the faith. I had pushed it with the chocolate, but this seemed overboard.

"Keep your eyes closed, Martin. Let's just try it. I'll just put some seeds in the batter and see what happens."

"Okay ..." I began. "Look, I don't think I'm up for the story this week." I wondered if this inertia involved my resistance to the next part of the tale. I really wasn't sure I was up for an adventure myself.

"No worries, Martin. Why don't you listen for a while. I know where we are. I'll go from here."

I was alarmed. "Oh, do you know about lemurs?"

"No, Martin. You can fill me in where I get it wrong. But I know where we are in the story."

How could she? This was my story. She was going to ruin it. At the critical point for Nikko. And for me.

Sammie was excited. "All right, Jane. You tell the story for a while. Then I can tell some, too. We can all take turns."

I woke up. The story would wind up on the North Pole with Santa, Nikko helping to pull a sleigh. "No guys. Let's wait until next week when I have a little more energy. It has been really stressful for me this week with this case."

"Close your eyes, Martin. I have an idea what happens next."

I wasn't sure if I could share my story with another storyteller. As far as I knew, she wasn't even literary. But she was stirring in the kitchen and dropping pomegranate seeds into the batter. She and Sammie were laughing. Nick came into the kitchen and saw the scene.

"You're putting pomegranates in the pancakes?"

"Come on, Nick. We need help peeling."

"That's crazy!" But he joined them in dropping seeds into the bowl.

"What do they taste like hot?" asked Nick.

"We'll find out," she said. Nick played basketball, shooting seeds across the kitchen and landing them into the batter. I enjoyed watching him shoot. If it couldn't be basketballs, at least it was pomegranates. He did have some sense of boyhood in him. Jane laughed as a seed splattered batter in her eyes.

"The rose is a rose, what's next, who knows? A pomegranate I suppose!" Jane laughed, wiping her eyes.

That was Frost. She knew Frost. And she had added to him. She had brought him right into my kitchen. If she could add to Robert Frost, she could add to my pancakes. She could add to my story, and start off Nikko's adventure. I relaxed into her words.

"Samaya had worked in Rosalie's kitchen for two years now …"

"Samaya, who's Samaya?" I was alarmed and threw off my blanket.

"Relax. You mentioned her a while back. So let's find out about her."

I was helpless. I thought again of chess and castling. The queen had broken through the pawns, and I was vulnerable. I watched her stirring and listened to her voice. It was deep and sultry, coming from a mysterious place inside of her somewhere. I watched her flip pancakes on the grill. She had pulled her hair back in a pony tail held by a pink rubber band. I glanced at her breasts as she leaned over to stir. I imagined for a moment gently caressing them. I imagined lying next to her, inside her teepee, on a wild adventure near her home in the Sierras.

That's when Nick broke in and altered our course. As if reading my mind, he changed it all up.

"I think we should tell the story in the teepee."

"What? No, Nick, I just want to relax."

"That's a great idea!" Sammie joined in.

"I really don't want to do that, okay? We've been telling the story in here. In the kitchen."

"Dad, I think it's time for an adventure."

I burst out laughing. "You what?"

"An adventure, Dad. We worked really hard on that teepee. And you haven't even seen it yet. It's just sitting there, and I think we should use it."

Jane smiled as she cooked. She was warming my heart. "I can pack us up and have us moved in just a few minutes."

"All right," added Samantha. The three of them went to work packing up the kitchen. I felt a bit energized, at least enough to get up from my chair. Nick gave me a hand and pulled me from the recliner, and the four of us ventured over to Jane's backyard.

The teepee was dark inside with an oaky smell. The skin was worn thin in places, and the light shined through. I stared up to the top. It rose nine feet into the air. Jane brought in a candle to give us some light. She had packed the pancakes, plastic plates and cups, and a carton of orange juice, all in a wooden picnic basket that she found in my kitchen. Sammie had silverware, and Nick carried the syrup.

"I have some nice pillows. I'll be right back." She left me with my two children inside a marvelous structure.

"I'll light the candle," Nick said excitedly. "Do we have a lighter?"

He knew that I did. The once former runner and preacher against smoking, now a nicotine addict. I pulled it out and threw it over to Nick.

"You know how to use that?"

"I've seen you do it like a million times."

I smiled as he worked on lighting it.

"Nick, you can keep that thing. You be the candle master. That way, I'll stay away from the cigarettes."

"Really, Daddy?" Samantha smiled. "Can't you just go get another lighter?"

"Well sure but …"

"Then give me the cigarettes." She knew I kept a pack in my back pocket.

"You going to smoke them?" I asked her. "You want to send smoke signals out the teepee?"

"No. I just don't want you to smoke them anymore."

I reached into my back pocket and threw her the pack. She dumped them onto the floor in front of her and reached for the carton of orange juice. I didn't stop her. She looked up at me.

"Is it okay?"

"Yes. It's okay." She poured the orange juice on the cigarettes. They didn't want me smoking anymore. As I watched her pouring the juice, I vowed to myself that I would never smoke again. I reached over and held Nick's hand as he struggled with the lighter. I helped him hold in the black knob, and the flame appeared as we held onto it together.

"Okay, I've got it Dad."

I let go, and he lit the candle, casting shadows and lights over the inside of the teepee. Jane returned with the pillows.

Red, orange, brown, all with different designs on them. Some of deer, some of bears.

"These were my mother's. We used to sit on these inside here. I forgot all about them."

"They're cool!" chimed Nick. We tucked them under our butts.

"Where's your mom now?" asked Sammie.

"Still in Carson City. With my dad." She paused and smiled. "It's been a couple of years since I've visited. Maybe you can come with me some day. You'd like them."

"Can I, Dad? Can I go to Carson City?"

"We'll talk about it. It's a long way for a little girl. That's a big adventure."

Jane smiled. I smiled back. We began to eat, and Jane resumed her storytelling.

Samaya and the Boat

Samaya was a six-year-old lemur and was Rosalie's most useful kitchen staff member. When Rosalie got frustrated, Samaya would save the day. She was resourceful and would stun the others with her ingenious ideas. Samaya loved to cook pancakes. More than that, she loved to feed others.

Samaya had been influenced by Rama when they worked together in the kitchen. She had loved the way Rama served pancakes, and she knew that Rama had wanted to feed as many as possible. Samaya believed that if she could have, Rama would have fed lemurs well beyond the boundaries of Paden's Patch. Rama might have sent her kitchen crew out on boats to bring pancakes and good cheer to the whole world one day.

Samaya was deeply saddened when Rama was captured. Though she was only two, she remembered that day well. She wondered where Rama had been taken, and if she had left Madagascar altogether. It is with this history that she approached the Indri lemur at the seaside, carving a large log with a knife. Beside him were some jugs of water and a sack.

"Watcha makin' there, Nikko? Is it a totem pole?"

"No, Samaya, I'm carving a boat."

She watched as he continued his work.

"What's in the sack?" she asked, trying to get his attention.

"It's food. Apricots, pecans, seeds …"

"Oh …" She watched as he carved. "Where did you get the knife?"

"I got if from Elliot. He found it. It belonged to Carlos. My father."

"Is that what he was searching for all of those years?"

"Yes it is."

"What's the hole in the top of the log?"

"That's where I'll sit." She watched him curiously as he worked.

"It seems like the boat won't be balanced. If you sit in that hole, there will be too much weight in the front end of the boat. How will it move forward?"

Nikko stumbled. He had built a boat that would sink if he sat in it.

"Well, it will be okay. I'll just lean backwards to distribute my weight."

"That's an awkward way to travel. With your knees in the hole and your back balancing the back end of the boat. Won't you get tired?"

"I'm a different sort of lemur, Samaya. I'm capable of such a stretch."

"Oh, Nikko, I don't doubt that you are. It just seems that the boat might balance better if you carve a second hole. More toward the back of the boat."

"It's a nice idea," answered Nikko kindly. "But how would a second hole balance the boat if my weight is still in the front?"

Samaya smiled at Nikko and he knew what she meant. "You want to come with me?" he asked her.

"Yes, I do. I want to come with you. Do you know where you're going?"

He paused for a moment. The idea of a companion was appealing to him, though he had become accustomed to being on his own most of the time. "I don't exactly. I just know that I'm supposed to go on an adventure. And that I want to find ..."

"Rama? Do you want to find her? Because I think she's alive somewhere. I never heard a shot that day."

"That would be a good adventure. But I also want to find the future. I want to understand what happens when we evolve, and if it is as bad as Elliot warns."

"Why do you want to do that?"

"I can't tell you exactly. I just need to know if it's okay to change. I keep thinking maybe there's something good about it, even though Elliot warns us otherwise."

"That sounds like a good adventure, though I would still want to find Rama."

"Why?"

"Because I would like to bring her some pancakes. So she can see how Rosalie makes them now. She would be proud. Maybe she can help us to spread the pancakes to other lemurs, beyond Paden's."

"Yes … that would be a good thing to do …"

"I'm not sure where she went. But I do know that she was trapped."

"By the Mofinko Trappers," answered Nikko. "I know that. Elliot showed me a piece of their jacket."

"Good. So we know where to go."

"But I don't know where that is. Mofinko. And I had a different idea in mind."

"What was your idea, Nikko? Where exactly were you going?"

"Well, I would like to find Rama, too. And Max. And the Argons forest, where I came from."

"Which will you start with?"

"I'm afraid that I can't search for those things. You get stuck if you don't move on from your past. I've watched Elliot suffering from loneliness in his tree house. And my father, stuck in one place on his search, until he died. Rosalie resentful in her kitchen. Jasper and Lionel, swinging through the trees. Ruining the lives of others."

"So then where …"

"So I thought I'd build a boat to leave altogether. I want to find the New World monkeys that Elliot has told me about from his books. I want to meet them. I want to understand what became of the lemurs away from Madagascar. And I want to meet what we become."

"I see. That's a big adventure. I've heard from Elliot's books as well. Those monkeys are frightening. Curious George. King Kong. Why would you want to meet them?"

"I want to see if we really turn into bad monkeys. I want to learn about destiny. And about evolution. About what happens when lemurs grow up. And most of all, I want to learn about taking an adventure, and if it's really as dangerous as Elliot says. "

"Are you afraid? To leave who we know and to cross a big sea?"

"Not really. I don't belong here, anyway. I never have."

"Are you sure you're not running away from something, Nikko?"

He looked down and carved more quickly. "Yes, I'm sure of that." There was quiet between the two, and he kept whittling with his knife.

"I think your boat will balance better with a second hole, Nikko. For now, that's all I know."

Nikko looked up at Samaya. "I think you're right."

"I will bring three pancakes in case we do find Rama. I think she'll appreciate that. One with apricots. One with spice. And one just the way she used to make them."

"That will be good. In case we meet her along the way. I'll have my knife. And Elliot gave me this book. He told me never to leave Madagascar. But when he realized that I was determined, he gave me this book. He told me it would help my adventure to have it."

Samaya looked at the worn leather book by Frost lying in the hole that Nikko had carved. Then she watched as Nikko moved to the back of the boat to begin carving a second hole.

"He doesn't want me to go either, you know."

"He wouldn't want any of us to go. For Elliot, we should forget all about adventures and stay safe here in Paden's." Nikko kept carving.

"No, me in particular. He's always taking extra care of me. Warning me about being careful. I don't know why. I don't think he knows what an adventure I can have. And that I can bring Rama back for all of us."

"He's just that way. He's afraid for any of us to leave the island."

"Funny thing is, I told him I was coming down to the

beach. To join your quest. He knew that you were leaving on an adventure. He was sad about it, but he told me that it was something you had to do. I told him that it was something I had to do, too. And for the first time, he told me to go. And I can't quite figure out why."

A Dream

Sunday night came. I told Nick that my shoulder was hurting from sleeping on the floor, and he assured me he would be okay on his own. As long as he knew he could come get me, he could sleep by himself. The gorilla hadn't come in nearly two weeks, and Nick thought maybe he was gone.

"I'm not sure he's so bad anyway, Dad. It's not like he ever tried to hurt me."

"Is that right?"

"Yeah. It's like he just wanted to get my attention. To play or something. He was always smiling."

"You might be right."

"Maybe he wanted to teach me to wrestle or something. Like Elliot and Carlos." Nick laughed.

"Maybe he wanted you to go on an adventure." I tucked him into bed and gave him a kiss. He rolled over and fell asleep as I picked the dirty clothes up off his floor.

I attended to my usual nighttime rituals. I turned on the dishwasher, locked the doors, and alarmed the house. I changed my clothes and settled into my bed.

Danny's journal was by my bedside, on the bottom shelf of my nightstand. The television was on, experts discussing the collapsing economy and the flooded housing market in Florida. I drifted off to sleep, and Danny came for another visit from somewhere deep in my mind.

I was up on a bridge. It was dark out. I looked out over the posts and saw my old friend calling to me. It was Danny again, his head bobbing up and down above the ocean water.

"Marty. Don't come in … It's too cold in here!" And he was pulled under the sea.

I screamed for him. "Danny!" And his head popped back up. I felt a force pulling me from the sea toward the bridge railing.

"Marty—stay out of the water. Stay on the bridge. Stay on the bridge. Live! Decide to live!"

His head disappeared again under the water. I screamed with all my might, probably out loud in my bedroom. And then a car came. It was coming down the bridge right at me again. This time I turned away from Danny and looked right at the oncoming car. I saw the driver, a young boy. Our eyes locked. And then he swerved his car. He nicked my arm and went on. I turned to the bridge and looked at the black ocean. Then the night turned to day. To a bright shining day. And I felt something in my pocket. It was something hard at the bottom of my pocket, right near my groin, something that hadn't been there before. I reached in and pulled it out. It was Danny's knife. I looked over the bridge. Danny had drowned. And there was no more force pulling me toward the edge.

I awoke in a panic and a cold sweat, disoriented. The sounds of the television grounded me. I looked around my empty bedroom, and I couldn't shake his voice.

"Live Marty. Decide to live."

My mind wandered to Frannie, singing in her club. And her words came to me. "Happy Birthday."

Charlie

Jane was a good storymaker. I'm not sure that if I had been telling the story I could have carved that second hole. In my world, Nikko would have set sail already and been toppled early by an ocean wave. Cursed by an attraction to water, hindered by a lack of know-how for paddling the ocean sea. But Jane had set this up differently. She had provided Nikko with some valuable assets for his adventure. He had a vision to discover what lay in his future and to face it head on. He was armed with a knife endowed from the heart of his father, a book of wise thoughts from an uncle, and three pancakes. He had built a balanced boat. And most of all, he had a passenger. A first mate. A co-pilot. Thank goodness Jane had taken over just then. I would have certainly set Nikko off to sea by himself. But now there was Samaya. And I sort of liked Jane's little lemur.

The following Monday morning, I dropped the kids off at school and drove to work along my customary route. I noted the beautiful people. The runners, the talkers, the coffee drinkers. I didn't feel quite the separation that I usually experienced. A slight charge of envy had been drained. I thought that I might go running that evening. It had been many years, but maybe I should run again. I was doing progressively better through intersections. The image of cars coming at me from the right was dissipating. But my shoulder still ached, the pulling from the base of my neck to my scapula. It wasn't crippling, but it was a bother. And a reminder of a past that still had a grip on me.

I had a bounce in my step as I got out of my car and headed into my old crumbling building on the VA lot. Today it didn't look so bad. It seemed more historic than it did institutional. I parked my car and looked at the veterans' horticulture garden, the garden I had noted from time to time outside my office window. The patients who worked there were psychiatric patients in a work therapy program. They cut flowers to take to offices around campus. I had never wanted any part of that, but today seemed different. Four months ago maybe those patients had been homeless. Now they were growing flowers to bring to other people. I don't know what happened to me in that moment, but I walked away from my office down toward the horticulture center. I had never been down this long dirt driveway. In my old sports coat and rumpled tie, I walked toward the flower farm, not sure why I had turned this way, except that I was compelled to follow the trail. I wasn't sure if I had an eight o'clock appointment. "So what," I thought. "I'll be a few minutes late." I chuckled to myself as I imagined old Elliot, winking at me, for taking Frost's road less traveled.

I didn't know any patients at the hospital. I usually tried to ignore the fact that my office was surrounded by psychiatric patients. Another part of my castling, I supposed. I walked into the horticulture office and looked around. Simple, but nice. There was artwork hanging on the walls created by veterans. Pastels, some oil paintings, and some photography. It was an impressive display. Some of traumatic scenes, some of nature, others still life. The public would have enjoyed it, but it was tucked away inside this small trailer. There were a few chairs by the door and a desk at the back of the room. Out the window of the trailer I could see the horticulture grounds. It was a large expanse of nearly three acres. I saw veterans at work tending to the garden.

No one was at the counter in the office. As I turned to leave, I heard footsteps coming in the back door. An older gentleman with no hair and no teeth appeared. He had deep grooves along the outside of his cheeks. He was shrunken to under five feet tall and had a notable tremor in his hands. He wore a hospital gown and a big smile as he greeted me. He spoke with a shaky voice, but I could understand him well.

"Hello there ... I've seen you before."

I had never seen this man.

"What's your name?" I asked him.

"Charlie."

"I'm Martin, Charlie."

"Do you like songs?" he asked me.

"Well, yes, I like songs." I thought he was likely demented. Maybe Alzheimer's disease. But I suddenly felt playful, a feeling that was growing now, rooted in a teepee.

"What song do you like?"

"Oh, I don't know. Just any song."

"I know a fine song. Do you want to hear it?"

"Why, yes." A smile came to my face. I was in the horticulture shop, suddenly charmed by a patient. I wondered if he had ever been to Spellman's. Maybe I could take him. He had my full attention. He was going to sing a song, and I was depending on him. Yes, I thought. Please sing me a song.

He cleared his throat. His mouth turned up again in a big smile, a smile with wisdom but no teeth. I could decode the tune, though he was wildly off key. Pat Boone. "Love Letters in the Sand."

I listened as Charlie sang to me with a toothless smirk stretched across his face. I heard his words, as though he had selected the song just for me. I pictured letters in the sand, washed away by the sea. In a moment, he struggled with the lyrics, and his smile dissolved into frustration. Without pause, I joined his tune and we sang together, there in the shop of the horticulture garden. Together we muddled through the song, down to the very end. And I gave Charlie a gentle applause.

"Thank you," I said to Charlie.

"Yes. Sure. You're a good singer," he said.

"Thanks." I smiled. "It's my first time in a while."

"You want another one?"

"No, I have to go back up the hill."

He began to sing again.

I laughed. "I have to go back up the hill, Charlie."

He stopped and smiled again.

"Is anyone here to sell flowers?" I asked him.

"I don't know. I don't see anyone," he answered me. "Just you and me."

They were probably all out in the field. I'd come back another time. "Thanks Charlie," I said. "Thanks again for the song."

I turned around and left the small trailer. I meandered up the dirt road, enjoying each step. And as I walked, I hummed Pat Boone and imagined a large ocean sweeping across the beach, clearing everything in its path. I looked behind me at the veterans in the garden. I thought of Tine the leper in the village I had visited in West Africa. Hers was the song that I usually played in my head. Now it was Charlie's. And it was hard to let it go.

When I got to the office, Dorrie was concerned.

"I was worried about you. It's ten after eight. Dr. Bradshaw called for your phone conference."

"I'll call him. I was down in the garden."

"You were?"

"Yes."

"Did you order anything?"

"No, no one was there. Well, someone was there, but no one to sell anything."

"Did you want me to order you anything?"

"Oh, sure. That would be nice."

I looked around at our office suite. The law books on the shelves, the federally issued furniture, and the posters.

"How was your weekend, Dorrie?" It was as though I had all the time in the world.

"Oh, it was nice, sir. I mean a little stressful. My son is doing better, though. He has leukemia. I don't know if you knew that. But Friday they told me it was in full remission and that he would likely make a full recovery. So it was a good weekend."

Leukemia? Her son has leukemia? I walked back and forth all these weeks without a hello. While her son had leukemia? We talked a bit more. She told me about the treatment he had received. I struggled to listen. I thought of Nick and Sammie, and I was terrified. But Dorrie was strong. How could she come to work every day and deal with this place while her son was at home with leukemia?

"Do you need to go home?" I asked.

She looked confused.

"I mean to take care of him."

"He's better now. Jack's better." She smiled. "Don't worry. It's been two years we've been dealing with this. He's back in school. I blocked time in your calendar for you to work on your case."

I wondered about Henry Dawson. Maybe he had a son with leukemia. Or a wife that left him on a motorcycle. Or a child who was upset and wanted to run away. Or a friend who jumped off a bridge. I was paralyzed. I knew I had to keep working for the kids. But at that moment, I didn't see how it was possible. I couldn't keep helping the hospital fire employees. It suddenly dawned on me that these were all people. People with real lives. I was going to have to figure out another angle.

"Oh, okay. Can you get Bradshaw on the phone?"

"Sure." She left for her desk.

"Oh Dorrie …" I interjected.

"Yes, sir?"

"Dorrie … can you call me Martin?"

I was in a boat. Headed across the ocean. One seat carved for me. And at that particular moment, Dorrie was in the back. Or was it Jane? Or was it Dawson? I wasn't sure … I could just feel the weight of my soul tipping back as though someone were there balancing it from behind. Yes, someone had certainly joined my boat. Perhaps it was Charlie. Or Danny. Or Tine. Or Frannie. Or God.

July 25, 1987

Yesterday was a trip. We got to this dock on the edge of the island of Komodo, and met this guy Apollo. He took us to a village where we bought a goat. Apollo killed it and strapped it to a pole. He gave us large walking sticks. Apollo told us it was a mile walk into the center of the island, where most of the Komodo Dragons were. "Walk carefully," he said. "Some of them run wild on the island. They have a deadly bite from the bacteria in their mouths. But you can poke them away with your stick." This was crazy. These things were 20 feet long with huge jaws. Poke them with a stick? Apollo said not to run from them. They're faster than us. So we walked on looking for the dragon pit. We looked from side to side, with Apollo as our guide, ready to poke. I thought we had finally gone a step too far on our adventuring. I didn't even really care about seeing these dragons. I don't think Marty did, either. Seemed we were looking for something, both of us. But I don't think it was Komodo Dragons …

I thought about fighting one off with my stick and slamming it in the face. Then I realized that I had my knife. If I could slow down the dragon, then I could always finish it off with my knife. I heard Marty humming a tune behind me. "Thank You for Being a Friend". I started laughing, and before long we were singing together. The guide warned us to be quiet, but we kept singing softly anyway.

Spellman's

"Marty!" Frannie greeted me with a big smile. "You're dripping wet. Come in and get warm."

"It started to pour as I drove over."

She looked older than I remembered. She wore a long blue silk dress adorned with pastel flower petals and butterflies, her neck wrapped in a matching scarf.

"Come, come. Sit here with me. It's my birthday." She coughed. I knew she was pretending. Every day was her birthday. It really was mine, though nobody knew.

"Mine, too." I smiled.

"Really? Horty, look, my boyfriend came. And it's his birthday."

I smiled as the pink haired lady rose from her table in the front.

"Marty! Shame on you. Frannie dear has been broken hearted for weeks. Where have you been? How could you stand her up like that?" They both giggled.

"Help's hard to find, you know. It's not easy getting out."

"I was worried it was another lady." Frannie smiled as we sat.

"Never," I answered. "Waiter, Roy Rogers please?" There was no alcohol in the bakery karaoke club, despite the clandestine nature of it all. Though the cokes and sprites added to the charm. I imagined the liquor license was just too much for Frannie to pursue.

"Certainly," the waiter answered me.

"What are you doing for your birthday?" Frannie asked.

"Well … I thought maybe I'd … Why isn't anyone singing?"

"It's free for the moment. Want a turn?" Horty asked.

"No, I …"

"Colonel!" called Frannie to the man at the karaoke machine. "My boyfriend Marty is going to sing." She had a spasm of coughing again.

The crowd clapped and waved their rhythm shakers. Frannie held my hand and brought me to the front of the room, where the colonel handed me the mike.

"Your father would be proud," Frannie told me.

I was confused. "My father?"

Frannie smiled. "Oh how he loved to sing!"

"What's it going to be?" asked the colonel. Frannie had sent my mind spinning. But there was no time to ask what she was talking about. I looked down at the menu and pushed the button through the decades of music, until I landed on Elton John. "Goodbye Yellow Brick Road."

"This one," I said nervously. I looked out at the crowd. Frannie and Horty stood ready to shake their rhythm eggs.

"Sing it, Martin!" cheered Frannie.

Horty whistled in my direction, and the music began. I thought of Charlie, had a buzz of confidence, and began to sing. I knew the words and embraced them. At first I looked at Frannie, and she encouraged me with her nods and grins. As the music unfolded, I moved about the room, singing to the patrons of Spellman's as though they were old friends. My voice cracked and I stumbled when I got to the first chorus, the only words that everyone knew. The crowd came to my rescue and sang along. I was having a blast. But when I looked back in Frannie's direction, she had disappeared. Horty told me afterwards that she had left to tend to some issues in the bakery. I wondered why she had gone, and what she knew about my father.

An Adventure's Beginning

Sunday came. I added some bananas to the pancakes. Jane packed us up, and off to the teepee we journeyed. Nick held the lighter and Sammie the syrup. I took back the role of story teller. I didn't know where I was going, but as we uncovered the pancakes and I stared at the smeared banana bits, they became my starting point.

Samaya sat in the front hole. The log was parked on the sand, the nose in the water pointed to the sea. Behind Nikko was a forest of palm trees. He stood crouched behind the boat, his hands on the back to push them through the waves. Samaya held a paddle that Nikko had whittled, and a second oar sat in the back hole. But before Nikko could push, they heard a loud hooting from the trees on the beach.

"Not even sayin' goodbye?" called Lionel. He and Jasper and others from the School for Swingers sat in the treetops. Jasper held a coconut in his hands.

"Oh, we must have forgotten," Nikko called back to the trees. "I said goodbye to Elliot, though. Didn't he tell you I was leaving?"

"He may have mentioned it … But Miss Rosalie ain't so happy about losin' her best kitchen hand. Her Mama Marisol weepin' so about a daughter just gettin' up and leavin'…."

"I left a note. Didn't she get it?" Samaya answered. We're just leaving for a couple of days. Just to see if we can find Rama. I don't see what the big deal is. I can't just work in the kitchen my whole life."

"Well your Mama Marisol has. She's expectin' the same from you," answered Lionel. Jasper was smiling and laughing with the others behind Lionel.

"Well tell them goodbye for us then," answered Nikko. He gave a big shove to the log.

"Oh, don't think that'll be necessary," answered Lionel.

"Here's a going away gift I made special for you," called Jasper. He threw his large coconut at the boat and it landed at Nikko's feet.

"What was that for?" yelled Samaya.

"They don't want us to leave. We have to go now."

The Swingers launched more grenades. Coconuts and bananas. The bananas made a mess over the log. One struck Nikko in the back but it didn't bother him. It was as though he were made of steel.

"We have to get out of here. No one wants us to go on an adventure. They're all scared to know about destiny. They'll have you cooking in that kitchen forever."

"But Nikko, Mom's upset. I don't think I can ..."

"It's too late. We can say goodbye when we get back."

"Nikko, look out!" she screamed. A large coconut barely missed his head and landed on the boat. The log rolled to the left.

"Five points," yelled Jasper.

Nikko rowed furiously, but it was difficult to move against the riptide. "Samaya, paddle. We have to get out of here."

She was upset. She hadn't considered the impact that her leaving would have on the kitchen. Or on her mother. She was paralyzed.

"Samaya ... paddle! There's a strong current. You need to paddle."

It felt like a meteor. But it was Lionel. He had jumped from the trees and landed on his belly, stretched out between the two holes.

"What are you doing? Are you crazy, Lionel?"

"The girl can't leave. I'm bringin' her home. I have instructions from the kitchen."

"Since when do you follow anyone's instructions?"

"Anything to please Miss Rosalie!" He laughed.

They had passed through the first series of waves. Lionel scooted toward the back hole of the boat and managed to get a paw on Nikko's chest.

"Get off of me. You don't have a ticket to ride. Keep paddling, Samaya!"

Samaya was shaken, but determined. She knew Nikko was right. If she didn't take this adventure now, she would lose all opportunities. In her heart she felt that she was doing right. No one had tried to save Rama that day long ago, and she wanted to try. She rowed with all her might. As she clutched the paddle with both hands, her box of pancakes slid to the side of her hole. The lid fell to her feet, and the top pancake fell out of the boat.

Lionel pounced on top of Nikko. He tried to throw him out of the boat.

From the moment that the pancake hit the sea, it sent a nice smell through the currents. It attracted a school of dolphins within the minute.

Samaya had never seen a dolphin before. "What are those?" Samaya hollered. The boat rocked furiously as the lemurs wrestled in the back hole. "They're coming up against our boat!" "Nikko I'm scared! I'm going to jump."

"Jump? Are you crazy?" he yelled as he stood up in the boat. He held on to Lionel as the boat rocked. Water lapped into the boat holes as it dipped from side to side into the sea.

"Put me down and take this thing home," demanded Lionel. Nikko held Lionel in the air and threw him from the boat. Lionel landed in the sea and yelled for help.

And help was there. The dolphins edged right up to the log and stopped the wild rocking. They brought it to a simple balance and began to swim along with it. The two lemurs floated in their log, balanced in the middle of a school of dolphins.

Two dolphins left the school and headed toward the floundering Lionel. They carried him back to shore and threw him to the seashore as the Swingers watched the scene from high above. Nikko and Samaya gazed back toward the island as they headed on their quest toward destiny. As Paden's Patch grew dim, they could see around to the north side for the very first time, around the western tip of Madagascar. Nikko thought he saw a lemur far away on the beach, waving at them.

Samaya saw him, too, as the craft carried on toward the north. "That's Max, Nikko. I think he's waving goodbye."

Nikko wondered if Max was collecting more things for his children. Maybe that's what a father does, he thought. Makes sure that their children have what they need to make it in the world. He felt for his knife and was reassured that he hadn't lost it in the struggle. And he watched as Max and the island disappeared from sight.

Nicholas

The kids were asleep, and I was studying case law. I needed a deeper understanding of the Hatch Act. I read about a sheriff in a small town in Arkansas, who was accused of violations of this statute. He had introduced a political candidate at a rally while in his sheriff's uniform. No federal or state employee was allowed to use their position to influence an election. But I couldn't see where Henry Dawson was doing that. It was late, and my mind began to wander. I remembered my father's stories of Sheriff Fred.

Like most dads, I had wanted to be a better father than my father had been for me. That didn't seem too difficult at first, since that relationship had ended in my father's death following years of estrangement. At this point, however, I was struggling to keep up with him. As I carried on his Sunday morning rituals, my earlier years were coming back to me. The years before my mother died.

My father had sat with his customers, staring at jewels under the microscope, showing them perfections or imperfections. He enjoyed doing the same with me, though I didn't share his passion for gems. My father wanted a special relationship with me, his only son. When I didn't share his interests, he tried other things. I recalled Dad teaching me to fish at Mammoth Lakes. When I snagged my line on the rocks or the trees overhead, he sat patiently retying my hooks and sinkers. I recalled his teaching me to ski down a mountain outside Lake Arrowhead. I held onto him tightly from behind and skied in his tracks. The memories of my early life with my father were coming to me. And with that I grew more despondent about our years of silence.

I recalled our family dinners before my mother died. She loved to cook. Lamb chops, lasagna, and I remembered glazed ham. Not particularly Jewish food. I remembered my mother leading us in saying grace as a child. I had forgotten about that, and it seemed unusual to me now. I hadn't met another Jewish family that did that. It wasn't in Hebrew or anything; it was just a simple thank you to God for what we had.

Then another memory. Driving in his car, a brown Ford LTD. His deep voice saying, "Are you all strapped in?"

In most ways, I couldn't keep up with him. Though we both were single fathers, I was raising two children, and he had raised four. I dragged myself to an uninspired office, where he studied his jewels with passion and grew his business into a component of a large department store. He managed to send us all to prestigious universities; that's where the money went. By the time he died, there was nothing left to help me raise his grandchildren. He played sports with me. We threw baseballs. Shot baskets. Tossed the football. I was never as good at those sports as I was at running, but it was a way that I connected with my father. In the years when I ran, I connected with no one. It was just me, running.

The difficulties started for me after my mother's death. My childhood had been filled with innocent times. After Mom died, I began to feel different from everyone else. I spent more time on my own, drawing pictures of alien planets and wondering about extraterrestrial life forms. Dad was less available, and I disappeared inside of myself. I came home most days to an empty house, often eating bakery products Dad had purchased from a local store, watching cartoons and *I Love Lucy* in the afternoons and into the night. My sisters weren't around as much anymore as they had all disappeared into activities outside of the home.

In high school, the runners on the team brought me out of myself a bit. I became a bit more social. We traveled to meets singing Grateful Dead songs. I preferred the hits from the '70s. Top 40 hits. "Love Will Keep Us Together." "Thank You for Being a Friend." "Angie Baby." "Up on the Roof." But I didn't dare share those songs with those guys. Not until I met Danny—he liked those songs, too.

As I reminisced, I became more aware of my failure to

connect with Nick. We shared some time together now telling stories on Sundays, and we had successfully chased away the gorilla from the ivy outside of his room. But I wasn't connecting with him as I wished I could. Not with baseballs or basketballs or footballs. He just wasn't interested. After his early sports failures, he just turned away from that world completely. And his asthma didn't help things. I thought he was pretty coordinated, and he had a good body to be an athlete, at least to be a runner. But he was a chess player, a logic lover, and a puzzler.

Nick's true gift was intellect. Supreme intellect. He was about the brightest child that I had ever met. His acumen for math was near frightening, and his teachers never understood how he knew the things he did. So at this point, in third grade, Nick was focused on pre-algebra skills with a plan for him to begin a course in algebra in the fourth grade. He brought home brain teasers and logic questions that I couldn't solve. So even in the realm of homework I was losing the ability to be with him.

The most difficult thing for me about Nick was that he seemed at times to have no skin. He was like an open heart walking around on the street, taking the bus to school, watching a movie … an open heart to which he had full and complete access. He had somehow not learned the secret trick that they teach us early in male school. The trick of taking your heart and hiding it away in a steel chamber so that no one can get to you. The trick of castling.

I seemed to have taken advanced courses in this subject. By the time Mom and Dad had both died, I really didn't feel much for anyone at all. After Danny jumped, I made a commitment that I would never rely on anyone again. After Lara left, I said I would never love again.

Where the leavings in my life had taught me to place another steel bar around my heart, Nick did the opposite. After Lara left, he became even more sensitive. That's why I was so surprised at what transpired the next day.

On the Tuesday following Nikko's journey to sea, the school called me and told me that Nick had been in a fight and was hurt. I couldn't leave work, so I called Jane and she picked him up. She brought Nick home to our house and took care of him until I got home. By the time I could get there, it was 5:30 and dark, and I carted in Chinese food. Though Jane had reassured me that he was okay, I was still a bit frantic on the drive home from work.

I bolted in through the door, red chicken and egg rolls in hand, sauces leaking out the bottom of my plastic bag.

"What the hell happened?" I yelled to the group sitting at the kitchen table.

Jane sat with Nick and Sammie, playing some kind of card game. They were lost in laughter as Sammie yelled, "Bullshit."

"What? Sammie, what kind of ..."

"It's a game, Dad. Wanna play?" asked Nick.

"Nick what happened to you?" I looked at him, a small scratch on his neck, a slightly swollen left eye. It didn't look as bad as I had imagined. But Nicholas was not one to fight. He looked more powerful now. His posture straightened, his face glowing, and I could see a little of his mother's wide cheeks and dark black hair.

"What happened, Nick?"

"Nothing, Dad."

"Tell him, Nicholas. It's okay," said Jane.

Nick looked up at Jane and back at me. He started slowly as he looked at his cards. "Nothing so much."

"Not nothing. Look at you. Something happened. The school said you got into a fight."

He avoided me and looked down at his cards again.

"Three eights," Sammie said, as she slapped three cards on the pile between them.

"BS!" exclaimed Nick. They all laughed as Sammie exposed her cards and took back the pile. I stood impatiently watching the group.

"Nicholas, what happened?"

He looked up at me from his cards. The light reflected off the shiner underneath his eye.

"We had a substitute today. And everyone was going crazy. I couldn't stand it. They were all yelling, the substitute was yelling."

"Aha ..."

He gripped his cards tightly in his lap and looked up at me. The intensity grew. "So Brian. He and Mickey were teasing Sharon in the back of the room like they always do. They were flinging these paper things at her. And she was screaming 'Stop it' and they wouldn't. And I was going crazy." Nick threw his cards across the room and started to scream. "I hate him! I hate Brian! Why does he have to be so mean?"

This was the Nick I loved. The Nick who was about justice and what is right. It stirred him deeply, and this is the part of him that I could truly find in me.

"I know, Nick. I know."

"So I told him to stop it! And he wouldn't. So he and Mickey and this other guy named Jason, they all just started teasing me then, too. But I didn't really care about that. I just wanted them to stop teasing Sharon. They just always do it and she hasn't done anything to them. And they won't stop it!"

Nick was crying now. And I felt myself starting to as well. "So what did they do to you?"

He looked up at me. "I couldn't take it anymore, Dad. So when the bell rang and we left the class, I got my stuff. Brian was outside, laughing with Mickey. So I dropped my backpack and I pushed him. Onto the ground. I kept pushing him, Dad."

"You pushed him down to the ground?" I felt a surge of pride in my chest. I couldn't help it. This was so unlike my Nick.

"Yeah. And I told him to leave Sharon alone. Then some other kids came over and started yelling at him, too."

"At Brian?"

"Yeah. Everyone hates him. Except Jason and Mickey. So I was on top of Brian and I pinned him to the ground."

"You pinned him to the ground? How did you do that?"

"I don't know. I just did it. But then Mickey came and pushed me over, and he hit me in the eye. But I didn't really care. So that's it."

I looked at Nick in awe. This was not the story I had imagined. He had never been in a fight in his life. He fled from conflict. What happened to him? I wasn't sure what to do. Send him to his room for starting a fight? Give him a high five for taking on Brian? I was stuck.

"Did you get in trouble?"

"No, I just went to the nurse and they said I had to go home after school. So Jane came."

"Are you in trouble?"

"No. The substitute came over and asked what happened and I told her. And she didn't do anything."

"Maybe she wished she could have pinned Brian to the ground." I was really floundering. What next? Should I suggest he beat up Mickey before school tomorrow?

"So what did Brian say when you left?"

"Nothing, Dad. He could get expelled if he gets into any more trouble." He looked up at me and saw my worry. "Dad, it's okay."

"I think he's okay, Martin. I thought about taking him to urgent care, but his eye just looks a bit swollen. We've been putting ice on it."

"Should I call Brian's mom?" I was lost.

"No, Martin. I think it's all okay," answered Jane. "Why don't you just take over my hand and I'll get dinner on the plates for you guys."

"There's enough if you want to stay."

"Oh, thanks. That would be nice."

I agreed. That would be nice. So she did. And we ate red chicken and egg rolls. And we played some more Bullshit after dinner. I didn't know if the kids had homework that night. Seemed like we were all doing enough work. I thought of Nikko, at sea with Samaya, steering a craft with knife in pocket having successfully taken on The School for Swingers. And my little Nick, taking on a few of his own.

July 27, 1987

We walked with Apollo for a mile until we came to a clearing. In front of us was a huge pit. There was a noose hanging over the center. And there we saw them. I counted 23 Komodo Dragons waiting there for their next meal. The noose was connected to a rope leading to a tree at the edge of the forest. Apollo pulled on it, and the rope swung back in our direction. As he did that, we felt the exhilaration from the reptiles. Apollo fastened the goat to the rope and swung it back into the pit. Marty yelled, "Dinner time! Come and get it!" Sometimes he just cracks me up with what comes out of him. The dragons swarmed for the food. They formed a perfect kaleidoscope image. Their jaws all attached to a different part of the goat. Their tails stuck out in a perfect circle. It looked like an image from a James Bond movie or "Raiders of the Lost Ark." Or maybe hell. Maybe this is what hell looked like. I was glad we came. It was really cool. As we watched them, I really got to like them. I thought to myself, it would be good to come back as a Komodo Dragon. And live in a pit for people to come see me with my friends. And I would eat the goat that they brought. But then I thought, maybe it's not so cool. I mean, they're stuck here in that pit. They're actually trapped. On this island, in that pit. It's the only place in the whole world where they live. Except in a couple of zoos. No, I wouldn't like to be on an island. I would rather come back as a bird or something that could travel and take adventures. We're sleeping in a science observatory station. It's an old wood room with spiders everywhere. It's pretty creepy. But fun.

At Sea

Sunday came. The kids were up early. We all waited for Jane before resuming our story. It was raining out, so we would have to settle for my kitchen. I was happy when she rang the bell right at 8:00.

"Jane!" Sammie yelled as she ran to open the door.

"Good morning," Jane answered.

Jane looked different somehow, and she was holding something in a brown paper bag. I wasn't sure what it was, but Sammie knew right away.

"You're wearing lipstick," Sammie said to her. "And mascara."

"That's a big word for a seven year old," Jane said. I thought I saw her blush as Sammie pointed this out so expeditiously. If she were wearing make-up, it was subtle, but it made her stand out even more beautifully in my doorway.

"I only wear it for special occasions. I know that Nikko and Samaya are headed out to sea this morning. So I thought I'd do something special." She smiled. "Can I come in?"

"Yes. We already have a place set for you."

"I brought this special maple syrup," she said. "They make it in this small store on the North Shore of Lake Tahoe. They run out of it as soon as they put it on the shelf, that's how good it is. It's my last bottle."

"Good morning, Nicholas," she said to Nick as she walked in. She saw that he had returned to playing chess after setting up the pancake ingredients. "What are you working on?"

"This move. It's a trap."

"Will you show me later?"

"Do you play chess?" he asked her.

"Oh, I love chess. I usually lose, but I love it."

She walked into the kitchen, and we started to cook. I was taken by Jane's make-up. She was taking the story as seriously as I was. Something was happening for her, too, and I believed this was her way of showing me that.

We sat down to eat. The syrup was tasty. The pancakes were better than ever, and I began.

—⟋⟋⟋⟋—

The log rocked back and forth across the Indian Ocean, balanced by the dolphins on each side. Samaya threw bits from the second pancake to keep the dolphins close. Though Nikko had warned her not to use up all of the pancakes, she knew how important it was to keep the dolphins by their boat.

"Seems I can throw pieces forever," she said to Nikko.

"Well you can't," responded the Indri. "If you ever want anyone to taste those, you'd better stop feeding the dolphins."

"I've been throwing pieces for days, and I still have the whole pancake."

"What do you mean?"

"I mean just that. I keep throwing pieces, expecting to get to the last pancake. But I'm still using the middle one. Maybe when you feed a dolphin, your pancake can go on forever."

"That's crazy."

"Well maybe it's what they do. Pancakes. Maybe they just feed. Like dolphins help."

"I think you're getting sea nutty, Samaya. When a pancake is eaten, it's done."

"Not this one." She twisted toward the back of the boat and showed him the basket. Then a booming sound rang out from behind them.

"What was that?" screamed Samaya.

Nikko looked behind them. He saw a large black ship with sails approaching their little craft. It looked like a pirate ship that Nikko had seen in one of Elliot's books. The ship moved quickly with the wind. Another shot fired out, this one splashing the water near their boat. Samaya nearly lost hold of her pancake basket.

"Row, Samaya, row! They're coming for us!"

"What do they want us for? Who are they?"

Nikko read the side of the boat. "Look at that! It's the Mofinko Trappers. They want to trap us like Rama."

Samaya rowed backwards to slow the boat. "What are you doing, Nikko? That's what we're here for. They probably have Rama on that boat. Or they can tell us where she is."

"Samaya, no. Rama is gone. If she's alive, they've taken her somewhere else. They had her four years ago."

Samaya kept rowing backwards toward the ship. "Well, who else will know where she is?"

"Samaya, they'll trap us. If they don't kill us first. They'll send us to a zoo or to a safari park somewhere. You'll never be free to cook another pancake."

"You don't know that. Let them come and get me." She threw her oar into the water far from the log.

"Samaya. You fool! I don't have strength to row for us both. At least feed the dolphins, then. Maybe they'll swim faster."

"Nikko, just stop. Let them catch us. This is what we're looking for. I just didn't believe we'd find them so soon."

The ship had gained considerable distance on the lemurs. A horn rang out from the big boat that sent Nikko shaking. Samaya sat clutching her basket, excited to board. It grew closer and closer and the lemurs could see the humans aboard the ship.

"Lower the nets," cried one.

"There are two of them. They're looking for a home," said another.

"Well, drop the nets and let's find them one." The men's laughter sent pains to Nikko's soul. He would have preferred to take on Lionel and Jasper's School for Swingers. He couldn't possibly defend the two of them against this large ship. There must have been twenty humans on the top deck. He eyed rifles and a cannon off the back of the boat.

"See that, Nikko. They want to find us a home. They're cordial."

At that, a large net fell over her. It tightened around her until she was squeezed into a tight ball.

"Nikko! I can't move. What's happening?"

"Samaya! They want to take you away somewhere. They're not friendly."

The net was attached to a large pole off the edge of the boat. Three men stood at the back of that pole holding a large crank. They wound it and wound it, and Samaya was carried into the air. She was squeezed like a small balloon rising up above the sea. Nikko rocked wildly without her weight to balance the front of the log.

This was not a friendly boat. Nikko knew it from the start, and Samaya knew it now, too. She clutched her basket of pancakes inside the net. She thought of dropping bits down to the dolphins. Maybe they could get her out. She struggled to open the basket. Her dismay grew when she looked down. Just one pancake left. The middle pancake was gone.

"Nikko! The second pancake," she screamed. "It must have fallen."

"I think it's finished," he screamed back. "It can't do what it wants to do up there."

The dolphins had stopped swimming. They just froze there at the side of the log. Nikko let out a low minor-pitched sound over the sea currents, and it rang out over the waves. He looked up at Samaya screaming, hoisted higher and higher above the ocean waves.

Nikko felt around in his pocket. There it was. The knife that Max had given to Carlos. The knife that Carlos had died for. The knife that Elliot had found. The knife that Elliot had released to Nikko's care. He looked up at Samaya and his heart sank. The idea of traveling alone at sea was too much to stand. Even worse was the thought of Samaya on the ship, surrounded by a band of heartless trappers.

He clutched the knife and pulled it from his pocket. He looked down at it and recalled its history. He opened the largest blade and wondered how deeply it could cut. With his left hand he held to the side of the log for leverage. And with his right, he launched his knife into the sky.

It sailed with an open blade toward Samaya, trapped inside the net. It sailed just above her head where the blade met the rope just below the large knot. And as if powered by a special battery pack, it severed the knot holding her above the sea. Down she fell, the netting releasing from around her. And before she could land on the waves of the sea, a dolphin jumped up to catch her from the nets. She struggled to hold on to his slippery body as he swam away from the ship and back to Nikko in the log. Nikko's knife had completed its flight and landed in the water with a gentle splash before beginning its descent down through the murky ocean waters.

Nikko grabbed Samaya from the back of the dolphin and hoisted her back into the log. With his great strength, he rowed and rowed as Samaya panted heavily. The ship disappeared from behind them as the Indri powered the log westward.

Nikko sat in silence listening to Samaya breathe.

The two were quiet. They heard only the sound of the waves and the tones of the dolphins. Nikko gazed out at the sea as the knife that he had so briefly owned floated to the bottom of the ocean floor. He wondered what would become of it. Perhaps it would land on deep coral and grow barnacles. This was not what Max had in mind when he brought it as a gift for his son. This is not what Carlos would have wanted had he ever found it. This is not why Elliot gave it to him in such ceremony. The lemurs before him had not given him his knife to throw to the bottom of the sea. But there it was. And no dolphin was retrieving it. They had retrieved only Samaya and brought her back to the log.

Nikko wondered if it was a good trade. He could not help the rage that swelled inside of him. Had Samaya listened to him, he would not have lost his knife. What trouble would she cause him next? What trap would she lead them to next time? He wondered if he weren't better off floating alone.

But it was over. He had cast his fate. He had traded the knife of his forefathers for the friendship of the ring-tailed passenger. Somehow she still had her basket. Somehow she still had one pancake. Nikko knew that the last pancake wasn't to feed the past. It was to greet the future. He would tell her to save it to meet the monkeys on the coast of Mozambique. There would be no more discussion of Rama. They could not float looking for the past. That's where his knife was. In the past. It was no more, and he tried to forget about it. The past could only trap you. They had to let it go somehow. They had to set their sights on what lay ahead, to the coast of Mozambique.

Samaya rested and recovered as the pair floated under the moonlight that evening. She ate apricots and nuts, and Nikko gave her sips of water. There was quiet between them as they listened to the water lap up against the side of the log. Try as he could, though, Nikko could not forget his knife. And as he closed his eyes, he dreamt about the knife, open blade, on the bottom of the sea.

Love Letters

The fall rolled along. It was a Thursday evening, and we were approaching November. It was cold and rainy out, and Nick and Sam were in their PJs preparing for bed. Jane had been over for dinner, and we all talked about Nikko's knife. We wondered where it was and if he would ever get it back. It sent me secretly wondering about my knife, the knife that Danny had given me.

"Maybe a sea turtle found it. He could polish his shell with it," was Sammie's idea.

"Oh yes," answered Jane. She always said that. Oh yes. Not "I don't think so," or "that doesn't make sense," just yes. And magic always came of it. I watched her as she mused with my children about the places that the knife might have gone. And as they considered the destiny of the knife, my thoughts turned to Danny, up on the bridge, and I wondered why he jumped.

Nobody knew. He didn't call anyone. He just left a note on his computer. "It got to be too much." What got to be too much? Damn it, Danny, why didn't you call me? I would have met you up there. What if all he needed was someone he knew to show up there that night. An old friend to tell him that his feelings were alright about whatever it was that drove him up there. So he could cry. Instead of jump.

Now Danny was gone. And all that I had of our friendship was his journal documenting our adventures, his sleeping bag, and his knife that I had misplaced somewhere. Danny's adoptive father had given that to him before he went to camp when he was nine. I think that was his very first adventure. He treasured that knife wherever we went. He used it for cutting ropes and whittling. He ate with the spoon and the fork. He used the can opener to open soup cans, and the bottle opener for beer bottles and colas that wouldn't twist. He even had it in his pocket when he got married, to protect him on the adventure.

I recalled the memorial. "He wrote a note, Marty," his mother said. "He didn't say why he did it. Just that he had to. He wanted you to have this knife. I brought you his sleeping bag, too. I wasn't sure what to do with it. It doesn't feel right throwing stuff away." I couldn't imagine much worse than your son jumping off a bridge. She was tearful. I wished I could have cried, but as had become my custom, I couldn't feel a thing. I took the sleeping bag, and I put Danny's knife in my pocket.

For a while I kept the knife in my glove compartment to hold him close. But gradually his memory faded, as did the spirit I had felt on our adventures. And so did the knife. I had moved it to a bedroom drawer. Then into my jewelry box. I had no idea where it was now. It was a ghost for me. Something that I treasured, yet something filled with horror. I wished he hadn't left it for me. I thought one day I might bring it back to him and bury it in the ground by his grave, though I knew that was not his desire. He wanted me to do something with it, but I couldn't imagine what. As the kids laughed with Jane that night about the possible adventures that the knife might take, I alone knew the truth. The knife was lost. Danny was gone. And with them had gone my spirit of adventure.

The kids went to bed, and Jane went home. I wondered if she might want to spend the night. She had become more attractive to me with each passing day, but I couldn't imagine how we would evolve past our friendship. She was a friend from next door who had come to join the family. We tacitly agreed that she must go home each night. When she left, there was never a hug, never a kiss, just a goodbye, though it was growing more awkward. She lingered longer each evening. She did very well in the role of Mary Poppins. I was scared of anything that might alter that. So I said goodnight to her again at about ten that evening.

It was eleven when the doorbell rang. I had gone to bed and was in my pajamas—my fifteen-year-old boxer shorts with holes growing from the waist band, and an old blue and yellow

UCLA Law School T-shirt that barely fit. I wrapped myself in my trusty bathrobe and walked nervously toward the door. Maybe it was Jane. Maybe she could read my mind and had decided to spend the night. I looked through the peep-hole expecting to see … anyone but her. Anyone in the whole world but her. Lara. She was standing at the door, wet from the rain.

I caught her image through the peep hole. She wore gold hoop earrings that looked like they had been hand crafted. Beads of water ran down her hair and neck. The shoulders of her white T-shirt were soaked, and her bra showed through. I froze there at the door, as she rang again. Against all of my instincts, I opened the door. She probably had a key anyway. Or maybe she had tossed it off the back of Major's bike into the Grand Canyon en route to Colorado …

"Hi, Martin …" she looked at me and smiled. Her shirt read, "Martha's Café, Pagosa Springs, Colorado." She wore a pair of tight jeans and leather boots. She had lost too much weight. She was worn, like she had been on one too many bike rides.

"What are you doing here?"

"I've missed you. I thought maybe we could talk, see where things went wrong. You know?"

"It's the middle of the night."

"I'm soaking wet. Can you at least let me in?"

I had no choice.

"Okay. Come in. Dry off."

She crossed into the entryway, dripping water.

"I had to walk from the bus station. I didn't have money for a cab."

I followed her into the kitchen. She moved quickly now and made herself at home. "Do you want some tea or something?" I asked her.

"Jesus, the linoleum's peeling off the floor. You need to get that fixed. The front door needs painting, too." She opened the pantry where she knew we kept extra towels. I hadn't reorganized much since she left. She dried her body and wrapped the blue towel around her head to dry her hair.

"He threw me out, Marty. Major threw me out. I found him in bed with another woman. I found them naked, fucking in my bed when I got off my shift." I noticed her hands tremble a bit as she wrapped her shoulders in another towel. She walked into my house as if she had an invitation to reenter the kitchen, the pantry, and our lives.

"Fucking asshole. Just hops into bed with some slut. Do you have a cigarette?"

"No, I stopped smoking."

"It's something, taking a bus from Colorado. I sat slammed against the window next to this 300 pound dirtbag all the way to LA."

She opened the small kitchen drawer where she had kept her Marlboro packs. I had forgotten about those when I cleared the cigarettes from the house. She lit it up in the middle of the kitchen.

"Lara, we don't smoke anymore in …"

"I couldn't even breathe sitting next to him. I didn't mind walking home, even in the rain. It was good to get some air after being in that bus."

"Home?" I stared at her in disbelief as she exhaled smoke.

She looked up at me. "It's really good to see you." She exhaled smoke. "How could he do that to me? Where did he think I would go? He introduced me to his new lady. Pia. He met her at a fucking bar."

Lara was different. She moved faster, she talked faster, and she was even more self-involved than the woman I had remembered marrying.

"We got in a big fight. Fuck! I scratched him down the side of his face. Then he threw me against the wall. I got a big bruise on my back." She turned to lift her shirt. I could see her ribs. "Fucking Pia just watched and smiled."

"The kids are sleeping. Please be quiet."

"Oh, sorry." She blew smoke.

I was angry. Angry that she had left, angry that she had come back, angry that she wanted me to take care of her.

Angry that I had lost the relationship with my father for her. And Danny, too.

"Well, fuck him, Marty. Can you get me a shirt? This one's soaked." I grabbed a T-shirt off the top of my laundry stack. It was from a 10K I had run 20 years ago. She put it on and squeezed out her hair. "Anyway, I'm home. It's good to see you. It'll be good to see the kids. How are they doing?"

I was losing my mind. Lara didn't give a shit about any of us. She didn't care about me, and she didn't care about the kids. Lara cared about Lara. The rest of us were just objects in her mind. Not real people with real feelings. I wondered what had happened to her. I suppose "oh, yes" would have been the cordial thing to do. But you have to earn "oh, yes." And Lara had earned something else.

"Lara, you have to leave," I said.

"Excuse me?"

"You can't stay here."

"This is my house, Marty." I saw the agitation in her face.

"It's not your house. You wanted no part of it. You wanted no part of any of us. Every breakfast, every lunch bag, every piece of homework, every doctor's appointment, every dental cleaning, every hurt feeling in our children … you handed them all to me."

"We can talk about it in the morning. I'm really tired."

"There's not going to be a 'we' in the morning."

She started toward my bedroom.

"You have to leave, Lara."

Part of me wanted to help her. How great it would be for Nick and Sammie to meet their mother. But not like this. Not this mother. The Catholic girl from Alaska I had married was gone. She had been replaced by a desperate woman, clinging to a place she didn't belong.

She turned to face me. "This is my home."

"This is not your home. You have to leave."

"But I spent all my money. Major didn't have much. We lived off my trust. I worked in a restaurant, carrying fucking dishes for people." She started to cry.

"I thought you had a quarter million dollars in that trust. And I thought you were living in Major's house. You said he owned it."

"He just always needed the money."

"What did he do with it?"

"I don't know. We spent it. I don't even have money for a cab."

"What did you spend it on?" I looked at her again. She was gaunt, worn, and trembling a bit. "Was it drugs? Cocaine? Meth? Heroin? What?"

"You asshole. So we partied a little. What's the big deal? What are you, my dad? I thought you'd be happy to see me."

"You need help. Look at you." I picked my wallet up off the counter and counted out the five twenty dollar bills I had just taken from the ATM.

"Here's money for a cab. You need to get help."

"I just need some sleep. It's been a rough couple of days. I just need a place to sleep for the night."

"Then go to your Mom's. You can't stay here. Not like this." I couldn't believe it. I wasn't going to save her.

"My mom's! Nice, Marty."

"She'll take care of you."

"Oh really. Like she would know how to do that."

"Lara …"

"Damn, Marty. You have some crazy notion about my mother. My sister wrote me that Mom just had another course of shock therapy."

"I'm sorry … "

"She still blames me for that. As if her depression and all those overdoses were my fault, because it started when I was born."

"I've called her a couple of times. The kids don't have a grandparent and I thought she'd …"

"Well don't bother. When she's not depressed, she's toiling away writing her fucking romance novels that will never be published. She doesn't give a damn about anyone else."

"Runs in the family, I guess." I was too angry to contain myself. I wasn't going to save Lara. If she wanted to, she could save herself. I wondered how she could let this happen to her. Maybe it was drugs. Or maybe this was just Lara. Somehow she had slid from the prep school Catholic environmentalist I had once loved to a waitress doing drugs, living with a biker. Maybe it wasn't all her fault, but I couldn't let the kids see their mother like this, and I couldn't lose anything more for Lara.

She took the money from my hand. "I just need a place to sleep. Anyway, I can't wake Mom in the middle of the night."

"Then go to a motel. You can't stay here. Write and let us know how you're doing."

I found an old down jacket that I had had in college. That was it, 100 dollars and an old jacket. She sat down at the breakfast room table, the table that had become sacred for making stories. That was it. "I'll call you a cab. You wait outside. There's a Motel 6 up the street."

"Marty!"

"The kids needed you. Nick cries if I mention you. Samantha desperately wants a mother."

"Okay, so maybe I wasn't made to raise kids."

"You could have hung in there. We could have gotten you help. Just because you were depressed didn't mean you had to leave."

"Do we need to get into that right now? It was more than post-partum depression. You know why I had to leave."

"No, I don't."

"Oh really? You know, if you could have loved me, I would have stayed." She got up from the chair. "If you could have fucked me, Marty, I would never have had to get on that bike!"

"Lara that's enough …"

"I wasn't going to turn into my mother. Depressed and raising kids. Some kind of a nun with a husband who can't keep it up long enough to love me …"

"Get the hell out of here. I don't want you in my house."

"You're really going to throw me out?" She got little tears in the corner of her eyes.

"You walked out seven years ago."

"Where am I supposed to go?" She started to sob. I was paralyzed standing there, holding my old college jacket in my hand. I felt bad for her.

"Lara, later, if you want to visit, maybe we can set that up. I know the kids would love to meet you."

"Meet me? I'm their fucking mother! What do you mean meet me?"

"They don't have a mother right now."

She grabbed the jacket from my hand. "How old are they now?"

"Nick's nine, Sammie's seven."

"How are they?"

"They're doing well. They're doing just fine."

She put on the jacket. "And you? Are you still alone?"

"No … I'm seeing someone." This was a trick I had seen Danny do many times. He called it "storymaking."

She put out her cigarette, got up from the table, and slammed the chair against it. "Is she here?"

"Not right now."

"Then I could just spend the night." She stepped toward me. I stepped back. At that, she flew into a rage. "You're a creep, you know that? What kind of a guy would throw a woman out on the street?"

"I guess one like Major, and one like me."

"You're such an ass."

She knew she didn't belong with us. She knew she was only looking for a place to land before she would carry off to some other kind of adventure. Lara's adventures were killing her now. Her adventures were about escape. They were not real adventures. She was running from the terror of reliving her mother's life. She had become depressed after Nick's birth, and it got worst after Samantha was born. She was running from the dread of repeating her mother's story. I realized right then that an adventure can't be about running from something. Or running to grab on to something. To be on a true adventure, you had to be exploring, with curiosity, and with an open heart. But Lara was just running, looking for someone to take care of her.

"Okay, Marty." She put out her cigarette. "You live with it on your conscience."

"I can manage that."

"Tell the kids I miss them." She moved toward the door. She was half way out before she turned. "Are you managing to fuck her?"

I said nothing.

"Are you? Are you fucking her?"

"As a matter of fact, I am."

"You're a liar," she answered. She slammed the door behind her and left the house to wait for a cab outside.

I watched her out the kitchen window. She was there five minutes before a cab picked her up and rolled off into the night. She would probably never write another letter. I thought of Charlie. His song wafted into my thoughts. I sang quietly, as I wandered back to bed. And I imagined love letters sinking to the bottom of the sea.

July 18, 1988

We're in Guayaquil, in Ecuador. We're here for four days, then our boat leaves for the Galapagos. Marty seems excited to get there and wants to leave port already. He has been talking all about evolution, and that stuff gets really boring. We met a girl last night in the bar, Melanie. She was hot—blonde hair, blue eyes, perfect body. She's from San Diego, and here on a mission. I think she's Mormon, but she didn't come out and say that. I started pretending again, and at first it pissed Marty off. I liked it when he joined me in storymaking. That's when we're at our best.

I told Melanie I was on a mission, too. That I was an FBI agent on a top secret assignment. She could see through my stories, but she let me go on with it, and just kept asking me questions. I told her about my secret spy gear. That I was chasing down an arms dealer from Nicaragua who had come to Ecuador. I told her I had been trained as an assassin, so I could protect us all if we needed. By the end we were pretty drunk and cracking up. I didn't know Mormons got drunk, but she was. Marty tried to talk to us some more about evolution. He was really serious and intellectual, explaining Darwin's theory. Melanie and I just cracked up at the bar laughing to his lectures. She sprayed beer out her nose, and Marty finally loosened up. Melanie explained that she didn't believe much in evolution. She asked us if it were true, why we humans had stopped evolving. She asked what had happened in the last many thousand years to prove that this survivor of the fittest thing was still happening. We couldn't think of anything. Then Marty got into storymaking with me. He explained to Melanie that I was an example of evolution. He explained to her how I had evolved to become a perfect sex partner to assure the survival of the human gene pool. That's when I really loved Marty. Not only was he telling a story, but he was helping me out.

Later that night, I went with Melanie to her apartment. We had awesome sex, and she told me to tell Marty that he was right. But when I told her I had to go, she got angry. She wanted me to spend the night, but I told her that I couldn't and that I had a girlfriend. I told her I thought we were just having fun for the night pretending and shit, but she wasn't too happy about that. She called me a pathological liar and to get out of her home, so I left.

Spellman's

The seasons never change in Los Angeles. The lawns stay green all year, protected from aging, just like the people. Sometimes it bothered me. Everywhere I had traveled, it was the elders who were revered with wisdom. Not here. Though Frannie's crowd seemed to embrace their birthdays. I was excited to see her as I opened the door to her shop. Her white apron draped all of her little body, and her hair was streaked with flour.

"Morning, Martin!" She smiled.

"Morning, Frannie. How are you?"

"I'm good. I didn't expect to see you so early in the morning."

"I thought I'd get some coffee cake for the office staff."

"You're in luck. I have fresh blueberry streusel."

"Sounds great."

She went to work behind the glass counter, coughing.

"Has anyone checked that cough?" I said.

"I don't believe in doctors. They get in the way of a good day." She was reaching for the pastry.

"Where did you go last week? I couldn't find you after I sang."

"Oh, I was tired. Can't stay up like I used to."

"Oh." I paused. "I was afraid it was my singing."

"Honey, you sang perfectly. I was so proud of you." She looked up at me. "Did you enjoy it?"

"Very much," I answered. "I haven't sung like that in a long time."

"Well come back this week. Once you start singing, you want to keep going. It's good for you. Breaks up the day. That's what I think. Did you want the whole streusel?"

"Sure." A moment of quiet. "Frannie, did you say you knew my father?"

She kept to her task. "I did. He came in sometimes. Long time ago now."

"Really?"

"First I wasn't sure. When you came into the bakery a few

years back. You looked familiar. I thought maybe I recognized you from long ago."

"I came in here before?"

"Yes. Years ago. While your mom was dying. Your daddy brought you in. I made you a birthday cake—a space cake with planets. You said you wanted aliens on it. It was quite a cake!" She came out from behind the counter. "When you signed your check Grossmark a few years back, I knew it was you. Nearly forty years ago now I made you that cake."

She coughed some more.

"I remember it. That was my last birthday party. My alien party." My smile quivered.

Frannie put the streusel into a box. "He just brought you by a couple times. You looked sad back then. I knew he was trying to make you happy."

"I don't remember ever being here."

"Well, it was years ago. There. They'll love this. My secret recipe."

"What was he like?"

"Like you. Always doing something kind for people. Like bringing breakfast over like you are. I tried to sell him challah, though, and he was never interested."

"He liked to cook pancakes." I wanted someone to know that. I wished he were around, and that I could have another chance as his son.

"He liked singing, too," she added. "He had a good voice, like you. But he just sang quiet, while I put together his orders. I teased him to sing louder. He got bashful, though."

I tried to imagine my father bashful.

"He always sang that song. Under his breath, but I could hear it. "Goodbye Yellow Brick Road." 1973. I knew his wife was dying. Your mom. I thought this was his way of saying goodbye. Who knows, maybe he just liked the song."

I was up against a memory that wasn't there.

"He stopped coming later that year. I imagined after your mom had passed," she said.

I spied the door to the left. "Did you have your club back then?"

She was ringing me up. "No. I opened that twenty years ago. I needed some place I could gather with my friends. Besides those country clubs. I always felt like I was dying when I walked into those."

"Oh. The people who come … have you known them for a long time?"

"Oh, yes." She pushed the box toward me. "I've known Horty for fifty years." She smiled. "You know, she's been through all kinds of hair colors. It's been pink for a good twenty years." She had a spastic coughing fit that concerned me. "The colonel and I met gambling at Hollywood Park. Shortly after the war."

"How did you stay in touch? I mean with so many people."

"It's difficult. That's why I opened the club. To have a place where I could meet my friends each week."

"I see." I hadn't stayed in touch with anyone in my 42 years. "I'm glad to be your friend, Frannie." I took the box in my hand. "Can you get that cough checked?"

"I don't worry about it." She smiled.

"What if it's serious?"

"I told you. I don't believe in doctors. You can't spend your years worrying about how to live longer. You should just spend them living."

"You don't worry about dying?"

"No. Just about living. That's what to worry about, Marty. Worry that every day you spend it living. Then dying's not such a problem. Sing a song. Cook something. Did your daddy teach you to make pancakes?"

"Yes." I smiled.

"One day, make some for me. If they're any good, we can sell them here."

"I need to practice a bit more." I turned to leave.

"Is your father still living, Marty?"

"No. He died of a heart attack years ago."

"Oh. I'm sorry to hear that. Do you miss him?"

"Sometimes. I miss a few people."

"Come back to the club and sing some more then. It makes the missing easier."

"I will."

"And enjoy the streusel!"

I walked the street toward home clutching Frannie's pink box. Just down from the bakery, I passed the small men's clothing store. Arnold's. I recalled Bradshaw's advice to me, and though it had been hard to hear, I considered that he might be correct about my attire. So into the store I wandered.

At Sea

The next Sunday morning, we were back in the teepee. The air was fresh and crisp, and we were warm inside the cover of the structure. We never cooked at Jane's. She hadn't invited me in. It would have been easier. The pancakes cooled down in the walk over, even when we wrapped them tightly in a towel. Something was changing for me. After all the years of living in my own world, I had now developed a yearning to be in hers. I wanted to cook in her kitchen, to sit in her den, and to sleep in her bed. The kids were ready for our story, and I began to narrate.

The log rocked back and forth, balanced by the dolphins, and Samaya had become their friend.

"Did you know that Slickie swam here from the coast of Mozambique?"

Nikko was quiet as he listened to her talk.

"He says it's nice there on the coast. He has been to our island, too. He prefers Mozambique to Madagascar. He says there's a village at the seaside where the drums play most evenings. He likes to swim to the rhythm."

Nikko stayed quiet. He pictured his knife at the bottom of the sea. He was irritated with Samaya. He wondered if she understood what he had sacrificed for her.

"He said they're guiding us there. The village is called Gbamandu. It's a little way up a slope on the top of a cliff at the seaside."

Nikko said nothing. His heart grew colder as she spoke. He wanted to move on, but he was mad. He had only one possession left in the world, so he turned to it for help. Nikko found Elliot's leather book at the bottom of his hole. It was wet but had fared generally well on the passage so far. Nikko knew nothing of this Frost, but he hid himself from Samaya as he opened up the book.

A Minor Bird

I have wished a bird would fly away,
And not sing by my house all day;

Have clapped my hands at him from the door
When it seemed as if I could bear no more.

The fault must partly have been in me.
The bird was not to blame for his key.

And of course there must be something wrong
In wanting to silence any song.

Samaya kept going. "This one is his sister, Marybelle. She's gone on all kinds of adventures. She says we're on the best current. We have to stay a little south as the water up north gets too choppy for a log like ours."

He finally spoke. "How do you know what they're saying?"

"I just listen."

"But all I hear are sounds."

"I noticed on the first day we were floating that some sounds were different than others. The more I listened, the more I understood what they were saying."

He was impressed. "You're like a spy, cracking a code."

"It's quiet out here. Especially these last two days. You haven't said one word to me. I know how mad you are. I would be, too. I didn't listen to you. I almost got trapped forever. And you lost the one thing that mattered to you to save me. Well, there's really no way for me to thank you. All I can do is let you be mad. So I've listened to the dolphins to learn their language."

"Can you talk back to them?" His heart softened as he listened to his talented friend. How nice it was that she understood his feelings.

"No, I've tried. They don't understand my sounds. I can't click and chirp like they do."

"Oh." He was disappointed. He had hoped that he could request that Slickie dive down for his knife.

"Why do they stay with us, Samaya?"

"They enjoyed the pancake. Now they want to help us to shore."

"Why do they come and go like they do? Have you learned that?"

"Sometimes one of them wants to go on an adventure. Sometimes they get mad at each other. Sometimes they need alone time. But they always know that they will come back to the group."

"Have they seen a knife?"

"I haven't heard that. I'm sorry. But I'm going to find it for you."

Nikko laughed. "You are, are you? How might you do that?"

"I don't know. But you saved my life. So somehow I'll find your knife. Even if I have to dive down to the bottom of the sea."

"A shark might eat you if you do that."

"It's a risk I might have to take."

"The current might be too strong for you to get back to the log."

"Then I'll throw the knife to you. And hope that Marybelle sees me struggling."

"And what if she is mad at that moment. Mad at Slickie. What if she won't bring you back to the log?"

"I'll carve you a note. With your knife that I find. I'll carve it on a piece of driftwood floating out at sea."

Nikko's anger passed. He felt touched with this storymaking and chuckled. Something unfamiliar was bubbling up inside of him.

"What would it say? What would you carve in the driftwood?"

"It would say … 'Dear Nikko. I've found your knife. It was a difficult swim. I had to wrestle a moray eel. I am bruised and

174

battered from the coral. A shark chased me and bit my ring tail. But a big green sea turtle found me struggling and swam me down to it. I've found your knife. And that's how I'm carving you this note.'"

"That's a lot to fit onto one piece of driftwood."

"Yes, I would have to wait for just the right piece to come by. But Marybelle would balance me while I waited."

"You don't really understand the dolphins, do you?"

"No. But it's fun pretending."

Nikko was smiling in the back of the boat. It was the first time that he ever recalled feeling joyous. He had smiled a social smile in line at Rosalie's kitchen when greeting the others. But this was a different sort of smile. It started as a warm feeling in his heart. It was a smile he couldn't stop.

"I guess it is. I haven't done it much."

And that's what they did. They pretended and pretended. Two lemurs. One pancake. One worn leather book. Seven dolphins, sometimes six, sometimes five. Headed toward somewhere, perhaps Mozambique. Hopefully south of the dangerous waters. Pretending and pretending as they floated on the Indian Ocean.

Nikko wondered about this book. He thought perhaps it was a magic book. Elliot must have held it close for some reason. He was careful with it now and clutched it in his lap. No more water across the pages. This was his last secret weapon. His last tie to his past. And he rehearsed the poem again in his mind as they pretended.

Pain Relief

The darkness of the mornings grew longer as the year came closer to an end. I woke up early Sunday morning to review case law. I was having difficulty finding an argument for Bradshaw. For the first time, I couldn't toe the party line. Bradshaw had wanted a quick answer, and I had dragged this on for months. Though he had become distracted by other issues around the hospital, I knew I had to get him something soon. I had scoured case law. I had churned federal statutes. I turned to the computer again and reviewed the provisions of the Hatch Act. There really seemed to be no case.

Thoughts of Lara still disturbed me. I wondered if there was more I could have done, though I knew I couldn't do much for anyone who didn't want to change. But I had wanted to, I really wanted to. That was the feeling that was growing inside of me, a feeling of wanting to help someone.

My shoulder ached badly, and I was having difficulty turning my neck to the left. I thought about the accident. I remembered rolling, glass shattering, and turning to see my kids in the back seat. I thought about the boy, asking me to drive him home.

The police report had included his name. John Cameron. On a whim, I broke from my work and searched his name online. Nothing came up. I opened my accident folder, filled with documents that I had scanned into the computer. The insurance claim, medical receipts, the police report. There I read his parents' names, Cynthia and Peter. I searched Peter Cameron online, and I discovered a small newspaper clipping from the *Culver City Observer*.

Peter Cameron, marine and veteran of the Persian Gulf conflict, in jail awaiting trial for prescription fraud. Cameron allegedly forged prescriptions for Codeine and Demerol under a physician's name. Bail set at $10,000.

Scumbag. No wonder this kid was messed up. His father was strung out on drugs. I took satisfaction in the justice of this, but it didn't last as my mind began to play tricks. I wondered about Peter Cameron and why he took pills. Maybe he had pain like me. He was a veteran. I wondered if Henry Dawson had ever met him. Was he one of the many veterans he wrote about?

Maybe this wasn't him. I had to be sure, so I searched some more. Peter Cameron. I clicked on Culver City Track Club. He was the coach. His picture was there, with a monthly coaching blog. His son was the top 800 meter runner in Los Angeles. I stared at a photo of John, winning the race. It was him. The boy who hit me. I read about the practice schedule. The upcoming meets. The awards various kids had won, including John.

Nick woke up early and brought an end to my thinking.

"Jane said we can cook at her house this morning."

"She did?"

"Yes." He headed for the kitchen. "Come on, Dad. We need to get stuff together."

"Nick, it's 6:30 in the morning."

"I know, she said we could come over at 7."

"She didn't tell me anything about cooking at her house."

Samantha joined us in the kitchen. "She did, Dad. She said it was getting too cold out to carry the ingredients in the morning."

"But we can still use the teepee," Nick said, gathering the flour and sugar in a large metal bowl.

"She doesn't want us to get sick from the walk over in the morning."

"Oh, I see." I joined them in the preparation. "Well, if you say so."

I expected Jane's house to have frills and laced curtains and maybe a floral wallpaper print. Her kitchen was far from that. It looked like the inside of a mountain cabin with wood beams overhead and a rust-colored tiled floor. The walls were painted light green with pictures hung everywhere. I marveled at a photograph of the Sierras, a picture of a buffalo carved in a rock, and a black and white image of a wise Native American woman with a wrinkled face and a bright smile. Jane had an old black stove in the corner of the kitchen. There was a small table where only two could sit, and there was a large leather chair in the corner of the room. That's where I sat.

"I'm going to watch you all cook." I looked at the small black stove next to the chair. "What's that?"

"It's how I heat the house in the winter."

"Really? You don't have a heater?"

"Not in this half of the house. Only in the bedrooms. That's how we heated our home in Carson City. I liked it that way."

Nick and Sammie went to work, and Jane helped them find what they needed. They loaded Jane's picnic basket with fine china plates and silverware, the likes of which I had never seen. Her silver had intricate carvings on the handles and seemed worthy of resting on King Arthur's table. I thought of Rama, insisting on the finest kitchenware.

The inside of the teepee had transformed. Nick and Sammie had spent much of the week drawing pictures of our lemurs, and they taped them on the teepee walls. There was one of Elliot in his tree house reading books and sipping coffee. There was one of Rosalie making pancakes. There was another of Jasper and Lionel throwing coconuts from the tree. Another showed two lemurs in a boat, Samaya in front, and Nikko in the back. This morning Sammie taped another picture of Samaya swimming deep under the sea to retrieve a knife off the ocean bottom. Her artistic abilities were impressive. They hadn't drawn Carlos. I imagined that was a scary picture to draw.

"We can't put that one up," Nick protested. "It didn't happen."

"She said she was going to get it. So if she said it, it's part of the story."

"But it makes it look like she got it."

"Well I think she will," Sammie said back to him.

I didn't mind the fighting anymore. I admired the passion. I admired the hell out of it.

"Leave it up," I interrupted. "It's a beautiful picture, Sammie. I didn't know you could draw like that. We'll see what happens to the knife. Maybe she will find it."

"But Dad …"

I put my arm around Nick. "Tell me which drawings are yours."

He calmed down a bit. "I made the one of Jasper and Lionel throwing coconuts. And Elliot in the tree."

"They should be hanging in the Louvre. I'll send copies and a letter of inquiry."

"We'll send them directly to the curator," Jane added.

Nick lit the candle, and the flame brightened the images of lemurs all around us. We devoured the pancakes. They tasted better on Jane's china. I inhaled the smell of buffalo skin emanating from the inside of the teepee, and I caught a glimpse of Sammie's knee. The ointment had worked. The red around it had faded leaving only a faint scar. I continued right where we had left off.

—⟋⟋⟋—

Nikko was thankful to have his companion with him in the front of the boat. He enjoyed pretending with her as the days passed. They ate apricots, nuts, and bananas, though their food supply was running low. Nikko enjoyed reading his book in quiet times. He wondered about Elliot; how he and the others were doing. He hoped that they were not too upset that he and Samaya had left.

As the days passed, Nikko wondered if they would ever come across their future. But he gave up worrying about it to enjoy his present moments. They listened to the ocean lapping against their boat. They enjoyed talking to each other and making up stories. They liked to imagine the place that they would land, and what they would say to whomever greeted them.

Nikko enjoyed living this series of present moments. He thought of home. Rosalie burdened by the future, cooking for the troop. Elliot worrying about the future, warning of its dangers. And Carlos. Sacrificing every present moment in search of a past. Nikko looked down at the leather book. He opened to a page and he read ...

Oh, give us pleasure in the flowers today;
And give us not to think so far away
As the uncertain harvest; keep us here
All simply in the springing of the year.

He liked this poem. Elliot's book knew exactly what to say at the right time. He enjoyed being here with his companion in the boat. As Nikko considered these words, the boat began to rock. The dolphins had left their side quite suddenly. The two lemurs were left to balance on their own, and they had little practice in this.

"Where did they go?" asked Nikko.

"I don't know," answered Samaya.

"I thought you understood them."

"I told you I was pretending."

"Well, shift your weight forward and to the left. I'll lean back and to the right."

"But it keeps changing. The waves keep changing where we need to lean."

"Okay then. I'll tell you where to lean. I'll steer the boat, you do the leaning."

"Should I paddle?"

"No. Just lean. Lean left. Lean far left, Samaya!"

She leaned far to the left. But a current came from the other direction. "Lean right, Samaya. Lean all the way to the right."

Samaya leaned right. "I'm leaning as far as I can!"

"I am too. Now go left again."

She leaned to the left and as she did she saw something in the sea. Samaya couldn't believe her eyes.

"Nikko, look. They're beautiful!" Samaya pointed to thousands of small purple jellyfish. The boat rocked furiously as she gazed in amazement, stunned by the translucent purple bodies. Samaya had never seen such a beautiful sight.

"Nikko. They're beautiful." But no response came from behind. Samaya looked over her shoulder at an empty hole.

Nikko had been thrown from the log and was struggling to keep his head above the water. He had always been able to do most things, so he had assumed that he could swim. It had never occurred to him that it was a learned skill. He popped his head above the water.

"Help, Samaya!" He paddled uselessly. "Ouch! They're stinging me! And I can't stay up!" The current dragged him under.

Samaya grabbed Nikko's oar from the back of the boat and reached over the left side of the log. As she did, the log tilted wildly from side to side.

"Grab on, Nikko!"

His head popped up again. "They're all around me. They're stinging me. Get them off!"

He couldn't reach Samaya's pole, though he managed to paddle to keep his head up. He hollered and screamed from the painful stings.

"Swim a little this way," she called. "And grab the oar."

"I can't move through them," he hollered back. "Get them off of me!"

Nikko moved his arms and legs as fast as he could. He discovered that this movement kept his head above water. But it also kept him bumping into these strange creatures. His leg. His shoulder. His face. The thought occurred to him that this might be his destiny, and that he would join his knife at the ocean floor. But Nikko kept paddling and kept his head above the sea. He thought to himself, "Live!"

I surprised myself with that, and I paused for a moment.

"Daddy, what's happening?" Samantha exclaimed.

"Don't worry, Sammie ... I'll tell you ..."

Samaya recalled Nikko's warning never again to throw an oar off the boat. She looked into the back hole where she saw a worn book. She grabbed it, hoisted it over her head, and slammed it into the ocean next to Nikko. The book sent ripples through the water, carrying the jellies further away from Nikko. He was left in a clearing, the jellies floating a good distance from him now. Elliot's book opened then submerged under the sea, slowly falling beneath the waves.

Samaya reached again for the paddle, balanced carefully, and stretched to reach Nikko. He grabbed on and maneuvered himself through the circle of jellies toward the log. He reached the side of the boat and struggled into his hole. Nikko cried out from the pain of the stings. He looked off to his right to a sea of jellyfish floating, beautiful yet deadly. In the center of their circle lay an open book sinking beneath their translucent purple beauty. Mr. Frost was joining the knife at the bottom of the sea. Samaya had thrown the last remnant of his past, and it, too, would soon be gone forever. Yet Nikko knew that it was a good trade, the only one available. His past had been swapped for a future that only the tides knew.

Nikko continued moaning in pain. Samaya reached for her basket.

"Here. Have some of this. It will make you feel better."

He was moaning the minor key tone of the Indri. "It's the last pancake. We need to save it."

"We need to save you."

"The pancake won't save me."

"It might. You don't know."

Nikko nibbled on the pancake as they floated through the sea of jellyfish. And as he ate, the pain dulled.

"It's helping."

"Just keep eating."

"But we won't have any more pancakes."

"We'll have to get along without them. We'll make do with what we have."

"But we don't have anything left." He was amazed that the pain was going away.

"Yes, we do."

"What?"

"We have pretending."

Nikko grew quiet, and the pain subsided. It was a magic pancake, indeed. He ate all but the last bit and put that back in the bamboo box.

"Thanks for saving me, Samaya."

"You're welcome."

They came to an end of the red and purple band of jellyfish, and the seas calmed a bit. Samaya looked up from the front of the boat and couldn't believe her eyes.

"Land! Nikko, I see land!"

They paddled on. Nikko had lost everything—his knife, the book, and all but a small crumb of pancake. But now they could see a future. And they paddled straight into it with all of their might.

July 30, 1988

Guayaquil is a cool place. We spent the day at the docks arranging our trip to the Galapagos. We met a cool kid there named Tomas. He's eight and he works on the dock. He lives in a village with his mother. He speaks perfect English and Spanish. He had a soccer ball, and we kicked it around. He wanted to take us up to his village, but Marty told him that we had to catch the boat early in the morning to the Galapagos. The kid was bummed. I asked him how he got back home, and if his father would pick him up. He said he didn't have a father, but that someone always gave him a ride back home to his mother. I felt bad for him. I had this weird feeling for a little while that I wanted to take him home with me. I thought about being a father for him. Then I realized I couldn't do it. It sounded good, but I'm not sure that I could ever be a father. The whole idea freaks me out. He followed us around all day. He seemed to know everyone on the docks. They all smiled when he came by and yelled, "Hola, Tomas." He reminded me of myself when I was eight. I wished he would come to the Galapagos with us. But to be honest, I was relieved when he got a ride back to the village. The whole thing scared me. Marty's back talking about evolution, and I'm feeling lonely. I wish he could get what a waste of life all that thinking can be. And it seems like he's doing it more and more on this trip.

Dr. Bradshaw

As the Chief of Staff, it was Dr. Bradshaw's job to assure that staff performed effectively and professionally, that outstanding and timely care was delivered, and that measurements of quality and satisfaction were ahead of the national curve. It wasn't an easy job, but he had moved from Oklahoma back home to L.A. to accept the position.

I wasn't particularly looking forward to today's meeting, though I had done enough research at this point and I had no choice. Henry Dawson had not violated the Hatch Act, and I could not pretend that he had. I had cancelled my meeting with Jerry altogether. There was nothing to discuss. I didn't have a case.

Dr. Bradshaw sat at his computer desk facing a bank of windows and a large conference table. That's where I sat down while he responded to an e-mail.

"Hi, Marty. Take a seat. I'll be right there. Damn these people! Don't they know anything?" He stared intently at his screen as he typed furiously. "Is everyone around here just an idiot?" I braced myself for the conversation to come. He got up from his desk and got a bottle of water from a small refrigerator by the wall.

"Want a drink? I have water, soft drinks, iced tea."

"No, I'm fine."

He approached the table and sat down at the head. I had known not to sit there. It was marked as his spot by the white jacket hanging from the back of the chair with a stethoscope dangling from the pocket. He opened the bottle and drank half of it while I watched.

"Sure you don't want a drink?"

"I'm sure."

He picked up his pen by the yellow pad at his seat, gazed at me intently, and smiled. "New tie, Marty?"

"Oh, yes, actually."

"Very nice. Bright colors look good on you. And your shirt?"

"What about it?" I was uncomfortable by his perceptions, though I had followed his advise.

"No wrinkles. Is it new?"

"It is, actually."

"Much better."

"Oh, thanks." I had taken his advice, and now I felt awkward.

"Now you need to join a gym. Then you'll be peeling women off you."

I was half tempted to mention Jane, though I bit my tongue. "I'll think about that one."

"So where are we?" he asked, picking up his pen and turning to the yellow pad. I felt a chill run through me as I struggled to speak.

"I want to talk to you about Henry Dawson." I saw flowers on the bookshelf against the window behind him. "Are those from the horticulture garden?" I asked.

He nodded. "Yes. I have a patient there."

"Is it Charlie?"

"Yes. You know Charlie? I didn't know you lawyers left your bungalow."

"I went down there. What's wrong with him?"

"He's a Korean War veteran. He has brain injury from combat."

I wanted to tell him that I sang with him, and that he knew the words perfectly. But I supposed that would threaten my professional image. Maybe he had seen us through the window, me and Charlie singing Pat Boone, while he gripped his wrist strengthener.

"Tell me about Dawson. This administrative leave is getting expensive. I'm ready to let him go."

My palms sweat in my lap. "I've researched this."

"Yes. For months now."

"Okay." I ignored the jab. "I believe he was making a public health statement. He stated that the best treatment for PTSD would be to prevent the trauma."

"Go on."

"That's like advocating for exercise or smoking cessation to prevent a heart attack."

"Of course it's different. He's using his position as a federal employee to make a public political stance."

"I don't bclicvc it's a political stance. I believe he made a statement about the toll of war. On soldiers. I can't find the politics."

"He's trying to influence others by using his position as a VA employee."

"But you would have no objection if he wrote to advocate smoking cessation. Or exercise. Or sunscreen. Would you? Is it wrong to let the public know about the problems caused by war?"

"Suddenly you're the anti-war guy? Get a new tie and you're into leading causes?" He clamped down on his jaw and gave a squeeze to the water bottle.

"No. I just understand what he wrote now as a public health statement."

"Oh, Jeeze. This is not what I was expecting." He put down his pen and thought for a moment. The room smelled of his musk and my sweat.

"My father is a Korean War Veteran, Martin. It's not like I don't know the impact of war. It's not like I don't know what that can do to a person. It tore him up."

I was caught off guard by his disclosure. It was unlike him and I wasn't sure how to respond. "I'm sorry."

"Oh come on, it's not your fault."

"I know. Just sorry that he had to go through that."

"I am, too. At times, when I was growing up, he was lost in the memories in his head. He lived in a world of private thoughts that haunted him. But he never would talk about it to us."

"Right, so …"

Bradshaw got up from the table to look out the window bank clutching his water bottle. "He would sometimes just fly into a rage. He would yell at us, just for no reason. We all knew he was struggling with some kind of memories." Bradshaw paused for a moment. He appeared lost in thought. "But he was a proud man. He was honored to have served. That's why I did it, you know. It's really something to take a stance for your country. In that way, I'm proud of him. And proud that I followed in his footsteps." He paused again. "We all knew he was struggling with some kind of memories. So I know about war, Martin. I know what it can do. That's why I'm in this job. And it's a hell of an honor."

I was quiet for a moment, and slightly embarrassed that I had never served. And more than that, I was ashamed that I had failed to honor those who had. My thoughts about our facility and about my job were changing. I was discovering a respect for military veterans and for the people who helped them. I found my voice and wondered out loud. "So what do you have against Henry Dawson?"

Nothing. I respect the man. It's Central Office. Are you willing to take them on?" He looked back over at me squarely in the eyes.

"Yes," I answered. "Is there any reason you want him removed?"

He swigged the bottle until it was empty. "No. I admire him, frankly. He's got balls, putting his opinion out there."

"Is there some kind of problem with his job performance?"

"No. Not at all. Like I told you, he's a devoted doctor with outstanding performance appraisals for over two decades. He treats my dad." His eyes watered for a moment.

"I see."

"Whatever you want to do," he said, regaining composure. "I'll support your understanding of the case. But you're swimming in dangerous waters. I can't help you if Central Office disagrees."

"They won't. There's no case here. Dawson didn't do anything wrong."

He looked out the window. "Okay then. Do you have anything else?"

"How do you treat PTSD?"

"Since when does a lawyer care about treatment?"

"Well, I was just wondering. When you have memories coming at you. And you can't stop them. What do you do?"

"You just talk about them. Over and over again. And you cry a lot. If you can cry, I think it helps. Problem is, with our guys, like our Marines, they don't grieve. That's not what they were raised to do."

"You mean if you can just cry, then the memories stop?"

"I don't know. I think it helps. It's a hell of a lot better than the alternative."

"What's that?"

"Not to remember. And not to feel. Then you're really in trouble. I mean, I think the memories are bad. But if you can't remember, and you can't feel. That's worse."

"Why's that?"

"Then you're all alone with it. Like on an island. Doing things to keep the memories away. Things that cause problems."

"Right." I was sure he could see into my mind. "So it's okay then. I mean to call Central Office and tell them that I don't think they have a case."

He was thinking and staring out the window. "I wonder if Charlie really has brain damage. Or what's wrong with him. Or what he did out there in Korea."

"Excuse me?"

"Well, speaking of islands. I guess that's what we are. We're like an island for a lot of people. Who can't make it out there in the world."

"It's good we're here," I said. And I was starting to believe that.

He laughed a little. I could see him struggling with something. He had lost a bit of the composure I had come to know. I supposed it was thinking about his father.

"Right. Everyone needs a home they can come to. That's what we are for Charlie."

The word home sent my mind adrift. "Can you give me a ride home ..." John Cameron standing by my vehicle, smoke enveloping the two of us. I imagined he was at home now, probably with his mother, and his father was in jail. I wondered if he ever thought about me the way I thought about him. If I were in his dreams like he was in mine.

"I have a question," I said.

"Sure."

"If I do know someone, a combat veteran, and they need help. What do I do?"

"Bring them here."

"Okay. Whose name should I give? I mean how do they get in?"

"Give them my card. I'll get them in. He was still staring out the window.

"Okay. Is that it? I'll write a response to Central Office explaining there is no case."

"That's fine."

I got up to leave.

"And Martin ... thanks for hearing me out."

"Sure thing."

"There's a woman now. Isn't there."

"Excuse me?"

"In your life. You're dating."

"Well, no. I'm working on it though." I was stunned at his perception.

"I thought so ... It's good to get back on the horse. Good for you."

"Oh, well thanks I guess." I felt awkward again. "I'll send you a copy of the response to Central Office."

"Good plan." He was still staring out the window. "And don't forget what I told you about exercise."

"I'll give it some consideration."

"Good. I'll see you later, Martin."

Part

III

Greeting
Destiny

August 1, 1988

I haven't written for four days. The boat ride over was rocky as hell. Felt a lot better when we got to our first island, Pinta. Marty seemed more alive when we got here. There are so many creatures. Beautiful. So much to think about. It's a little scary to me. The whole idea of evolution. I started to think that I never wanted to do it. I never want to evolve. You lose something in the process. I got hung up on that thought. I like the way my life is now, going on adventures, meeting new people. I realized on the boat over that it would all be over if I had taken Tomas home. We're talking a lot about Darwin. Especially after we met this tortoise—Lonesome George. He's the last pure Pinta tortoise in the world. He's similar to other tortoises on the Galapagos, but they're all different, and that's what inspired Darwin's survival of the fittest idea.

I feel bad for George. He's like 90 years old. If he doesn't have sex, then his balls will shrivel up, so they try to keep him in shape with other tortoises. We watched him with a female tortoise next to him, but he just sank into a mud puddle and wasn't interested. Poor guy. Just doesn't want to have kids, I guess. He's going to go extinct. That doesn't seem to bother him, though. He just wants to bathe in the mud and have a good time. I guess I can relate to that.

Jody wants to have kids some day. We talked about it. After today, I'm sure I wouldn't make a good father. It's too much to deal with. The whole idea puts me up against this dark place in my mind. It's something about being given up in the beginning. It makes me nauseous. I'll have to convince Jody that we can have more fun with each other without kids. I don't know how she'll take that. The whole idea is tripping me out today. I guess I don't care about survival of the fittest. I'd rather hang like George in the mud puddle and have a good time. Even if my blood line does go extinct. I don't even know what it is anyway.

On Shore

I woke up early Sunday morning to the sound of pounding outside my bedroom window. Bang, bang, bang. It sounded like construction, and I was pissed. I stormed into the kitchen and stomped on the bump in the linoleum. It was really starting to bother me. Out the kitchen window I saw Nick shooting baskets in our driveway. That was the pounding sound that was so new for me that morning. His shots were pretty good, better than I remembered. I decided to join him.

"Hey there, stranger. What are you up to so early in the morning?"

"I felt like playing." He took another shot. It went in—swoosh.

"You're pretty good. I was watching you out the window."

"I don't know." He took another shot. It banked off the backboard, hit the rim, and went straight to me. I took a shot and missed the basket altogether.

"Better than me."

"That was on purpose, Dad."

I smiled. "I wish."

Nick took the ball and dribbled around the court. He was pretty coordinated.

"Where did you learn that?"

"I've been playing at recess."

I couldn't believe it. "How did you blow up that ball?"

"I found a pump in the garage." I watched Nick as he shot. Some went in, others didn't. When the ball came to me, I took a shot. We shot baskets together for fifteen minutes before Sammie came outside in her PJs.

"Are we making pancakes today or what?" she asked.

"Yeah," I answered. "You want to get started?"

"Are we cooking here or at Jane's?"

"We can cook here."

"Is she coming over?"

"Of course she is."

"Okay." She went back inside.

Nick and I kept shooting. It was a moment that I thought would never come.

"I want to play in the park league."

"You do?"

"Yeah. At Rancho. Signups are this weekend. Can we go?"

"Are you sure?"

"Yes. I'm getting pretty good."

"I see that. Do you know anyone playing?"

"Yeah. A bunch of kids. They told me to sign up."

"Kids at school?"

"Yeah."

I took a shot and missed. "Do I know them?"

"I don't know." He took another shot. "Brian said he was playing, and he told me I should, too."

"Brian—the kid you wrestled to the ground?"

"Yeah. We're friends now."

"You are?"

"Yeah. He's been cool to me lately."

"I thought you hated him," I answered. My shot missed the basket.

"No. I hated how he treated Sharon. But he stopped." Nick smiled up at me.

I was so proud of him. He was teaching me something now.

"He's not very good. Think I'm better than him."

"I'll bet you are. You're getting these all in."

"Will you help me practice?"

"Every day. I can come home early sometimes and we can go to the park."

"Okay." He smiled and then looked down at the ball as he dribbled around the driveway.

"I'm going in to check on your sister."

"Okay. I want to keep practicing this shot." He threw the ball up and into the basket. I thought maybe I was hallucinating. He was really good.

Sammie wasn't cooking. She had returned to her bedroom, and I went in to find her. Her bedroom wasn't the classic little girl's room. Soccer posters covered the walls. But she still had her princess tent bed, and I dreaded the day she wanted to give it up. She had taken her stuffed animals out of the closet and put them into piles.

"What are you doing, kiddo? I thought we were going to cook?"

"I formed a club. I'm giving away some of these old stuffed animals to whoever joins." She looked up at me. "It's called Samaya's club. People ask what it means, but I tell them I'm the only one who knows the secret."

"I see." I watched her pile her stuffed animals out from her closet. "Why are you giving those away?"

"Well, I really only need this one." It was the one she had gotten at the scene of our accident. "The rest I can give away."

"But why do you want to?"

"I don't need them." She went back to her sorting.

"But do you like them?"

"Sure. But if I give them away, then people will want to be in the club."

"Won't they want to just be in the club anyway?" I got down on the floor next to her.

"Maybe. But also, I think good things happen if you give things away."

"You do? Like what?"

"I might find something else."

"Are you looking for something else?"

"Maybe."

"What is it?"

"I don't know. I just like the idea. You give stuff away, and then you get something new."

"Oh, I see." I scratched her back.

"Is Jane coming over or what? It's already 8:02."

I got it. "She's coming. Of course she's coming. She always does."

"Should we go to her house to make sure?"

The doorbell rang. "There she is. I told you." Sammie ran to the door. I followed down the hall. Without asking who it was or looking through the window, she threw open the door. Sammie greeted Jane with a big hug.

"You're late!" she said to her.

"I am?"

"It's 8:03. You always come at 8:00."

"Oh, I was getting dressed."

Sammie stepped out of Jane's arms, and I looked on from the edge of the hallway. She was wearing a gold necklace. I had never seen her with jewelry. There was something hanging from it, and I couldn't quite make out what it was. Sammie saw it immediately.

"That's a beautiful necklace," Sammie commented.

"Oh, thanks. I suppose that's why I'm late. I was searching all over for it."

"What's hanging from it? It looks like a little monkey."

"It is. It's a little monkey. I think it might just be a lemur."

"It is! Nick, look. Jane has a lemur necklace!"

Nick came in from the driveway and Jane showed it to him.

"That's really cool," he said.

"It's very nice," I added. "Where did you get it?"

"I've just had it around for years. I haven't worn it in a very long time. I hoped it might come in handy one day."

I loved to watch Jane with my children. She helped me realize what treasures they were. We went into the kitchen and went to work. We cooked the pancakes and took them to our backyard temple next door. Nick lit the candle, and I began.

The shore line looked similar to the beach they had left five weeks before. But it was less rocky than their harbor back home. Just a strip of charcoal colored sand. Beyond the beach was a palm forest similar to the edge of Paden's Patch. Nikko scanned the tree tops as he walked step by step from the ocean onto the sand. In one hand he held the basket, in the other he guided the log until it beached just beyond the waves. He continued to scan the trees.

"Watcha lookin' for in those tree tops?" Samaya asked him.

"I want to make sure there are no coconut throwers."

"Why would there be coconut throwers in these trees?"

"I guess I just want to make sure it's safe."

"Do you think Jasper and Lionel swam all this way?"

"No, but there may be others."

"Maybe they swam all this way in your mind, Nikko."

"What are you talking about? I haven't given them a thought since we left."

"Well, they're your first thought when we hit shore. It seems like you've held them close!"

Nikko was struck by her perception. He had seen her as a free spirited adventurer. She was resourceful in a pinch, but likely to walk right into trouble. But now her words rang with wisdom and a familiar tone. He thought of Elliot back in the great oak, reading his great works and learning. Nikko knew that Elliot had spent special time with Samaya, and that he had read to her since the time she was young. He believed he heard the semblance of Elliot's voice coming from his fellow drifter. He continued to scan the tree tops.

"Nikko, can't you see? These are different palm trees. Do you believe we have come full circle? Look. The sand here is different. It's not white. And there are no boulders. This is a different beach. We have crossed the ocean. There is no School for Swingers here."

Nikko was anxious. He felt his heart beat in his chest.

"I know that. But we still have to be careful. Perhaps there is another school here."

"The School for Swingers is from the past, Nikko. You can't live in your past, remember? It'll trap you. You have to let them go now. They are still in the tree tops drinking palm wine. In Paden's. On Madagascar. We are somewhere else now."

"But without my knife, without my book … I don't have any protection."

"You mean you don't have anything from your past," she answered him. "Except whatever memory you put into those trees. And me. "

He was quiet. She was a wise lemur, indeed. Nikko was certain that she must be Elliot's daughter.

"They're not there, Nikko. They're gone. There's no School for Swingers in those trees."

Nikko's heart softened as he listened to her words. It was the first time anyone had truly understood him. He felt a strange new feeling. It was warm, and it started in his chest. Then tears came to his eyes.

"They're not here, Nikko."

And he cried. She was right, Elliot's daughter. They weren't there. His unknown parents. His grandmother, Rama. Carlos. The knife or the book. Elliot, Jasper, Rosalie … none of them. They weren't there. And for the first time ever, he cared about that and wished they were.

"I can't seem to stop looking for them in the tree tops." He paused. "I guess it's hard to let the memories go." He cried some more, and she stood quietly close by as his tears helped him say goodbye.

The minutes passed, and the tears eased. Nikko felt better. He wiped his eyes and looked around the beach. He saw the treetops, and they looked spectacular. He could see there was no School for Swingers there.

She smiled at him. "Maybe we should explore. I think I hear something in the distance. It sounds like drums."

Nikko heard it, too. He clutched the bamboo basket holding the last crumb of pancake. They walked together up the sand bank, and Nikko turned his gaze away from the trees. More tears came to his eyes, and he wasn't sure why. He had never cried until today. But Samaya seemed to understand it, and she put her arm around his shoulder as they walked. Her comfort brought a warm feeling to his body, and more tears to his eyes.

They discovered a dirt path at the foot of the palm trees and followed it toward the drum beats in the distance. Nikko looked over his right shoulder and noticed that the tide had come in and loosened the log from its spot. The sea stole one last thing. He watched as the log splashed far beyond the beach, drifting back towards Paden's Patch without a passenger. He watched as they lost their only way home.

Nikko felt it again, the warmth from his chest and the tears in his eyes. It grew more intense as his friend held his hand. He searched for a name for the experience but couldn't find one. He thought one more time of Elliot seated at the desk in front of his great window. In honor of Elliot, he decided to call this feeling "evolution."

The Doorbell

I lay in bed that night recalling the image of Lonesome George. Nick found me lying in bed, reading Danny's journal.

"Dad, I can't sleep," he said as he entered my room.

"The gorilla?"

"No, I just can't sleep."

"Me, neither," I answered him.

"I wrote this letter. It's to Mom. Can you send it to her?"

I sat up from bed. Nick handed me a letter, addressed to Lara Grossmark in Pagosa Springs, Colorado.

"I can try to mail it kiddo, but I'm not sure where she is right now. I'm not sure if she's in Pagosa Springs anymore."

"She's probably in town. She was here the other night."

I paused. "How do you know that?"

"I saw her. She was yelling all those bad words. It woke me up, and I saw her from the end of the hall."

I froze at his words. "I'm sorry about that," I said to him. I was angry at Lara all over again.

"She didn't even want to see us."

"She did, Nick, she just …"

"She didn't. Even you thought she was on drugs."

"Nick, I'm sorry. I don't know how to … "

"It's okay. We know she doesn't care about us." He looked right at me. He was becoming a strong young man before my very eyes. "Just find out where she is and send it to her, okay?"

His eyes watered a bit, but that didn't sway him from his course. He had developed a new armor and was becoming a different boy, one able to assert himself into the world. I think our time with Jane was helping him feel more powerful. I thought maybe I had something to do with it, too.

"Okay. I'll find her. Now get some sleep."

"You promise to mail it?"

"Yep, I will. Whatever I have to do, I'll find out where she is. Do you want her to write you back?"

"No. And if she ever does, don't show it to me."

It was Saturday night. Six days since Nikko's boat had floated back to sea. There was no going back to the past for him, and Nick didn't seem particularly interested in meeting his past, either. Sammie had long gone off to bed, and now Nick joined her. He fell off to sleep, and I opened his letter.

"Dear Mom – we wanted you to know that we are doing okay. We are both happy now. We are doing well in school. But please don't come home. We talked about it tonight. Sammie thinks you need to go to mom school first, then maybe you could. And you should learn there about taking us places. Like the zoo and the beach. And growing vegetables and putting pomegranates in pancakes. And telling stories. And building teepees. When you are done there in mom school, then please write us a letter and then you can come home."
From Nick and Sam

I looked at the letter and wondered where to send it. I wasn't sure if she'd open it. She probably wouldn't write back. One thing was becoming clear. Jane had successfully won the hearts of my children. I felt compelled to visit her. I would only be gone a few minutes. I had to see her.

I put on my bathrobe and walked through my kitchen. I opened the garage, greeted the chilly night air, and walked next door. I could see my house from Jane's front porch, so I wasn't too worried about leaving my sleeping children for just a moment. Hers was a small pale blue house, adorned with blue shutters and roses and impatiens blooming in the flower boxes around the home. I rang the doorbell. I rang again. It was nine at night, and I assumed she would be awake and home. Maybe she went to bed early and I would wake her up. That would be okay. I needed to talk to her. I was no longer afraid of my growing affection.

No one answered the door. I rang and I knocked. But no one answered.

August 4, 1988

We're on the plane home. Marty told me he's going to law school next year, and he wants to go to UCLA. I told him I was sticking around in Boston to finish my Master's, and then I'd try to find a teaching job. I was thinking about going back to L.A., too. I'm not really wild about being near my folks, to be honest. I get nightmares thinking of dinners with them … My mom telling everyone "location, location, location" … My dad just sitting quietly in his chair. I do miss the weather and the beaches. And Jody wants to spend some time on the west coast. We celebrated that we might wind up in the same place and that we could continue our adventures. I told him he was in charge of the next one. He said he really wanted to go to Alaska. We made a deal that we would go there next. Thank God for Marty. These adventures are the best times in my life. Even though sometimes he reminds me of Lonesome George, like a stick in the mud, even when there's hot girls around. But he's got it in him, I know he does. He likes to take adventures. That's how he and George are different. Marty likes me to pull him out of the mud.

Sunday Morning

Jane didn't come over. She had been over every Sunday for months now, but this morning there was no Jane. Our story was stuck without her, and we all knew it. I feared she had been in a car accident, and I imagined her rolling, all alone. Perhaps she was in the hospital. I wasn't sure who would be by her bed or who the police would notify. I struggled to develop other possible scenarios. She might have gone to see her parents in Nevada, or she might have taken her class on an overnight trip. These scenarios were unlikely. She would have told us she was going away. I looked at the phone, and I saw the red light flashing. Someone had left a message in the middle of the night. I played it, and we all listened.

"Hi everyone. It's Jane. Listen, I'm not going to make it over this morning. I'm really sorry. Something's come up for me, and I'm so sorry. I'll try to come over later. Okay? So you can catch me up on the story. Well … I'll see you later." Click.

I looked at Nick and Sammie. We were all quiet. And a little worried. I told Nick and Sammie that I would go check to see where she was. I looked for my old puffy royal-blue ski parka to put over my pajamas. I recalled that I had given it to Lara.

"Damn it," I said out loud.

"What Dad?" Nick asked with concern.

"Oh, just I lost my jacket. No problem, I have this one."

I grabbed a wind breaker, too thin to keep me warm. I put it over my PJs, and I ventured out into the morning, where I saw a blue Subaru parked in front of Jane's home. This wasn't Jane's car. She parked in the garage. My thoughts took off. Perhaps it was someone to help fix something in the house. Perhaps it was a relative. Maybe something had happened to her car, and this was a rental. I wasn't convinced by any of these possibilities. It was early to ring the bell, but this had become our unofficial time together. I couldn't help myself. I needed to see her desperately.

I rang the bell and stood on the porch for a good minute. Then came the wrestling with a lock from inside, and the front door opened leaving me behind a screen. It was Jane, in her nightgown. Her hair was a mess, and her eyes were slightly swollen as though they were just opening.

"Hi, Martin. What are you doing?"

"I'm not sure. I just thought...it's Sunday morning. And we're cooking pancakes. You know. I didn't know if you wanted to come over. We were going to tell our story."

"Oh, Martin, I'm sorry. Didn't you get my message? Were the kids still expecting me?"

I looked curiously at Jane. Expecting her? She had become a permanent fixture at our Sunday morning table. Of course she realized the sacred spot that she had come to assume. While some went to temples and church, we were praying together to a lemur colony over pancakes, and we were a congregation. The four of us.

"Oh. They were. I guess we all were."

"I'm sorry. I can be there tonight if you want. We can tell the story tonight."

We couldn't tell the story tonight. That would have been like going to church on Sunday night. The story was told on Sunday mornings. Or sometimes Saturdays in emergencies. And she knew it. This was not the Jane who had come for visits, shared my story, and stirred the yearnings of two children for a mother. And me for a lover. It was as if she didn't know me anymore.

"It's just that I have company over."

"Oh. I'm embarrassed. Oh. I came to see if you wanted to come over last night but you weren't ..."

"You did? I was at the James Taylor concert. With Marco. He's ... well, he's still here. I really should ..."

"I'm sorry, Jane. I didn't know."

"Why don't we tell the story tonight, Martin?"

"I have work tonight. I can't. Maybe another time if you want. But you don't have to."

"No, we have to finish the story."

"No, it's okay. It's just a story. We don't have to finish it. Really."

"I'll come over tonight."

"It's okay, Jane."

"Maybe we can tell it next week, then."

"Maybe. Yeah. Maybe."

I thought about Marco. I was desperate to know who he was. He was probably lying in her bed, wondering who I was. I feared he might come bounding out in his underwear, or maybe nothing at all. I didn't want to see Jane's lover. I couldn't bear the thought of him making love to her all night. I thought about Major, flashing me a peace sign, and I had to get out of there. I had to get out of there forever. I had allowed it to happen again. I couldn't believe I had set myself up this way. I had sworn there would never be another leaving. But here was another one. Another leaving. And I left.

We never made pancakes that morning. The batter sat in a blue bowl, and I found some frozen waffles in the freezer and threw them in the toaster.

"Isn't Jane coming over?" asked Sammie.

"No, she can't. She's sick. Maybe she'll come over when she's better."

"What kind of sick?" asked Nick.

"I'm not sure. She just has to stay in bed."

"Why don't we make pancakes and bring them over to her?" Sammie asked.

"No, honey. She can't eat them right now."

"Why not, Dad? Was she throwing up?" asked Nick.

"No. I think she has a sore throat."

"We can make pancakes and freeze them for when she feels better," answered Sammie. The tension was mounting in the kitchen. I took the waffles from the toaster. Still cold.

"Dad, I don't get it. We have the batter already. Why are you making those?"

"I just feel like frozen this morning. Is that okay?"

My grumpiness was escalating and they knew something was wrong.

"I'm going over to see what's wrong," chimed Samantha. And before I could do anything, she was out the door. My little spy, Samantha, determined to find the answer.

"Wait, Sammie. I'm coming," called Nick.

I couldn't stop them. They were in motion, and I was frozen. The kids were in charge of the scene, and I couldn't move.

"Grab the batter, Nick. We can cook them in Jane's kitchen."

"Damn it, she doesn't want to cook this morning!" I screamed. "Didn't you hear me? She's sick. Leave her alone."

The kids stopped at the rage in my voice. Nick held the batter in his hand, and Sammie held the door leading out of the garage. They looked at me frozen in the kitchen.

"Daddy, what's wrong? Did something happen?" asked Samantha.

"No, honey, nothing happened. Nothing happened. Jane's just not feeling well. And we have to let her get better. Sometimes you have to just let people be alone. Okay?" I felt a rush up my back as I looked on at Nick and Sammie. I tried mightily to hold the tears back from my eyes.

"Dad, should we make the pancakes here?"

"Yeah, Nick," I told him. "Let's make the pancakes here." The tears were coming.

"Are you sad that Jane's sick?" asked Samantha.

"Yep. I'm sad she's sick, kiddo. And that she'll miss the story. But we have to tell it, right?"

"Right, Dad," answered Nick.

You can't stop going to church or synagogue just because something bad happens. Maybe it's best to go when things aren't just right. Nick took charge in the kitchen. He was heating the griddle, and he poured the first pancake. It probably wouldn't be very good, that first one. It rarely is. But Nick, he had turned out well. He was the first pancake, and he had turned out very well. He was in charge now, helping me, and he knew it.

I glanced out the kitchen window at the teepee. It was empty, with pictures of lemurs hanging on the walls inside. I sat down at the table, and Nick delivered a plateful of pancakes. Sammie brought the silverware to the table.

"Okay, Dad, what happened to Nikko and Samaya?" Nick asked.

I struggled to get there, but I did.

Beyond the Path

The two lemurs followed the trail. Samaya's excitement helped Nikko find the courage to walk, despite his fears. Together they walked toward the sound of a drum playing in the distance. The path took a left into the palm tree forest. The path grew muddy at times and difficult to find. When they lost the path, they would follow the sound of the drums. Nikko wondered what he would say when he met his future. He imagined a group of chimpanzees playing the drums in a circle. He hoped that they were friendly. He thought of Elliot in the tree, his warnings against leaving, and his cautionary tales of evolution.

"Come on, Nikko. I hear them this way," shouted the joyful Samaya. She was excited to find the source of the rhythm. They wandered over streams and a makeshift log bridge until they came to a dense clump of palms. Samaya held her basket tightly as Nikko took the lead and cleared the way for them to travel. The path disappeared in this tree clump, and beyond it was a clearing.

Nikko gazed out between two large palms and over a large clump of scrub brush. There he saw a group of humans gathered in a circle, dancing. They danced around a drummer who played the rhythm. They were children, dancing, singing a song that rang out into the forest, matching the rhythm of the player in the middle. On closer inspection, Nikko saw that the drummer had no drum. It was a woman with no fingers, playing on an old tin container with the remnants of her burnt hands. The children sang out as they danced under the setting sun.

"Ba Ma Sa Kedio, Ba Ma Sa Kedio, Ba Ma Se Kewah." They sang this line over and over as the two lemurs looked out onto the clearing.

"I think they'd like some pancake."

"No, Samaya. They are humans. They trap lemurs. We must stay away."

"No, Nikko. Look at them. They're singing. They're children. I think they're friendly."

"Where there are children, there are grown-ups. They'll trap you. We must stay under cover. They can harm us."

"Not if I offer pancakes, Nikko."

"You only have one crumb."

"Maybe it will last. Like with the dolphins."

"You can't go out into that clearing. They will see you running. They will catch you."

"Nikko, I have to go. I have to find someone to enjoy what Rama …"

"No, Samaya. Listen to me this time. There is danger out there!"

"The danger is in your head, Nikko. Jasper's coconuts are back home. You told me to stop searching for the past, but you keep bringing it with you."

"I was right the last time. You remember when you jumped out to the ship? Or have you forgotten that?"

"Nikko, if I don't try, I'll never share this pancake. Maybe if they try it, the children can help me find ingredients. We can set up a kitchen together and cook some more. I know what we need. I just have to give them a taste so they will trust me."

Samaya sprang over Nikko's large shoulders with the basket in one paw and wrestled over the Indri and into the clearing. She ran toward the circle. Nikko stood frozen and watched.

—⟋⟍⟍—

"No Daddy! No!" yelled Samantha. "No, no, and no!"

Samantha had stopped eating. She knew what I was up to, and she stopped me. She stopped the story right in its tracks.

"Samaya is too smart to run into the clearing and you know it. She already learned not to just run away."

"Yeah, Dad. And Nikko wouldn't just stand there. She saved his life. He knows you can't just stand there and watch someone you care about get hurt. That's what Elliot did."

My kids had found themselves in the story. And they were helping me to guide it in the right direction.

"You're right," I answered.

"Of course Nikko wouldn't just stand there. You're right, Nick. He went after her. He tackled her down. He used a move he had learned at the School for Swingers. He stopped her at the edge of the forest, before she could run out into the clearing. She realized then that he must be really serious. That he was right last time, and that sometimes you have to be really careful. And she realized, too, that he wasn't going to let anything bad happen to her. That he really cared about her a lot.

July 14, 1989

It's our fourth day in Alaska; we're in Juneau. We've got a job for the summer working for a tour company. It was Marty's idea to come. I wasn't so into staying in the States, but I wanted Marty to have a good time. Today we met a girl, Jeannie, who showed us around the park. She's a ranger, and I wouldn't mind spending the summer with her. She's got long brown hair, a nice chest and ass. She's a real outdoors girl, and I can tell there's no messing with her. I tried to tell her that I was a geologist, but she saw through my game in a couple of minutes. She asked me about plate movement and stuff I knew nothing about. We laughed when she called me on my bullshit.

It's not bad to be away from Jody for a bit to see what's out there. I'm glad she lets me go traveling. She seems to know that I have to. Marty gets pissed off at my storymaking, and he preaches to me about love and honesty and shit. Today I told him that I'm not married yet and to back off. I know he likes making stories too when he lets himself. But he forgets that sometimes. I figure that's my job, to keep reminding him how fun it is to be in a story.

We've been to many places, but this one has blown me away the most. It's green everywhere, against the blue water. The Mendenhall glacier is wild. We saw it caving into the ocean, and Marty asked about global warming. Jeannie said it grows as fast in the back as it caves in at the front. I wondered if that was some sort of storymaking they use up here to protect Alaska's image.

She took us through the park. We got to a bridge over a small stream, and I saw something that I just can't shake. I just can't get the image out of my head. There were hundreds of salmon swimming around in this shallow stream. They were pale and weak. Jeannie said this was a spawning ground. The salmon had swum upstream from the ocean. I watched on as some of them just died. Their bodies drifted down the stream. Jeannie said that they spawn here. She said that only the fittest salmon can make it up the river, and that they jump small falls to make it here. The males often fight with each other to find the best mating ground. The female digs a small hole and lays eggs, and the male spreads milt right over them. Then the two move on and do it again.

Both of them die, and the eggs hatch in three or four months. I watched as she told the story, salmon dying in front of me and drifting down the river. I thought it was just the females, after they laid their eggs. I couldn't believe it when Jeannie said it was the males, too. I didn't understand it. I asked her if she was sure, and she smiled at me. She said she thought it was something that maybe we lost in evolution. She wished that men cared as much about their kids as male salmon did. They fought to have them, and then they died for them. And then the bears lived off their dead bodies. I had always wondered how the salmon knew how to return to their streams from the ocean to lay eggs. Now I wondered why they did it. What drove them to swim all that way, just to die. I couldn't shake Jeannie's words. They were chilling me. Marty saw I was disturbed and he kept checking if I was alright. I lost sight of Jeannie's breasts and butt. I didn't care about that the rest of today. All I could think about was that these fish did anything to have kids. Made me think about my father, my real father, and how he just gave me away.

Marty started reciting poetry as we watched the dead bodies floating downstream. He told us this one I want to remember. It bothers me, but I like it. It summed up the story of the salmon. He said it was Robert Frost. "Home is the place where, when you have to go there, they have to take you in." Makes me think of my mom—"location, location, location". But she sold houses, not homes. It makes me wonder about my other home, my first home, and how my mom died to have me, and how my dad wouldn't take me in.

Marco

We cleaned up the kitchen in silence that morning. Our story was stuck, with two lemurs at the edge of the clearing, looking at a future that was too dangerous to join. They had no way back to their past. And they had lost their spirit of pretending and storytelling.

It was nine at night, and the kids were asleep. I watched an old episode of *I Love Lucy* on television, not sure quite what to do with myself. It was my favorite episode where Lucy drinks the Vitametavegamin, advertising it as a great elixir. That's what I needed now—a great elixir to rid me of my feelings.

The doorbell rang. I couldn't imagine who it might be. I hoped it was Lucy, with a few bottles to sell. I gazed through the peephole at Jane standing on my porch. She was wrapped in a blue wool coat, holding it tightly to protect herself from the cold. I considered leaving her right there and ignoring the doorbell. I considered just returning to my friend Lucy, drinking away. I had nearly killed Samaya, and who knew what I might do if I opened the door. But I opened it. Against my impulse to castle, I opened the front door.

"Hi, Martin," she began.

"Hi." She didn't bring anything with her. Just herself. "It's late," I commented. I was more than mad.

"I know. But I told you that I'd come over and finish the story tonight."

"The kids are asleep."

"I figured."

"So then we can't ..."

"Can I come in?" she asked.

I paused, stuck as my lemur friends at the edge of the clearing. But my anger dissolved a bit with the softness of her smile. And despite my hesitation, I said, "Oh, yes ... Sure. Come on in. Yeah, come in. Do you want some tea or something?"

"That would be nice."

Jane followed me into the kitchen. I went to work and filled our old tea kettle with water as she put her coat down over the breakfast room chair.

"Did you tell the story this morning?" she asked me.

"Is that why you came?"

"Yes. I wanted to know what I missed."

"The kids can tell you. Nothing too much. Just Nikko and Samaya are at the edge of a clearing. But they can't go into it. It's too dangerous."

"What about the drums?"

"Well, they saw some children dancing around in a circle. Around a drummer. In the clearing."

"I see." She was thoughtful.

I wasn't sure why she cared about the story. I went to the pantry for tea bags I had bought after sending Lara away. "I have blackberry and chamomile."

"Blackberry sounds good."

Jane sat pensively at the kitchen table. We were both quiet.

"I'm not involved with him, Martin."

"Involved? What are you talking about?" Of course I knew what she was talking about. At least I hoped I did. But I was braced against hopefulness.

"With Marco. We're not involved."

"What do you mean?"

"He's an old friend. I've known him for twenty years. He helps me with my loneliness."

"Your loneliness?"

"Since Jake died fourteen years ago … Jake—my husband. Marco looks after me. He and Jake were good friends. So now we go out for a few laughs. He spends the night from time to time."

"So you're not …"

"No," she said. "Marco doesn't get involved with people. We have fun together from time to time. And that's all." She looked shy and embarrassed, and I wondered why she was telling me this.

The water boiled. I poured some into my cup, and some into hers. I followed an impulse.

"Do you want to sit in the living room?"

"That would be nice." We moved from the kitchen and sat down on the gold couch under the glow of a faint light. I hadn't sat there in many years. It was the kind of sofa that embraces you like a womb when you sit down. I sat up against one end, she against the other, with a full section of couch empty between us.

She continued. "He's wild, Marco is. He always has been, always will be. He was with Jake the night he collapsed in the restaurant. Sometimes I wonder."

"What are you talking about?"

She struggled to talk.

"Oh, I don't know. I have my ideas. Marco lives the fast life, always has. Jake was moving fast, then, too. He was out most nights with clients. He was trying to make it big. He had been an assistant working at a desk of a top Hollywood super-agent. Jake was on his way up. He was working on some of his own independent clients. They were going to promote him soon. To be an agent, I mean. Marco worked in the industry, too. They met through work and he came over often."

"So what do you wonder?"

"Marco did quite a bit of cocaine. I think they used it that night. Oh, it doesn't really matter anymore." She sipped her tea.

"You think he died from the cocaine?"

"I don't really know. I wonder about that. I even wonder if they were involved. He and Jake. I never asked back then. I still don't. I just suspect it. Sometimes the way they looked at each other. The way they smiled at each other."

"Marco's bisexual?"

"I think he's just sexual. I don't think it much matters who he's with, as long as he's with someone. It's never for very long. I've never known him to be in a relationship. He moves too quickly for that. But not with me. We've never been involved in that way. I think he knows I suspect that something happened that night. That he knows something that he hasn't told anyone. And I think he feels guilty. So he comes to keep me company. He takes me nice places sometimes. And I don't mind the company."

"Does he want to sleep with you?"

She smiled at me. "Probably. But he doesn't dare try. If we stay out late and he's had too much to drink, I tell him to stay and he sleeps in the other bedroom. That's where he was this morning, when you came to the door. In the other bedroom."

"And why do you let him come over? I mean, if you suspect ..."

"It's the one thing I have that reminds me of Jake. He's the one other person who knew him well. So we talk about him. We talk about what Jake might have said, what he might have thought. Truth is, by the time it happened .... well, Jake and I had drifted apart. He was living his life. He wanted me to live it with him. To become the wife of a Hollywood super agent. But I wasn't up for it. I just wasn't. I couldn't. That's not me." She sipped her tea again and smiled. "I guess it was too much for me. I'm the girl from Carson City, and I always will be."

Jane sat on her palms and her hand wandered under the couch pillow.

"I'm sorry," I said.

"It's okay. It's been a long time. I'm mostly through it. Besides, I was on my own even when he was alive."

"I see ... "

"Most of the time I enjoy it. Being alone. I was an only child." She smiled. "So I learned to entertain myself. So that's what I do now. I just get lonely from time to time. And Marco entertains me then."

I looked around the living room and then at Jane. "Why did you come over tonight?" I asked her.

"I don't know. I was going to sleep and figured that would be the customary thing to do. I knew you were angry with me. And I figured I could just get mad back at you. I knew you were assuming something that wasn't true."

"Most people would …"

"I know. So that's why I came. I also wanted to apologize for being so abrupt at the door, and for not coming over this morning. I missed the story. I missed it very much."

"The story missed you, too." Then I felt it. The elixir I needed, stirring in my body. A shiver up my spine, and a welling in my eyes. I tried mightily to hold the tears back.

Jane moved her hand under the pillow. She turned it in a little circle as though she were fishing for something. Then she brought it out for me to see. She was holding something that she had discovered, something that she had uncovered from under my sofa pillow, something that she had fished out of the sea.

"What's this, Martin?"

Jane was holding a knife. She was holding my knife. Danny's knife. The knife I hadn't seen in many years. And Jane had discovered it now, buried deep inside the couch, poised to begin a new adventure.

My mind left, for a moment to follow dirt paths in Nepal and Africa. Then to Danny's funeral. I had felt nothing that day. So many of his students were there. They were angry and confused, and I was, too. Everything seemed in slow motion. The walls seemed like they were moving in and out, and there was a ringing in my ears that distracted me during the eulogies. I recalled Danny's mother giving me a long embrace.

"I don't know why he jumped, Marty. He didn't write anything about that. Just that he was very sorry. And that he had to go. Do you know? Do you have any idea? I can't figure it out." And she wept. I just remember backing up and wanting to get out of her arms.

"No, Mrs. Thorton. I don't. I don't know why. He didn't call me." I knew that was because I had stopped returning his calls. Then she retrieved his knife he had left for me. And his sleeping bag. I recalled the last time I had sat in the living room. It was the night that Lara left, seven years prior. That's when I lost my knife.

The image of Danny's memorial played on. But it played a new scene, one I had managed to forget. Now I recalled Jody. She was there, in the front row, dressed in black. She held a baby in her arms, a baby she couldn't settle. I had forgotten the baby. I never said hello to Jody that day. I felt too bad that Danny and I had lost touch.

I looked on at Jane exploring the blades of the knife.

"I was wondering where that went."

"It looks like Carlos' knife."

"Yeah. It is. It is Carlos' knife. The one that killed him."

"The one that's buried at the bottom of the sea." Jane smiled.

"Right." My voice was quiet and a little shaky.

"It's nice." She took out the blades. "There's a spoon. A knife. A fork. A can opener. It's pretty rusty. It looks like it's had a lot of good use." I think she was relieved to change the focus back to me.

"Yeah. It has." I was very, very quiet.

"Where's it from?"

I looked at the beautiful woman seated by my side. Just a couch pillow between us. She in the front of the boat, and I in the back. She had recovered the knife from the bottom of the sea.

"It belonged to my friend. His name was Danny. He was a really good friend. The kind you always hope to find. He went to high school near here. I met him at Bradbury College. He was my first friend after I left high school."

"Did he give it to you? The knife?"

"Yes, sort of. We made a deal. We decided one night that whatever happened in life—you know, I mean wherever we wound up—that we would always take an adventure together. Every year. We had taken adventures during college. We went to Africa to a small village in Sierra Leone. With a group. We worked on a water treatment facility so they could have clean water. It was in the middle of the jungle there."

"Were there lemurs?" she asked.

"No. There aren't any lemurs in West Africa. Well Danny had that knife there. And he liked to use it to eat. We had utensils, but he liked to use that. He liked to be able to take care of himself. And he liked to always be prepared to cut things. And to eat. So he always had that knife. Even at school. And he had it when we went to Nepal. On a trek to a village there. And he had it when we went to Komodo, to see the Komodo dragons."

Jane looked around the room. "Is that where this is from? All these wood carvings? And pictures?"

I looked around the living room. The bright multi-colored tapestry from Guayaquil. The two large carvings I had brought from Gbamandu. The Kallah game. The drum. The totem pole I had brought home from Alaska. The wool woven tapestry I had carried from Nepal. The Indonesian wood carving of three monkeys. Three New World monkeys.

"Right. It's from my adventures. The ones I took with Danny."

"Where is he, Marty? You don't talk about him."

"He's gone. He killed himself."

She paused and scooted closer. "I'm so sorry. What happened?"

"Can I see that?" I asked. Jane handed me the knife, and I held it in my hand. I held it, and I brought it up to my heart.

"I'm not sure. He had been teaching in a school, and I was in law school. We had both gotten married, and we lost touch. I thought he was happy." I looked at the knife. I could hear Danny singing in my mind. Hiking up the steps in Nepal, drunk on a song. "Thank You for Being a Friend." "Thank You for Being a Friend." I looked at Jane, watching me remember.

"I don't know what happened. I only know the story that I heard at the memorial. Danny wandered late one night to the Colorado Street Bridge in Pasadena. About ten years ago now. A stranger saw him there, up on the bridge. A homeless man, wearing wire-rimmed glasses. It was about ten at night. The man tried to talk to Danny. But Danny only smiled, said some words, and jumped. He jumped from the top of the bridge some hundreds of feet down to a little stream below. They found him there. Bare chested." I gestured toward the knife. "His mom gave me this. And I never knew what to do with it. It was a bad memory. Danny's leaving without saying goodbye."

"When did you see him last?"

"We had lost touch. My ex-wife, Lara, didn't want me going away with him. The last time I saw him, I met him in a bar. In Venice Beach, not far from here. We ordered margaritas. He brought a map. He wanted to go…." I felt a tickle in my throat and started coughing.

"You okay?" Jane asked concerned.

The coughing had become a spasm and my eyes watered as I struggled to speak. In a hoarse voice I answered her. "Yeah. Just a cough." I settled down.

"Where did he want to go?" She asked me.

"Well he wanted to go to Madagascar." I paused. It was getting hard for me to talk. "I told him that night that I couldn't take adventures anymore. I broke our deal. He was mad at me. I told him that Lara didn't like me going away. He was pissed and told me I was whipped. I think he was trying to help me, but I was stuck. I told him that I just couldn't go. He called me Lonesome George, stuck in a mud puddle. That's a tortoise we saw in the Galapagos. We talked from time to time after that, but our lives went separate ways. I was busy in law school. And he was teaching. He started adventuring with Jody. I stopped adventuring completely."

"Do you miss him?"

I spoke softly. "I miss him a lot. I dream about him some nights. I wish he had called me. And I just keep losing and finding that knife. It shows up. Then it goes away. And now it's here again." I smiled through tears. "I thought it was lost at sea."

"You okay?" she asked.

"Yeah. I'm just figuring."

"What are you figuring?"

"That this room. It's been frozen in time. And this knife just comes and goes. And Danny stays somewhere between here and gone in my mind. Somewhere between … between alive and dead."

There, I had said it. Danny was dead. And I started to sob.

"I don't like that word. I don't like dead," I told Jane as I cried.

"It's okay." Jane moved over, and she gently rubbed my back. It was the first time she had touched me. She moved her hand slowly in reassuring circles. "I don't like it either."

Dead kept coming. I had tried to push it out for a long time, but dead was greeting me. As I cried, the memories of Danny turned to others. The death I didn't want to feel that had kept me running for decades. Through mountain villages and meetings with drum makers and Komodo dragons.

"I don't like dead, Jane. I didn't like it when they found my father. Dead in the dirt in front of our house pulling weeds. We hadn't spoken in many years, since I had married Lara and he disapproved."

She was having a tougher time now. Jane's cheer was fading and her hand stopped moving. She held it there, at the base of my left scapula, at the point that had plagued me since the crash. "I don't like it either."

"I could've tried to talk to my dad. But we were just both stubborn. We were stuck with our horns locked."

I remembered my father looking passionately at his jewels.

"Danny was my friend. He was my fellow adventurer. But I was running. Running from my home, where I had left my father all alone. The four of us had left him, after he raised us all by himself for so many years. And in the end, I just stopped talking to him, because he rejected Lara. She hated him for it. I haven't been able to visit his grave. It's around the corner, and I haven't gone."

Grief welled up from my belly and I sobbed. Jane moved her hand again, and then she held onto me. She wrapped her arm around my shoulder and pulled me closer, like a child. And the next memory came, the one I had truly been running from. I had been a very little boy when she passed. It was hard for me to picture her; I could more easily hear her voice. I could hear her wooden spoon again mixing lemonade. But now as Jane sat with me, I recalled Mom's last days in the hospital, dying of breast cancer. It had been a horrible two years for my father, my three sisters, and for me. I recalled the last time I saw her, thin and wasted in a hospital gown.

"There you are, little one," she had said to me quietly. Now I remembered.

"Hi, Mom." I wanted to stay away from her.

"Come on over here, Marty. It's okay. I'll be out of here soon. When I get home, we'll make some lemonade to sell, okay? It will be so good you and Margaret can charge a dollar a cup."

I remembered walking to her bed.

"Come on over. It's okay."

I recalled the feeling of her embrace. I lay my head on her chest. I wanted to stay there forever.

"It's so good to see you, Marty. Just stay here for a while." Her voice was weak and trailed off. "Right here. Right at home with mommy." We both closed our eyes.

Those words called another from my mind. Like a collision in an intersection, the image of my mother was replaced with a jolt by the picture of a 15-year-old boy standing by my smoking blue Jeep. "Can you give me a ride home to my mom?"

I sobbed harder.

Jane held onto me as my head lay on her lap. I sank into her as more tears fell. I thought about Danny again. Of our adventures. Then up on that bridge. He had been running, too. We didn't talk about the things that were painful, We were just looking for good times. I wondered if we had really ever been on any adventures at all. Maybe we had both been running from our pasts all those years. Running and pretending.

Jane reached over and held onto my hand. I felt the knife in my palm, and I gripped it tightly as I held her. Then something odd began to happen. My body started responding, even though sex was the last thing on my mind. I felt blood rush to my groin. I was embarrassed, but I surrendered to the feeling.

"I'm sorry," I said.

"For what?" she asked me.

"For all this crying … And for this. I don't know what's going on down there."

She smiled. "Maybe Danny would've wanted that for you." She had tears in her eyes, too.

I smiled back. "I think maybe."

Jane unbuttoned my pants, and I pulled them off. She took a look at my old boxers.

"They have a lot of holes." She giggled.

"I know. I keep meaning to get some new ones."

Jane pulled off her jeans and threw them on the floor.

"I don't know if we should do this. The kids," I warned.

"They're fast asleep. Right?"

"Sammie's a good spy."

"Her spyware hasn't come yet, has it?" she asked, as she pulled off her underwear.

"No, not yet." I smiled.

"Then she'll never catch us."

Jane sat down on top of me. She rocked gently back and forth, and I gazed up at her glowing face. Behind her stood the large wood carving I had carried home from Africa, a large woman with naked breasts. We danced there together, rocking back and forth on the couch, discovering the rhythm that emerged between us. A slow gentle dance leading us both to surrender and both to orgasm.

Jane fell down on top of me. We lay there quietly. I thought of drums beating in a village in Africa and lemurs crossing a great sea. I smiled at her.

"Watcha thinking about?" she whispered.

I kissed the tip of her nose. "Jungles," I said. "Me Martin, You Jane." I kissed her again and she laughed gently with me. We fell asleep, and it was 4:30 in the morning when she awoke.

"I better go home," she said.

"Okay. I guess that's right," I said.

"Better they don't find us here."

I smiled at her. "Maybe. Maybe not." She got her coat and prepared to leave. I didn't want her to go. Sammie and Nick would be happy to find her there in my arms. But she was preparing to leave.

"What will you do with the knife?"

"I don't know. Maybe put it back under the sofa."

She laughed. "No more burying it and no more losing it."

"Okay, I'll put it in a safe place."

"With Nick?"

"He might like a knife." I considered it.

"Will Samantha be jealous?"

"She doesn't want a knife. No, she won't care."

She picked up the teacup to bring into the kitchen.

"Well what would she want? If you gave Nick a knife."

"Well … if I gave Nick this knife, she would probably say she needed something new, too. That's all. Just that she needed something, too. To be fair."

"And what would she want?"

"Maybe pomegranates," I answered. "Maybe someone to finish the story. Definitely someone who knew about putting ointment on a stinging knee. Maybe just to find you here when she woke up."

Jane was caught off guard. I had put it out there. I didn't care about coconuts coming at me anymore. And she knew that it was not just Sammie who wanted her to stay. She took off her coat.

"Okay then," she smiled at me. "I don't want it to be unfair on my account."

Jane and I finished the morning hours asleep in my bedroom. I woke up to make pancakes. I would surprise them all. No school today. Just pancakes. I needed a do over from the day before.

When Samantha woke up, Jane and I were already in the kitchen. She was seated at the table, and I was mixing batter.

"What are you doing here?" Samantha asked with a smile.

"Well …" she started

"We had a sleepover," I answered her.

"Really? On a school night?"

Nick appeared in the kitchen, his eyes barely open, his black hair flying in every direction.

"Did you use the sleeping bags?" he asked.

"No, we just shared the bed," I answered him as I mixed the pancake batter.

"Can I have a sleepover tonight with Jane?" Sammie asked.

Jane looked at me. "Well, I love sleepovers. If it's okay with your dad, I would love to have a sleepover with you, Sammie."

"We could have it in the teepee," Nick chimed in. He seemed to be well past his fear of the gorilla outside.

"We certainly could." Jane smiled.

"Maybe this weekend," I answered them, as I poured batter into the large pan simmering with butter.

"Dad, what are you doing?" asked Nick. "It's a school day. We can't make pancakes."

"I didn't think we should wait all week. I thought we should see what happens to Samaya and Nikko at the edge of the clearing."

"But we have school," Nick answered.

"Maybe we could skip it today. What do you think?"

"Yes!" Sammie answered.

"Cool!" Nick added, nearly simultaneously.

They were tickled at the idea of a day in pajamas and staying home from school. I wanted Jane to take over the story. I wanted the narration to conclude in the hands of someone with loving precision. But she refused.

"I missed the last bit, Martin. I can't just take over from here."

"Yes you can …"

"You do it, Dad. You know where we were," Nick said with full confidence.

"Yeah, Daddy. You can do it."

And so for Nick, Sammie, and Jane, I took the helm.

The Clearing

It was a large clearing, the size of two football fields. And despite the danger, the two lemurs ventured beyond the trees and ran toward the sound of the drums. Nikko led the way, and Samaya held onto the basket as the pancake bit rattled inside. It was the last crumb they had from their past, and she held onto it tightly. They stopped several yards from the circle and gazed at the humans dancing under the bright, full moon. They watched as children fell to sleep right on the grass. Nikko and Samaya stayed low in the tall grass.

As time passed, child after child lay down under the moon. The woman in the center kept drumming. There was no slowing her down. Samaya and Nikko moved in closer. Samaya could no longer contain herself and she burst through the grass toward the woman. Nikko had no choice but to follow his companion through the ring of sleeping children to the feet of the drummer. The woman took no notice of the lemurs, who were now right at her bare toes.

Nikko recalled Elliot's warnings, but here he was. He sat at the foot of evolution. It didn't seem bad, this evolution. He saw the humans lying on the field of grass, unafraid that coconuts might be thrown at them in the night. Some lay with their heads on the chests of others. And this human, this drummer, continued with her lullaby beat. This was different than Paden's Patch, where everyone lived alone in their own trees and he had been treated so differently his entire life. The humans lay in the grass like the flocks of birds he had seen so many times flying together through the sky. And then she stopped, the drummer stopped, and she smiled down at her feet.

Samaya said hello, but her words fell on deaf ears. The woman could not understand the cracks and whistles of the lemur. She smiled and put her tin can down on the grass beside her feet. She stared into Samaya's eyes and then turned to Nikko. This was Tine, the village musician, who suffered from leprosy since early in life. But she was not treated as an outsider, as Nikko had been. She played her rhythm, even without fingers, and the humans rejoiced in her sounds.

Samaya flipped the lid of her bamboo basket and reached for the crumb. It was soggy and very cold. She took it in her paw, and she held it out to Tine. The human took the crumb, the only offering the lemurs had. And she ate it, right in the middle of the clearing under the moonlight. And to Samaya's delight, she smiled.

As Nikko watched his friend, he knew this must be it. This must be evolution. To reach out to a stranger with what you have, with the spirit of generosity. But to do so, he was learning, it must first take a clearing. It would have to happen in a clearing. Without fears of the past or the future. It takes a great generosity of spirit. With no concern that this was the last bit of pancake. He wondered what would happen now. He only knew that it would be different, now that Samaya had reached out to the stranger in the field.

Behind Bars

The traffic was clear that morning as I drove East on I10 toward downtown. It was 8:00 on a Tuesday morning, and I was supposed to be at work. But I couldn't help myself. My palms sweated on the steering wheel as I drove. Most of the cars around me were headed to work, but I was going somewhere else.

I had never been to a jail before. Even during law school, I skipped the tour that the class took. I focused on tax and estate planning, contracts, and organizational law. I went straight to the federal government for my first job. So I was nervous when I went to visit Peter Cameron. I wondered what he would think when they told him that he had a visitor, and that his name was Martin Grossmark.

I parked my car and stared at a large sign that said Los Angeles County Men's Central Jail. My heart sped as I walked under the sign to the front door. It seemed like the largest jail in the world, and somewhere in here lived a man I needed to reach. I wondered what he looked like, what he sounded like. I approached a security check where I flashed my VA badge and was let through. A guard scanned me with a wand, and my old briefcase went through a scanner. I approached the information desk, told them I had scheduled an appointment with Peter Cameron, and was led through a series of four corridors to the visitors section.

There were seven others already seated, waiting to talk to their loved ones. I took a seat in a hard orange chair. The walls around us were white and bare. In front was a wall of glass, divided into five sections. Each booth had a desk, a phone, and a number on the outside door. On the other side of the glass there was the same—a desk and a phone. I watched as two others entered these booths and spoke to a person on the other side. One woman was in tears on my side of the glass.

"Martin Grossmark?" called a guard.

"Yes?"

"Room 4," he directed me.

I got up and entered room 4 where I sat for the longest five minutes of my life. My heart beat ferociously. Why was I doing this?

A man entered on the other side. I looked at him, my heart racing, and he stared at me. Pete was a foreboding presence. Like the others, he wore an orange jump suit. He was a strong, large man, about a foot taller than me. Maybe 250 pounds. He had thick brown hair flipped back over the top of his head, shining from the fluorescent bulbs above. His hair was shaven on the sides and around his ears and stood straight up like iron filings. He had a ridge from his lined forehead down toward his squinting brown eyes, his eyebrows furrowed as he stared at me. He chewed a piece of gum, highlighting the jaw muscles beneath his stubble-covered cheeks. His right forearm was decorated with blue and red ink. His left forearm read U S Marines. He sat down slowly in his chair and gazed at me through the piece of glass. He shifted uncomfortably from side to side. He spoke first in a raspy bass voice. I was playing with fire.

"Who the hell are you?" he said to me. He continued moving in his chair.

"I thought you might recognize my name."

"Did my lawyer send you?"

"No."

"My wife?"

"No. Nobody sent me. I came on my own."

He finally settled into a position. He appeared in pain. "We have eight minutes. Who are you and what do you want?"

"I met your son. He almost killed me. He ran into me in an intersection. My car rolled, and he almost killed me and my two children."

His expression didn't change. "I'm not talking about that shit." He clenched his jaw and got up from his chair.

"I'm not here to talk about that. That's just how I know who you are."

My heart was pounding. I thought he might slam his fist through the glass as he stood and faced me. I imagined shattered pieces in my lap, just like the day of the car accident.

"You're in pain. I can tell by the way you're moving."

"I don't need pity."

"Right. Shit. I'm not here to pity you. I'm sorry. I'm not doing this right."

He faced his chair searching for a better position and sat back down. "Do you do this often, visit strangers in a jail cell?"

"No. Never. I wanted to try to help you."

"Help me? I don't need any help from you."

"Okay …" I paused. "I wanted to meet you then. Would that be alright? For seven more minutes?"

"I'm in fucking pain. What do you want from me?"

"I don't believe you belong here. I read in the paper that you're here for prescription fraud."

"That's right. And I did it."

"Okay. I just wanted to know the story behind it. I read you're a veteran. I work with veterans. Anyway, I wanted to understand what happened to you."

"What do you want to know?"

"Why are you in here?"

"I forged fucking prescriptions. You just told me that you know that already. For pain meds. Because no one would treat me." He paused and stared right through me. I got a chill through my body.

"How about here? Are you getting care here?"

"They say I'm an addict. I'm a clean son of a bitch now. Off any meds since I got here, six weeks ago now. But no one gives a shit that I can't sit down."

"How did you get the pain? That's what I want to know." I felt the back of my shoulder aching as I leaned closer toward the glass. It was a reminder of who I was talking to.

"Protecting my country. That's how."

"Excuse me?"

He held out his left arm for me to read behind the glass.

"See that? I served my country. And this is what they give me back."

"Were you injured?"

There was a long pause. Peter looked down at the floor. He softened, and I imagined that he was deciding whether to trust me with his story. He scooted his chair back and took a breath.

"You really want to know this?"

"Yes. I really want to know."

"How come?"

"Maybe I can help. And maybe you can teach me something."

"I was in the Gulf. In Madain. It's a small village along the Tigris River about 20 miles Southeast of Baghdad. I don't even know why we were there." He had a far away stare as he spoke.

"I was driving our armored vehicle. There were 20 troops in the truck with me. We had driven through the desert for a couple of days. In Madain, right in the middle of the village, there was a girl standing in the road. She must've been about seven. I stared at her through the windshield. I honked and flashed the sirens. She didn't move. She just stared at me through the window. I slowed down. Johnson was directing the operation; he told me to run her over."

He paused. He licked his lips and sighed. He was staring right through the glass and right through me.

"She wouldn't get out of the way. She stared at me through the windshield as I drove the truck toward her. I couldn't run her over. So I pulled the truck to a stop. Johnson asked what I was doing and ordered me to drive. I jumped from my seat and out of the truck, to tell her to move. Johnson yelled at me about disobeying an officer. That's the last thing I remember. They've told me the rest. When I got out, some guy opened fire from behind me and shot me in the back. The others from inside the truck opened fire back on a group of insurgents behind us. They told me the girl ran away. And that we're lucky that she didn't blow up our vehicle."

Peter paused for a few long seconds. "I have this pain in my back that won't go away. I can't get anyone to treat me. They say I'm addicted to pain killers. So I started doing the only thing I could. I forged prescriptions to get the medicine."

I looked on at Peter. He was an intimidating man. A marine. A father. He had tried to save the life of a little girl. And he was struggling in pain in a jail cell. We had a few things in common. We were both fathers. He had been a federal employee, just like me. We both supported our families through a relationship to the military. And we had both been castled. Though he was in a prison, and my own bars were self-imposed. I wondered which one of us was the freer man. He had served his country with honor and passion, and I hadn't done much to help anyone. He had saved the life of a little girl and risked his own. He had disobeyed an officer to do what he thought was right.

But someone was loosening my prison bars. In some sense it was my new lover who lived next door. Though it had really begun with the son of the man in front of me. He had jolted me from my isolation, from my prison cell, from my tree house. I was breaking free. Free enough to face the father of the boy who almost killed me. Free enough to face him without resentment, but with curiosity. I was about to hand what little morsel I could find in my basket to help a man I barely knew. A man who had tried to save the life of a little girl. And I wondered then what it must have been like when he heard that his son had hit our car.

"You planning to use my story in your lawsuit?"

"I'm not suing. How's your son?"

"He's okay now. He had a hard time after he hit you. My wife had a hard time with it, too. He needed us to hold him and tell him it would be okay. But we were angry at him. Particularly his mom. She yelled at him and kept telling him he could have killed you."

He stopped again and he looked at me. My heart raced as he stared at me in the eyes. "One night, I found him hanging in his closet. He had cut the seat belt from his car and I found him hanging from the top bar. Hanging by his seat belt." He swallowed. The light above highlighted a tear in his eye. "He didn't think he should live anymore after he almost killed you and your children. I don't think we helped, the way we treated him after the accident. I found him there. He had tied a noose around his neck and was hanging. Hanging from the closet. His face was blue. I unstrapped the belt and he fell to the floor. He took a big breath and started gasping. The blue in his face went away. He was okay."

I was having a tough time now. I didn't know what to say. I knew the marine seated behind the glass needed to get home to his son. He and I had another thing in common. In a pinch, we had both saved our children.

"I'm going to post bail for you. And I'll leave a card for you. There's a doctor's name on it. Dr. Bradshaw. Go to the emergency room tomorrow at the VA. You know where that is. Tell them that Dr. Bradshaw told you to come in. And if it doesn't work out, then call me, okay?"

"That's 10,000 dollars. Why would you do that? What do you want from me …"

"Will it help?"

The tear fell down his cheek.

"Yes. But I don't understand why you want to help me. My son nearly killed your children."

"You saved a little girl out there in the desert. You served your country. There's no reason you should be in here."

"She was trying to kill us."

"But you saved her. And you saved your son. And right now, I can help you. I can, and it would be an honor. You and I— we're both fathers. And our children need us. This place won't do anything to help with that."

"He had a hard time when I went overseas. He was scared that I would be killed. And he has a hard time leaving his mother now."

"Just go home and tell him that you're going to be alright.

Tell him I'm alright, too. And so are the kids. And that I know he didn't mean to hit us. "

"That's a lot of money. 10,000 dollars."

"One day, if you have it, and you want to, you can pay me back. I got the check from my insurance company. For medical claims. You need it more than I do right now."

I smiled at him. I wanted to shake his hand. I wanted to make contact. But I couldn't. We were separated by glass. I rubbed the back of my aching neck.

"From the accident?"

"Yeah, it hurts sometimes."

He looked at me through the glass.

"Thanks," he said quietly.

"When you get out, go to the VA. Get help for your pain. And for the memories. If you're in treatment, the court may even drop the charges."

Peter was crying.

"They're good people, the people who work there," I told him. "They're federal employees. They all could be doing something else with their lives. They could be doing many other things. But they've chosen to be there. To help people just like you."

Another Leaving

I got a card from Peter Cameron.

Mr. Grossmark- Thanks for bailing me out. I want to let you know what's happened since I saw you. I followed up at Pacific Rehab. I met a Dr. Henry Dawsom in the emergency room. He spent a lot of time listening to me, and he referred me to the pain management service. I've been getting treatment from a spine surgeon, and for the first time I can sit down without pain. I'm thinking about going back to work. Dr. Dawson also told me that I had something called post-traumatic stress disorder from fighting in war. I'm seeing a counselor about this now. I think talking about it is helping me to sleep better at night. Dr. Dawson also referred me to a team that's helping me with the court system, and it looks like the charges will be dropped as long as I continue in treatment. I wanted to apologize for what happened in the intersection, and I hope that you and your family are recovering from the accident. John is doing better. He is running track again, and I'm coaching the team. He told me that one day he wants to come talk to you and your children to apologize for what happened, but that he's not up for that quite yet. I hope he can in time. Anyway, thanks for all you did. I still don't understand why you did it all, but thank you. You have really saved me and my family. You and the VA Hospital.

Peter's note gave me energy. The feelings I had once had about working in the federal government had dissipated. I had become proud of where I worked and what we did to help people. Peter's note helped me just as much as I helped him. Most of all, I was satisfied that Central Office had accepted my response, and that Dr. Henry Dawson was back caring for patients, right where he belonged.

Jane often spent the night. The children were experiencing a mother now, one who cared about them deeply. December came, and we bought a Christmas tree. It was a longstanding tradition in my family to have a tree, usually right there next to the menorah. Many Jewish kids in our neighborhood had trees when I was growing up. I had a collection of ornaments stored in boxes in the garage. But before we decorated the tree that Sunday morning, the kids wanted to finish the story. So they pulled out the ingredients and started to mix. And as they did, I completed our tale.

Samaya found the necessary ingredients on the island to cook pancakes. The two lemurs returned to the clearing each night to hear the sounds of Tine in the field. The children learned to love the dancing monkeys, and they particularly loved their tasty treats. Each night, when the children fell asleep, Samaya and Nikko returned to a camp they had created in the woods at the edge of the clearing.

One night, Nikko heard a rustling in the bushes. He got up from his bed and walked a few steps further into the forest. There he saw a large monkey, the largest he had ever seen before. It was a gorilla, the kind Elliot had warned about. It was right there, just footsteps from their bed. Nikko grabbed a rock he found on the ground, and he prepared to launch it at the great ape.

"Good evening," the gorilla said to Nikko. "It's a beautiful night, isn't it? I've never quite seen the moon as full as it is this evening."

Nikko clutched the rock in his hand. "Who are you?" Nikko asked him. "Are you … are you evolution?"

"That's a strange name," answered the gorilla. "I am not evolution. My name is Daniel. You can call me Danny if you like."

"What are you doing here?"

"I live here," he answered. "Just down the forest, at the other end of the beach. It's a beautiful evening. I decided it was a good night for a walk. To take a little adventure." Daniel approached Nikko. "Are you a lemur?"

"Yes. I came across the sea. With my friend. She's sleeping."

"Was it a far journey?"

"Yes. And there were many dangers."

"Why did you come all this way?"

"I wanted to learn about evolution. My Uncle Elliot back home warned me about it. He told me that it leads to bad things, and that gorillas like you can kill small lemurs."

"Kill you? Why would I want to?"

"I don't know. That's what Elliot said."

"This Elliot, how does he know about evolution?"

"He reads about it. He lives alone in a tree house high above everyone else. And he reads lots of great books. Some about life. Some about history. And one about evolution."

"There's a lemur colony down the beach," Daniel told Nikko. "They've smelled your pancakes, and so have I. I was wondering if you ever share them."

"Is that why you came looking for us? To have some pancakes? Samaya will be happy to cook for you, I know that."

"No, that's not why. I saw you when you came to the island. I figured you had come a long way. On an adventure. I like adventures. And I like to hear about them."

"Do you ever take any?" asked Nikko.

"Sometimes. I haven't traveled very far. But I would like to. It's tough to do alone. It's good to have a companion."

"I know it is," answered Nikko.

"Want me to show you around the coast a bit?"

"Right now? In the middle of the night."

"Yes, why not?"

"Well, my friend is asleep. If she wakes up and I'm gone, she'll be alone and frightened. Why don't you come back in the morning for some pancakes. And we can plan an adventure."

"Okay," answered Daniel, and he left. Nikko watched as he walked, and he realized that Daniel had no intention of harming him. He only wanted to befriend him. Nikko considered what kind of evolution that would be, if evolution were about friendship and companionship, and if that were the result of the survival of the fittest.

That next morning, Samaya and Nikko cooked a feast. A group of lemurs came to their kitchen, and they enjoyed the pancakes very much. But Daniel didn't come. In fact, Daniel never returned. Nikko spent hours and hours during the day looking for him, but he couldn't find the friend he'd met that night. He began to wonder if he had really existed, or if he had dreamt him up in his sleep.

As the weeks passed, Nikko often turned his thoughts toward home. He wondered about Elliot. And Jasper. Rosalie and Lionel. He got homesick sometimes. He wanted to reassure Elliot that evolution was okay, and that it was good to take adventures. But he couldn't. He didn't have a boat to get back home. And he didn't have his knife to carve a new one.

Well one day, Nikko was walking down the beach looking for Daniel. He had nearly convinced himself that the gorilla never existed. As he walked, an object on the sand caught his attention, halfway up the beach. It shone from the reflection of the sunlight and looked as though it had washed up from the sea. Nikko approached it to get a closer look, wondering what it could be. He looked at it closely, buried under a thin layer of wet sand. And you see, when he got a closer look, he saw what it was. He saw exactly what it was. It had come up from the bottom of the sea. And somehow it had found him.

Nikko bent over and he picked it up. It was his knife. The knife that Max had given to Carlos. That knife that Carlos had lost to save his son. The knife that had cost Carlos his life. The knife that Elliot had discovered again and given to Nikko. The knife that he had used to carve the boat to travel away from Paden's Patch. The knife that he had thrown to save Samaya from the nets of the Mofinko Trappers.

And you see, Nick and Sammie, Nikko felt much better then. Now that he had the knife. Because now he knew that he could eat pancakes the way they are supposed to be eaten. With a fork and a spoon, like Rama used to insist. So that was good.

I put my arm around my children. I recalled our spinning in the car and walking away together. I thought of Peter Cameron taking his son down from the closet. I thought of my mom making lemonade with a wooden spoon. And my father telling stories and making pancakes.

So that was good for Nikko. That he could remember them back in Paden's Patch. And eat pancakes while he remembered them. The way Rama had taught them all. But that's not the most important part.

You see, now that he had the knife, he could … well, he could always carve another boat. He might, and he might not. It might have one hole in it, or two, or three, or four. It wasn't carving the boat that was the most important for Nikko. It was finding the knife, and holding it there, by the great sea. And knowing that now, if he wanted to, he could carve his way back home.

Frannie

When I awoke the next morning, I was determined to exercise before work. I found a pair of bright red gym shorts. It must have been twenty years since I'd worn them. At least I could loosen the drawstring to get them around my waist.

I decided to join the others in my neighborhood, running through the streets in Culver City. It was fun, moving with everyone, trying to stay young. I thought about my days in cross country, running up the dirt trails. I remembered racing and sprinting to the finish line. I had to remind myself that I wasn't racing, I was just running to get back into shape. Nick and Sammie were depending on me. Bradshaw would be proud.

I smiled at all the beautiful people. I wondered about their Botox, their facelifts, and their other desperate attempts to stay young. The attempts to avoid evolution. I felt part of them. For the first time in my life, I didn't feel like an outsider among the people that I passed. I thought to myself, growing old isn't so bad. I wanted to tell them that. But running with them, passing them by, I just waved hello. I just waved hello to lots of people. I thanked God that I was alive, and for every panting breath that I felt as I ran along the road.

I ran up the block to Spellman's to visit with Frannie. I wanted to tell her that I would come sing this week. A CLOSED sign was up in the window, quite odd for a Saturday morning. I looked through the window, and the store was bare. The glass counters had been removed, the tables and chairs gone. I pushed my face against the window. The door on the left wall was wide open, and the chairs and tables inside the secret room had been removed. Spellman's was gone. And Frannie, too. I feared she had run out of birthdays. I knocked furiously on the windows.

"Hello!" I hollered. Nobody answered.

A car pulled up and parked in the space in front of the shop. I watched as a middle-aged woman shuffled papers inside before getting out of the car. She came right toward the door of the bakery, struggling with her key ring before noticing me standing at the door.

"Can I help you?" she asked me.

"Oh, I…. I was trying to find out what happened here."

"Oh, the owner died."

"She did?"

"Yes. Did you know her?

"Yes. I mean a little. I mean I used to come here."

"I know. Seems like everyone did."

"Right."

"She must have been a busy lady. We've been cleaning the place out for three weeks now since she passed. I think over a hundred people have come by."

"Yes. Frannie was her …"

"Yes, I know. Francine Spellman. The shocker was the first Thursday night after she died. About 50 elderly people showed up, all dressed up ready to sing dance numbers. Did you know she ran a secret karaoke club in there?"

"I did actually."

"The people were adorable. I felt terrible having to tell them that she had passed. They were so torn up. They didn't know what to do or where to go."

"I see … How did she die?"

"Pneumonia I think. At least that's what I heard from her son. Good way to go … the old person's best friend. That's what they always say. Anyway, her son's trying to sell the place now. Ought to be a quick turnaround, you know? Great location here by the studios."

"Right."

"That's what it's about. Location, location, location."

Her words sent a chill through my spine as I envisioned Horty and her friends out on the street without a place to sing.

"Oh well. We've still got a lot of cleaning to do in here before we can get it on the market. Can I help you with anything else?"

"No. Thanks. I was just running by."

"Yes. I see that. And good for you. Great to stay in shape. Reminds me I need to exercise today, too."

I had never bothered to get Frannie's home phone number or information about anyone else who sang on Thursday nights. I ran frantically down the street and stopped at a coffee shop to catch my breath. It was a small place on the corner. The aroma was alluring, and I walked in. I needed something bold to help me sort through my thoughts.

I stood in line waiting my turn and considered how I might find out what happened to Frannie's friends. I could review the obituaries. I could visit hair salons inquiring about Horty's pink hair. I could wait outside the store until someone came by who knew something. I couldn't bear the idea that Frannie had died and I wasn't there. It had happened once again. Another leaving.

I thought back to the nights in the karaoke bar, sipping Roy Rogers and watching her sing. I wondered where the funeral was and what happened at the memorial. I wondered what I would have said if I had had the chance to memorialize her. And just above a whisper, I began to sing. "Come Fly With Me." The words came whispering out of me with a soft tenderness.

The others in line watched me, but I didn't care. I only thought of Frannie, and how she wanted me to sing. A man in front of me recognized the song and sang along quietly as we waited our turn. Our song came to an end, and he nodded at me. He got to the front and ordered his coffee. I noticed the brands for sale in a wooden bin beside me. Some bags were whole beans, some already ground. I picked one up and smiled as I read the name and description on the label. It was extra bold, and I whispered the name. "Madagascar."

As I waited my turn in line, I thought about my time as a patron of Spellman's. I was grateful that I had discovered the secret club and found my way back to singing out loud. I thought of Frannie at the center of it all, providing a place for so many to gather. A source from which people could evolve. I was grateful that she had helped me in my evolution. I was grateful to so many who had helped me. A neighbor. A Chief of Staff. A mother and father. A son and a daughter. A veteran in a garden. And some lemurs on a far away island. "What can I get you, sir?"

I held the bag of coffee. "I'll take this. Can you make me a cup now, too?"

"Sure, what size?"

"Oh, large I guess. Or grande. Whatever you call it."

"Large cup of Madagascar," he called. "That'll be right up."

"Is it good?" I asked him suddenly. "The flavor?"

"Yes." He was excited. "Really deep and bold. Makes me think of trips to faraway lands. You want to try some first?"

"No, I believe you." I had an idea. "Hey did you know Frannie Spellman? The bakery owner up the street?"

"Sure did." He paused. "She stocked coffee in her shop from us. We were all torn up when we heard she died."

"Yeah, I just found out."

"Well, you know, she lived a really great life. Hope I have that much energy at her age."

"Right. Me, too. Do you know if there was a funeral?"

"I think there was. Don't know anyone who went though."

"I see."

"Large Madagascar," announced a voice from the other end of the counter.

"I guess that's me," I said. I went to fetch my cup.

I expected to see a young person handing me my coffee. But the man was older, older than me.

"Large Madagascar?" he asked.

"Yes," I answered. I noticed the wrinkles in his face. The crow's feet at his eyes. They were alluring to me and reassuring. A mark of age that was so elusive in my neighborhood. A signal of evolution that Frannie Spellman had embraced so beautifully.

July 23, 1990

We're on the plane back from Thailand. All in all it was a good trip. I really liked Chiang Mai. Yesterday we took a raft down a river. Marty was a little freaked out—he was scared to touch the water. He said he had heard there might be schistosomiasis in it, some kind of parasite that can paralyze you if you touch it. He wore a long-sleeve shirt, jeans, and these full-length thick socks. He looked like he was dressed for a cold night, and it was 102 degrees outside! It didn't matter to him that we had seen people swimming at different points along the river. And he wouldn't listen to me when I told him how crazy he was acting. There was this beautiful river all around us, and Marty was just protecting himself from touching it. "Live a little!" I told him, but he wouldn't touch the water. I decided it was time to pull him out of his paranoid head. He always seems better for it when I do, and then he's my favorite person to be with. I rolled off the raft into the water and started to scream for help. I floated away from the raft and yelled at Marty for help. He didn't know that I was pushing myself along the bottom to move. It was shallow and the current really slow. Marty froze at first, but when he saw I was in trouble, he jumped off the boat in my direction, wearing all his clothes for protection! He couldn't believe how shallow it was. He was so mad at me when he realized I was just trying to get him in the water and then we wrestled around and had a water fight. Before long we were both laughing and we swam back to the raft. The water was cool so we stayed in it holding the raft most of the way down. Marty stopped talking about the damn schistosomiasis and saw how beautiful the river was, though he did keep his clothes on as we drifted!

Marty's quiet on the plane now. I can't figure out if he's pissed off at me or happy that I got him to jump. He told me he wasn't sure about going on a trip next summer with his going to law school. He said he just couldn't make any promises. I figure he's just perturbed. Giving up travels with Marty would be really bad. It would be like giving up my brother. But I know he'll come around.

A Dream

Danny's last entry disturbed me. There was nothing more in the journal. Our adventures were over, and there was no more to read. I lay in bed, thinking of that airplane ride flying home from Thailand. It made me feel anxious. Jane was asleep next to me which was reassuring. Somehow I fell off to sleep, but I awoke at one in the morning from a dream.

Danny and I were alone in the Bradbury coffee house. We had no map or paper, we were just talking. I looked out the window behind him and saw a shadow. I looked more closely. It was a life-size gorilla, waving at me from behind Danny. I gasped and felt a rush through my body. I was afraid. Danny asked what was wrong, and I pointed to the window. He looked, and he could see it, too.

"Tell me what it is, Marty. Tell me what it is."

I was too overwhelmed to speak. I yelled fragments of nonsensical sounds.

"Danny, what is it? What do you call him?"

The feeling of terror shifted as I stared out the window. I became awestruck at the creature out the window.

"Marty, tell me what you call it …"

"It's … it's living," I said. And I woke up.

The Bridge

I awoke with a feeling of fire. Jane was sleeping deeply, and I listened to the rhythmic sound of her breathing.

As I lay there, I became aware of another sound, a rustling sound that seemed to come from the ivy outside my window. I arose quietly from my bed to peer outside. I was afraid it might be a burglar, but I had a secret hope that I might spy the gorilla. The gorilla that had frightened Nick, abandoned Nikko on the beach, and now appeared in the Bradbury coffee house from somewhere deep in my subconscious. I knew this was crazy, but I couldn't shake the image from my dream. Jane remained asleep as I moved the window shade aside and glanced out.

I saw the leaves blowing in the wind and a fallen tree branch in the bed of ivy. I stared on, wondering whom I was really looking for. I thought perhaps I was looking for Danny. And I was sad as I stared and he was nowhere to be found.

I thought about the Bradbury coffee shop, Danny, and the gorilla that had joined us there. Living. I whispered the word out loud, ever so slightly, and a feeling of fire ignited me again. That's when I realized who I was searching for. It wasn't Danny at all. It wasn't my dad. It wasn't my mom. It wasn't Lara riding off on a motorcycle. I realized right then who I was looking for. I was looking for me. The part of me that yearned to be living, the part of me that had died. There was nothing to be found in the ivy, for living happened from inside of me.

I thought about the two lemurs that had crossed a great sea and had come to inhabit my inner world. They were evolving. They were growing up. They had dared to transcend Elliot's warnings and had left their isolated island. They were allowing themselves to connect with the energy of a great ape, a new world monkey, and as they did, I was filled with the energy of living. The energy, I supposed, of evolution.

I spied Danny's journal at the side of my bed. I had avoided this for too many years, and I had to pursue my impulse, right then and there. I knew it was crazy, but I had to do it. I kissed Jane on the cheek, and she awoke slightly.

"Watch the kids, will you? I have to go do something."

"It's one in the morning! What are you talking about?"

"It's okay. I'll be back in a couple hours."

"What are you doing?"

"I need to go say goodbye to him, Jane. I need to say goodbye to Danny once and for all."

"Now?"

"Yes, right now. Call me on my cell if you need. I'll be back by three."

I threw on my clothes, grabbed the journal, and jumped into my car. I strapped on my belt and pulled out of the garage. I drove through the neighborhood and onto Highway 10. The freeway was empty, and I could hear my car cutting through the wind of the night. I gazed at the buildings of downtown Los Angeles as I followed the ramp up the Harbor Freeway. I recalled the jail I had visited, nestled somewhere in those tall buildings. I thought of Peter Cameron and wondered if I would ever see him again. I was satisfied that he was home with his wife and son. He was free from prison, and now I was in the process of escape.

I passed the sign for the music center and Olvera Street. I passed the exit for Dodger Stadium. On I drove, through the darkness, following the 110 freeway. I knew that there was only one way that I could fully emerge from the bars of my own cell. My king had to move away from the protection afforded through castling. I had to step out of the tree house and leave my island. I had to say goodbye, and I had to do it from up on the bridge. I needed to see what it was like up there at the time that he jumped, when I wished I had been there to talk him out of it. The freeway ended in a street, and I followed it through Pasadena. I gazed at the street signs. California Street. Then Colorado Street. I turned left, and my heart raced. I saw the bridge in front of me. I pulled my car to the left and parked in front of a large white building.

I got out of the car and walked over a lawn toward the bridge. I passed two homeless men sleeping on the grass. My heart pounded as I turned the corner and faced the bridge. It was a formidable concrete structure built over ten expansive arches dotted with lamp posts that cast a yellow glow through the night. I had heard stories of the bridge through the years. It was said to be haunted with ghosts who wandered about, spirits of the people who had jumped. There were stories of strange sounds emanating from the top. I wondered if I might see Danny wandering about. Still living.

I walked down the sidewalk and onto the bridge, nervous and vigilant, clutching his journal in my hand. The wind swept past, and I peered down through the side rails. There was cement everywhere, hundreds of feet below. I knew this was not where he jumped. I kept walking. Then off to my right, across the street, I saw a patch of trees. The creek must have been there. I ran across the street to the other side of the bridge. I came to an alcove, with a small bench carved in the side of the bridge. It was a viewing spot with a lamppost exposing the setting far below. I stopped to catch my breath, stood on the bench, and looked down. I saw a stream running through the hillside and a small pool of water hundreds of feet below. There were five ducks swimming about on the surface of the pool. This was where he jumped. I watched the ducks swimming, half expecting to see Danny poke his head from beneath the pool. The air around me was cold and thick, my heart was pounding, and I struggled to catch my breath.

"Whatcha doing there, partner?" called a voice from further down the bridge. A man walked toward me. His body cast a long shadow in front of him. I was frightened and wanted to walk away. I wondered if he was real or some sort of apparition. He was tall, about six feet. As he approached me further, I saw his face. He had stubble for a beard, and his skin was worn from exposure. His head was covered in a blue knit ski cap. He looked about sixty. I couldn't see his eyes, as the light from the bridge reflected off his wire-rimmed glasses.

"Nothing. I just came to say goodbye to someone. That's all."

"Oh," he responded. There was a pause. "You planning to jump?"

I wanted him to leave. "I just need to be alone, okay?"

"No, not okay," he said back to me. His voice was raspy, and he coughed after he answered me. The wind blew by with a gust. Somehow, I wasn't afraid of the man. He was a large presence, but he had a helpful sense to him. He seemed concerned about me.

"Who are you?" I asked.

"Just a man. That's all." He came closer, and I was struck by a bad odor. It was the smell of sweat and homelessness. Now I could see his big brown eyes behind his glasses. He wore an old olive parka, unzipped and flapping around him with the wind. It was torn open on the right, exposing the stuffing inside. Underneath his jacket he wore a gray flannel shirt, marked and stained. Beneath that, a dark shirt. Dark green. His khaki pants were loose around his waist, held up by a worn leather belt A shopping cart at the other edge of the bridge held his belongings.

"You planning to jump?" he asked again.

My voice was shaky.

"No. I just need to be alone. To say goodbye to someone."

I walked away from the man and toward my car, but he followed me.

"Who you saying goodbye to?" he asked. He coughed a few times and spit what came up.

I wanted him to go away. "Do you live up here or something?"

"Yes. Sometimes the police come and take me away. They take me to the VA, but I usually make it right back."

"You're a veteran?"

"Mmmm." He paused.

"Well I work there. They can give you a place to stay."

"Don't want to stay there. They can't help me there anyway. All they're good for is a pair of glasses each year."

"I see."

"They want me to talk about Nam. I don't know why I would. I just need to be here on the bridge."

"Why?"

"So I can help. In case anyone comes up here trying to jump. Like you."

"I'm not jumping. I came to say goodbye to someone. My friend. He jumped."

I recalled Danny's memorial and the mention of a stranger on the bridge, a homeless man with glasses who talked to Danny. It had been almost a decade, but I wondered if this was him.

"Oh," he answered me. "I live down there. Underneath the bridge." He pointed, as though he were showing me around his house. I was struck by his conversational style.

"Have you been here long?" I asked him.

"Yep," he answered me. "Ten years now."

"Oh," I answered him. The wind howled past us.

"There's been a lot of people jumped off this bridge. They say over a hundred. Some say there's ghosts here. I never seen any."

He was quiet for a moment. So was I. Then he spoke. "Some people think I'm a ghost. At night, when I meet them. But I'm not. I'm just a man. A guardian."

"Guardian?" I asked him.

"I sleep during the day, and I stay up here at night. To watch, in case someone comes by planning to jump. I try to talk them down. Three times I've managed. The third one, he called me a guardian. The bridge guardian. So that's me."

I looked at the man towering in front of me. I caught sight of his eyes again, and his glasses, his wire-rimmed glasses.

"Ever seen anyone jump?" I asked him.

He paused, and he looked at me. "Seen a few … First night I stayed here, I saw a man jump. About ten years ago. I've seen two after that, but that one was the worst." He paused, and the wind blew his jacket from beneath up toward his ears. "That's the one I can't shake. He was a young man. Big green eyes. It was my first night living under the bridge, and I saw him up here. I still see his eyes. I talked to him, and his eyes kept pulling me toward him. I keep seeing them, even when I dream."

It was him. It really was him. I remembered the description of the stranger with wire-rimmed glasses.

"He was a good looking fella. Tall. Red hair. A crooked smile. He was wearing an adventure store shirt." The man grew quiet.

"That was him," I said. "His name was Danny. He was my friend."

"Oh …" he paused. "Well, you found the spot." He was quiet for a moment and looked out over the bridge. "I tried to talk to him that night. I asked him what he was doing. He climbed up on top of the wall. From right here on this bench."

"What happened?"

"I didn't know the right thing to say. I asked why he wanted to jump. I told him to get down."

"And what did he …"

"He told me he couldn't stay here anymore. He told me not to stop him."

I hung on to his every word.

"He told me that he was a father. That he couldn't do it, that he wasn't any good at it. That no one should have to be his son."

I was quiet.

"I told him that he wasn't thinking straight. But then he said … he said that it was nice to meet me. He smiled at me, a real big smile. I told him again to get down." The man looked down at the ground.

"He said his wife was with the baby all the time. All day, all night. They didn't need him around. He couldn't figure out what to do."

"I said, 'You'll be a good father. Just wait.' And he said, 'No I won't. I don't know how. It's not in me.'"

The man stopped. He looked away and over the edge of the bridge. He leaned against the railing and watched the small stream below. He turned his head back toward me, still hunched over the railing, the corners of his mouth tight as he talked.

"Then he looked over the bridge and down at the water. And he said, 'Home. Home is the place where when you have to go there, they have to take you in...'"

My heart sank. "Robert Frost. I taught him that. In Alaska. When we were watching salmon spawn at the end of the river."

The man looked down and then back at me. "He said that poem again. And then ... before I could ask him what he was talking about ... he jumped."

I was quiet and stared at the man, imagining Danny up on the bridge. "You saw him jump?"

"Yes. I still see it. Every night. I looked over the bridge after he jumped. I wish I hadn't." He paused. "I saw his body floating there. I could make out a pool of blood around him. He was face down and wasn't moving. There was a scream from under the bridge. 'Oh Shit!' It was another man staying down by the river bank. I watched, and soon there were three of them. They went into the water and grabbed his body. He wasn't moving. They brought him to the side of the river. I hiked down over the cliff, down toward the river. They had cut off his shirt, with a knife from his pocket. They tried CPR. There was blood everywhere. Coming from his head, his mouth, his stomach. He didn't move. Didn't say a word. The police came about twenty minutes later. And an ambulance. They took his body away. I talked to them a little. Told them what I had seen, what he had said."

He paused again. "Felt it was my fault ever since. Felt I could've talked him out of it. Wasn't the first man I'd seen die. It was like Nam, and it brought it back. The memories flooded me. They still do. I can't shake his eyes from my dreams. They're all mixed up with dreams from Nam."

I couldn't shake the image of Danny's bloody body at the bottom of the river. I tried to distract myself. "Why do you stay here?"

"Like I said, to get it right. Three times I have. A couple I haven't. But those don't affect me. Not like the first one. At least I know I'm trying now. And I've saved a few."

"I don't think you could have said anything …"

"I think I could have. Every night I practice to myself what I will say."

"You can't just live up here forever on the bridge. It wasn't your fault that he jumped."

"Maybe, maybe not. I'm in better practice now."

"Look, there's no use living your life up here …" I couldn't believe it. This man's prison bars were made of steel. Steel that Danny had manufactured.

He took off his jacket. Then he unbuttoned his flannel shirt. I saw the dark green shirt underneath. It was so worn I could see the man's skin underneath. But in the glow of the light I could make out the faded logo on the shirt. Adventure Outfitters. There was a zigzag stitching up the middle.

"Was that his shirt?" I asked him.

"I found it in the bushes. That's where they threw it. I sewed it with my kit. I try to wear it most nights, then I soak it in the river again. Helps me remember him. Helps me remember why I'm here."

I struggled to recall the poem by Frost and began reciting it quietly above my breath. "I sympathize. I know just how it feels to think of the right thing to say too late."

I stood with the man on the bridge as the cold breeze passed through us both. I continued to recite the poem, "The Death of the Hired Man." I came to the words that Danny had said, up on the bridge that night. "Home is the place where when you have to go there, they have to take you in …"

My eyes welled with tears as I felt Danny say goodbye. I recalled his desire for adventure, his desire for play, and for make believe. My friend, the storymaker. And right then, I decided to put his talent to use, to help this stranger, this veteran, locked away in a cell. I decided that I would do what it took to post bail. I decided to make a story.

"I was going to jump. Tonight I mean."

"Is that right?"

"I figured it was my fault he jumped. For not being his friend. So tonight, I figured it might be better if I joined him."

"You did?"

"I couldn't ever let go of it. I thought it was my fault."

The man smiled at me. Through his worn face, I stared into his eyes.

"I've spent ten years wondering what I would've said if he had called me that night. I don't think I would have known what to say."

"You're serious."

"Yes. Dead serious. And he was my best friend."

I looked at him through his wire-rimmed glasses. "So I was going to jump. Until you came over here. Now I feel better. Now that I know there was no stopping him. It was something he was determined to do."

The man smiled at me, and I smiled back. "I owe you one," I told the guardian.

"You okay now?"

"Yes. Thanks."

The man shook my hand, and he walked away toward his cart. I hoped I had eased his burden. I took Danny's journal in my hand, and I ripped out the first page. I wadded it into a ball, and I threw it off the bridge. The wind carried it into the river toward the ducks on the pool below.

And that's when I felt the sound of breathing next to me. I looked behind me. The man had returned, bare chested. "Want this?" he asked. He held Danny's shirt out to me. "I don't need it anymore. Maybe you want it."

I saw the flannel shirt and the parka on the ground a few steps from him. My first handout from a homeless man.

"Sure," I answered. We were both quiet. "You going to stay up here?"

"Probably. I have friends here. Don't know anywhere better to go."

"The VA has places to stay."

"Don't need a place," he said.

"They have programs for …"

"This is my best program. Helping people live. This is my home."

He dropped the shirt on the ground at my feet.

"Thanks," I said. He picked up the flannel shirt and put it around him, then the parka, and disappeared toward his cart.

I ripped the next page out. Page by page, I ripped, I wadded, and I threw. I was angry at Danny now. I had never been so angry, my chest filled with fury. I was angry about his not calling me, not calling anyone, and the many lives he had left frozen in time.

"God damn you! You son of a bitch!" I hollered off the bridge. I thought of this stranger on the edge of the bridge. I thought of myself, disconnecting from loving. I thought of his mother. Of Jody. And I recalled again the sound of the baby screaming at the memorial.

"You fucking asshole!" I yelled over and over again. "You were a God damn father! You could have at least called!" I screamed and threw pages, and I imagined myself pounding on his soggy dead corpse. Until my anger passed through me. And I wept like never before. With one last throw I took Danny's shirt and I tossed it off the bridge. I heard the faint sound of it splash into the water below. And I knew for the first time that Danny wasn't living anymore. Just me.

It was a long drive home. I pulled into the garage and slid quietly into bed. It was four in the morning. Jane was sleeping soundly, and I lay awake thinking about veterans. I thought about Charlie working in the rose garden. I thought about Peter home with his son. And I thought about the guardian up on the bridge. I was filled with honor to have entered their worlds, and a sense of horror at what their lives had become. War had set their lives on different courses, and I worked at a place that was trying to help them. I thought of the stranger on the bridge, free of Danny's shirt, wheeling away his cart. I wondered what he had done in Vietnam, what he had seen, and what stories he didn't want to think about. And I thought about Henry Dawson, his courage to write, and how correct he was. How many more injured veterans were there working in sheltered hospital programs? How many more ex-marines were locked away in prison cells? How many were homeless at the end of a bridge, locked in a private cell of survivor guilt? He was right, Henry Dawson was right. Primary prevention was all I could imagine. Somehow there must be a way to stop it all.

I imagined Danny on the bridge, and again I wondered why he jumped. Perhaps he was psychotic, lost in a peculiar meaning of Frost. Maybe he was up against the feeling of being alone, the feeling he ran from with me. Maybe being a father was just too much. I was disturbed as I considered the possibilities. But in the end, Danny had found a guardian. One who cared enough to try to talk him down, and one who was living a life in his honor. A veteran. Danny had met a veteran. Someone who finally cared for him like a father would. And I drifted off to sleep.

Chess

Spring came, and Nick made it into a national chess competition. He was going with his two teachers to Detroit for four days, and I wasn't allowed to go. The school told me they had sufficient chaperones and that he needed to focus on the game. In short, I wasn't invited. It was two teachers and four children. And Nick wanted to go.

The night before he left, he was worried. I had an old blue duffle bag, and I pulled it down from a garage shelf for Nick to use. We had a clothing list that we followed diligently. Four pairs of underwear. Four shirts. Three pairs of pants.

"I want to bring a sleeping bag."

"You do? It's not on the list. You're staying in a hotel. I think …"

"I can if I want. It'll help me sleep. Like when we're camping in here."

"Okay. Well, will this work?" I tossed Danny's sleeping bag out from Nick's closet where we had stored it.

"Yeah. That's good. That was your friend's."

"Sure was," I said. "It gave him a lot of good adventures. Drove away that gorilla, too."

"Yeah," Nick said. "Dad, I don't think we really finished the story."

"What do you mean?"

"I've been thinking about it. You reminded me when you said gorilla. The last thing was that they couldn't find Daniel on the beach. And Nikko found his knife."

"Right," I answered. "That's right. That was it, Nick. Nikko could go home if he wanted to."

"But Dad, what really happened to the gorilla? He just disappeared. I wasn't sure … you didn't say … is he out there? Is he alive? Or was he just in Nikko's imagination?"

"Well, what do you think, kiddo? You're the smart one going to Nationals. What do you think about that?" I wasn't sure of the answer.

"I think he's out there. He's definitely out there somewhere. I'm not sure why he disappeared. But I think he's really ... really living."

"I think you're right. I think he's out there. Living. But he got scared of something. Really scared."

"What was he scared of, Dad?"

"I think maybe he got scared when he met Nikko. He got scared when he looked back at where he came from. When he looked back over evolution. And so he disappeared."

"But why would he just go away like that?"

"Maybe that's what Elliot was warning about. It's not so much the evolving that's the problem. It's looking back at where you came from. And I guess, realizing that there's no going back."

"But Nikko could make a boat, Dad."

"Yeah, Nikko could. But not Daniel. In the end, when evolution was all said and done, he was all alone. You know, he wanted to be friends, and show them all around the forest, what it was like, how to take adventures. Like a father would. But he was used to being alone. Maybe he was afraid he might hurt them somehow. And he didn't want to do that. So he left."

"The gorilla doesn't come to visit me anymore. I check every night. Do you think he disappeared?"

"The gorilla?"

"Yeah, Dad. The one outside my window. I figured out that he was never trying to hurt me. He was just trying to tell me something. I'm not sure what it is. So I keep waiting for him to come back. But he doesn't."

"He might not, Nickie. Sometimes when someone decides to go away, they just don't come back. For whatever reason, they just can't." I walked over and looked out his window. The wind was blowing through the ivy. I saw a basketball and a tennis ball buried in the leaves. "Yeah, Nick. I don't think he's coming back."

"I miss him," he said.

"You do?"

"Yeah. I do. I think it would have been fun to play with him."

"Would you have him as a pet?"

"Maybe. Maybe I could get him to do things around here like clean my room. Maybe he could play chess with me."

"He might run away because you're too good."

"I would play easy on him."

"I think he would be able to tell." I smiled at him.

"Is that going to happen with us? Are you going away some day? Like Mom did?"

"No, silly. Of course not. It's you who's going away now anyway. You're the one leaving me."

"But you're going to die one day, Dad."

"That's true. But hopefully not for a long, long time. We already had our one car accident in our life. And I stopped smoking. So now you and I are going to die when we're very old. So we better get on with living, don't you think?"

"I can't, Dad. It's hard to get out of my mind. That something bad could happen again. I don't think I should go to Nationals."

"Of course you're going. Besides, I got you something. Look, it's right here." I pulled the rusty knife from my pocket. One with a spoon, a knife, a fork, and a can opener. "I figure you may need it, you know, in case they don't have any utensils there."

"That looks like the knife that …"

"It is, Nick. It is. It's Nikko's knife. The one that washed back up from the sea. Hold onto it tight for me, okay? It's been through a lot. But it will help you on your adventures."

He looked in astonishment as he held the knife in his hand. "You think it will help me in the tournament?"

"Yes, Nickie. It will help you do whatever you want. It will help you on whatever adventure you take. And more than that," I told him. "It will help you to remember that you can always carve yourself a boat and get right home to me."

I grabbed Nick and I held him tight. I wished I never had to let him go.

"Nickie … the gorilla did want to tell you something. I think you're right." I looked him in the eyes. Mine were tearing. "He wanted to say, 'Live, Nick. As big a life as you can. Spend it living …'" I held him even closer. "And know that I'll be right here for you in my tree house waiting to hear about it when you come home."

Last Night

The kids loved having Jane around and began to treat her like their mom. She drove them to school. She made their lunches. She helped them with projects. Sammie's zest for life seemed to grow the more that Jane was in our life. Sammie was becoming a master story teller herself. She and Jane told wild tales together. Tales of genies in India and settlers on the Rio Grande. And Sammie loved to hear the stories of Sheriff Fred that my father had once told me. But she took them in new directions, and it was a joy to let her recreate them.

Jane and I began a process of moving her into our home. It began with clothes in the closet. She added her belongings to the décor of our home. The kids slowly understood that she was moving in, and they were overjoyed.

Last night Jane helped me face my garage. It was filled with boxes and bags from my past. Many had belonged to my parents. We worked into the wee hours of the morning, sharing an excitement that there was a space growing inside my garage. I came upon a small white box with my father's writing on it. In a black marker he had written MARTY. In the mass of boxes I had hoisted from his garage, I had never noticed this one. I had never noticed that he had left anything special for me.

I opened the box, and in it were a few items. There were my old track medals that he had kept in case I ever wanted them. There were all of the certificates from my life. My kindergarten graduation. My citizenship award in junior high school. My high school diploma. There were letters I had written to him from my travels around the world. He hadn't thrown them away, even in those last years when we had stopped talking. There was an envelope at the bottom of the box. Under all of these old treasures, there was an envelope, and in a red pen in his writing, it said "for Martin."

Martin—

I'm writing you this note because I can't bring myself to have this conversation with you. I want you to know how painful it is for me that we don't talk anymore. I've tried everything I can think of, but I can't figure out how to end our war. So I decided to write down for you my feelings about this. Maybe I will send this to you one day, but for now, I will at least write it.

You know how I feel about Lara. She is not right for you, Marty. She will never think about you. She will never care about you. I can tell that when we interact. But I know you won't listen to me. I'm afraid that as time goes by, she will drag you further away from me. The thought of losing you is overwhelming. It's easier for me to stop talking to you for now, rather than you leave me like that. But there's more Marty. I've been bearing a secret that I can't yet bring myself to tell you. You may not think it's such a big deal, but for me, it is, because I've been living a lie with you and your sisters. And I can't bring myself to undo it.

Just like Lara, your mom, she wasn't Jewish. She was Catholic, too. And my father rejected her. And he rejected me. Your mother's family was so kind and understanding, but that's why you never knew my parents. They couldn't tolerate that I had married outside our faith. I thought if we pretended that your mom was Jewish, and we raised you all Jewish, that maybe my parents would talk to us. But they never did. Your mom was happy to help me with this, and she was more than happy to raise you all Jewish, though she wasn't up for a conversion herself.

In return, we held onto the symbols of her faith. Christmas trees, Easter eggs. She wasn't particularly religious, and she never went to church. There was just one thing that was very important to her. And that was her family tradition. It had started with pancakes on Shrove Tuesday, the day before Ash Wednesday, the start of Lent. Her family had a recipe, and they always made pancakes from scratch that day. It was a family tradition that probably went back centuries.

After your mom died, I couldn't talk about her anymore. It was too hard. All I could do is honor her every Sunday with her pancake recipe. When you and Lara got engaged, I guess it brought it all back. You were just like me, and I guess I became like my father. But I couldn't help myself. It hurt too much. It made me think about your mom, and I just couldn't. So I became quiet. Anyway, Marty, maybe I can send you this letter one day, but I'm not sure. I'm not sure I will be able to talk about it. I can't talk about your Mom, Marty. It hurts too much. But somewhere I had to get down that, despite what's happened to us, I love you Marty. I love you so much. And I wanted you to know that.

All my love,
Dad

I read it again. I wished more than anything that I could talk to him. The space that had grown between us now felt like a noose around my neck. A war that didn't need to happen. I showed Jane the letter. She read it slowly. She looked up at me with tears.

"Let's go inside, okay?" she asked.

"Sure," I answered. We went into the living room and sat down on the couch. Jane held onto my hand. I stretched my legs out, and she gently massaged my foot. I looked around at my artifacts. The wooden carvings. The rugs. The mandalah.

I was quiet as I stared around the room, thinking about my father. He had done everything he could to raise us. He had kept his pain a secret, and thrown himself into caring about us. I thought about his secret, how innocent it was, but how in the end it had driven us apart. If only he could have talked to me. Maybe things would have been different. Maybe I could have been there for him in those last years of his life, like he had been there in mine.

I realized as I lay there what a father I had had. He had cared about me from the day I was born. And he hid his own pains to try to make life okay for us. I recalled the salmon in Alaska and my conversation with Danny, about the males who swim up river, just for their young, and then drift down to die. I looked around the room.

"I don't have anything from Alaska," I told her.

"What are you talking about?"

"I mean I didn't bring anything home from there. From that trip."

"Why does that matter?"

"Well, that's where I learned about salmon. And that they will swim up the river. And do anything they can just to bear their young. They'll endure whatever pain is necessary. And then die. They just float back down the river, Jane. And the bears eat them."

She was quiet and thoughtful.

"I guess that's what's different for us, then. For people. From evolution," she said.

I looked at her eyes filled with wisdom. Like a woman who knew many sacred stories.

"People don't do that. You know? We don't lay eggs and then float away. That's not what we're meant to do. Because of evolution. We have to hold kids, right? Or else …"

"Or else how do they know that anyone loves them," I answered.

I thought of Danny up on the bridge. I thought of his son who would never know him. I thought of my father, withdrawing from me, bearing a secret that I would have loved to share. I thought of salmon floating dead down the river. Then I thought of Tine, singing a song for all the children in the circle. And of two little lemurs, offering her something new to taste. Jane sat with me as the images flew through my mind.

"What do you think old Elliot's doing back there in his tree house?" she asked.

"Probably reciting Frost. He knew his poetry pretty well. I'm sure he's writing down his favorite quotes."

She smiled at me. I had left my tree house, and was daring to face my own evolution. I had fallen in love with my next door neighbor. And I held onto her, all through the night, and I prayed that she would never leave.

But I knew that one day she would. Or I would. Because, after all, life is a series of leavings. From cancer and heart attacks. On boats or from trappers. From aneurysms or vultures. Running away or leaving for chess camp. On motorcycles or off bridges. Eventually it happens. We leave each other. And I realized that I needed to bear that thought with all of my might to truly love this woman who had discovered my knife. This was a new kind of adventure. It was about pancakes and pretending. Soccer spinners and walkie talkies. Dolphins and jellyfish. It was swinging from birches, not knowing where they led. It involved not knowing what was coming next. It was filled with music. And for this woman next to me a song came to my mind. It was a friend coming back to visit one last time. It was sent from Danny in my mind, struggling again in the ocean of my dreams. As I held onto Jane, I recalled a song from an old companion…. "Thank You for Being a Friend…."

We lay there on the couch, side by side. I held her, her face buried in my chest. We were both sweaty and hot from clearing out my garage. We were quiet for a long time, lying there in the living room.

I thought about Elliot swinging through the forest, now in a bright red bathing suit, with the rain falling all around him. Hooting for all to hear. My friend the lemur, coming to me off a cereal box, whom I had learned to tame in my mind. I imagined him surrendering himself to his own evolution, swinging wildly with Jasper and Lionel, soaked and cold and laughing up in the tree trunks. And as I considered the image, I noticed that he had fashioned a rope around himself. It secured him tightly while he swung, like a seat belt protecting him from falling should he have a collision. Elliot was learning to swing freely through the forest. But he knew to be careful of intersections and to protect himself. For one day, Samaya and Nikko might return from their adventure. And he would want to hear all about it.

About the Author

Jeff Katzman is a psychiatrist specializing in the area of human attachment and depth psychotherapy. He has been trained by renowned leaders in the field of attachment theory in the understanding of attachment, separation, and loss. His research has pointed to the impact of war in the development of psychological symptoms. Dr. Katzman is the recipient of numerous clinical and teaching awards, and his scholarly work has appeared in multiple academic textbooks and journals. Currently, he is a Professor of Psychiatry and Vice Chair of the Department of Psychiatry for Education and Academic Affairs at the University of New Mexico. Prior to this, he worked with veterans in various capacities and served as the Chief of Psychiatry at the New Mexico VA Health Care System for many years.